Texas Christmas

Texas Christmas

A Texas Legacy Romance

Holly Castillo

TULE
PUBLISHING

Chapter One

Republic of Texas
December, 1840

THE SCREAM ECHOED around the small home and out into the street. It was a scream of pain. It was a scream of fear. It was a scream that made everyone hold their breath.

Gabriella Torres tried to use her arm to wipe the sweat off her forehead and blew at a wisp of hair that draped down over her face. "Jerelyn, I know it is painful. But instead of screaming, this time, push! And push hard!"

Gabby nodded to the young woman's mother who wrapped her arm around her daughter's shoulders and encouraged her to bear down. "Now, deep breath, Jerelyn…and…push!"

Jerelyn's scream quickly turned into a high-pitched whine as she directed her energy to pushing. Her face was beet red, and she was covered in perspiration. She pushed for several seconds before letting her breath out in a sob. "I can't anymore. I just can't."

"You can, and you will," her mother said firmly.

Gabby rolled her eyes as she squeezed out the rag she was wiping Jerelyn's face and neck with, trying to keep her cool and comfortable. A pushy mother was the last thing they needed at the moment. Gabby had met Jerelyn earlier in the year, as she had been one of the few survivors of the Comanche War that had nearly taken her own cousin's life. So she had a special place in her heart for Jerelyn.

"Just take a few deep breaths. You'll feel the need to push again very soon, so breathe as much as you can right…" Jerelyn's face contorted in pain and she drew a deep breath.

"Don't scream…push. There you go, you're doing great! Push just a little more, just a little more…"

Jerelyn groaned low in her throat as she focused on Gabriella's instructions, and then gave a soft cry of relief. "Is it over? Is it over?" she asked with excitement, then cried out in surprise.

"You're almost there," Gabby said, though her voice trembled more than she wanted it to. "One more good push should do it!"

Jerelyn bore down again, then gasped, "I can't do it. I just can't do anymore!"

"Isn't there something you can do?" Jerelyn's mother demanded.

There was the sound of a small smack and suddenly the wailing cry of a baby filled the room, the little house, and filtered out to the street, where the people let out a sigh of relief and then cheered, rushing up to Jerelyn's ecstatic husband. He stood just outside the door of his home, silent tears of joy rolling down his cheeks and with a smile so large it nearly covered his entire face.

Gabby sighed with relief and joy as she carefully and gently wiped the young baby boy clean, then swaddled him and laid him in Jerelyn's arms. Same as her husband, she was weeping tears of joy, and so was her mother.

"He's perfect," she whispered, as his tiny fingers wrapped onto her finger. "He's so incredibly perfect."

"He looks so much like your father." Her mother beamed proudly.

Gabby smiled warmly at them, then finished cleansing the area, and cleaning Jerelyn. As soon as everything was clean, she went to the basin and scrubbed her hands and arms, and then tossed the bloody water out the back door.

When she came back, Jerelyn and her mother were watching her with grateful eyes. Gabby could feel her face flushing with a blush and avoided eye contact. Instead, she finished attending to Jerelyn and then pulled the sheet back into place.

"He'll be hungry soon," Gabby said softly. "So if you want your husband to see him, now might be a good time to bring him in to meet his new babe."

"Oh," Jerelyn said, as if she had forgotten entirely about him. "Yes, yes, of course."

Gabby smiled. "You were very strong, Jerelyn. And you're right. Your son is perfect."

"We couldn't have done it without you, Gabriella. This has been such a difficult pregnancy for her," Jerelyn's mother said, her voice thick with tears.

Gabby bowed her head in gracious acceptance of the praise. If only they knew that the babe wasn't breathing when it was born, as it had the cord wrapped tightly around its neck, choking him. But after she had pressed on his tiny chest, and then gave him a light smack to the bottom, he had let out the wail that brought so much joy to everyone, including Gabby.

She stripped off her bloodied apron and stashed it with her medical bag, then hurried to the door. When she opened it, she faced the anxious father. She smiled at him. "You have a beautiful baby boy waiting for you," she said encouragingly.

"You hear that, boys?" he shouted to the crowd. "It's a boy!"

As he ran into the house she heard some of the men outside whooping and hollering, and others groaning. Obviously there had been quite the bet going on whether it would be a boy or a girl. She smiled to herself and began towards the small shed where her horse was tied and she secured her medical bag. It was always an adventure and a joy to bring a new life into the world and she was beyond grateful that this babe had survived the difficult birth.

As she mounted her horse and turned towards the family ranch where she lived with her brothers, her smile broadened. She was about to embark on her own special adventure, and she couldn't wait to get started.

 ⚶

IT SEEMED THAT with every mile they covered, the temperature dropped another degree colder. But it didn't bother Gabby. She was so excited she was warm from the inside out.

She was finally headed home, or, at least, what she considered home.

San Antonio was where she had spent most of her young life. When she was thirteen, her father had inherited his uncle's incredible four-hundred-acre ranch in Corpus Christi where he raised some of the finest beef cattle in the state, if not the nation. Her father had jumped at the opportunity and gathered the family, some of their meager belongings, and headed South. Her whole world had changed.

"You're deep in thought."

The deep, rough voice made her jump, as she had been lost in her own world. She looked over at her brother, Raphael, and smiled at him. "I'm just very excited to be in San Antonio for Christmas. You know how much I love being with the family and in our hometown."

He smiled back at her. "I know how much you miss it. You've always loved the town and the people so much."

Gabby nodded, then snuggled deeply into her oversized cloak and settled in for the long ride ahead. It usually took five days to reach San Antonio, but Gabby was in a hurry. After having already been on the path for three days, she encouraged her bay mare into a smooth canter, taking advantage of the early morning light, then she would drop her down to a trot to regain her breath and cool down a little.

She had been worried that Raphael would protest the fast speed, but he seemed just as eager as she to get to San Antonio. It was the following day, just as the sun was beginning to crest, that they were finally coming to the outskirts of San Antonio, and Gabby's heart swelled.

As the houses became closer together, it was obvious that a lot of work had been put into some of the elaborate decorations that adorned the exterior of the homes, with pine and cedar branches interwoven to form ornate garland that was draped over the doors and windowsills. Beautiful wreaths had been created with flowers and fruit and Gabby wanted to run up to them and smell them. Poinsettias were bunched at the front doors, and through the windows you could see families working on more decorations as well as preparing delicious foods.

"I don't know why you are smiling so big," Raphael said, even though he had a lopsided grin across his own face. "It's cold enough out here that your face could crack like ice."

Gabby laughed. "To be honest, my face feels like ice! But I couldn't stop smiling even if I wanted to. Can't you feel it in the air? Can't you feel the joy?"

Raphael's grin turned into a full-blown smile. "Yes, I can feel it. It is good to be home."

"Yes," Gabby said breathlessly. "Home."

As they rode into the town further, they turned down a familiar street where there was a home with fragrant smoke billowing up into the air and catching on the breeze. Gabby turned her smile onto Raphael. "Home."

They quickly tied their horses to the post outside along with several other horses already standing in the cold breeze, waiting for their masters. "Business looks good," Raphael observed, but Gabby was already headed towards the door. He hurried ahead of her and opened the door for her, and they were greeted by the soft jingling of bells that hung on the door.

"Welcome! I'll be right with you," Angie's joyful voice called from the kitchen. Gabby didn't wait as she quickly shrugged out of her long cloak and scarf and stuffed her gloves in the pockets of her cloak and shed her fuzzy hat, trying, but failing, to calm her wild hair. She didn't hesitate before heading to the back where the kitchen was creating the incredible concoctions that were pleasing the palates of everyone in the small restaurant.

She came through the swinging doors and nearly collided with a beautiful woman balancing several plates in her arms. They both gasped in shock, then laughed once they recognized each other. "Let me put these out, and then I'll come back so I can give you a proper hug hello!"

Gabby took a few plates from her cousin's arms and nodded towards the dining room. "Lead the way."

Angie looked at her with gratitude, and together they made quick work of getting the plates out to the hungry patrons. Once they were back in the kitchen, Angie pulled Gabby into her arms for a warm, firm embrace. Raphael had already escaped out the back to be with the men grilling the delicious meat, not wishing to be a part of the overly emotional greeting.

Gabby closed her eyes, enjoying the hug that she had waited so long to have. With one final squeeze she released her cousin and brushed a few wisps of hair out of her face. Unlike her cousins, Gabby felt she had not been gifted with classic beauty. She thought of herself as plain when she compared her own skin and hair to their flawless olive skin, and long, shiny locks. Their smiles would light up a room and even after giving birth, the women returned to their hourglass figures quickly.

She turned quickly and began to head down the hallway towards Olivia's room. "It's time for me to check on my special patient."

"Oh!" Angie exclaimed from behind her.

Gabby didn't stop walking but cast a glance behind her to see Angie wringing her hands nervously. Gabby frowned. "Has something happened to Olivia? She's overworked herself again, hasn't she?"

"She always does that. There's no way to stop her. But this pregnancy has been hard on her, Gabby."

Gabby began walking even faster to Olivia's room. "And none of you thought to contact me? What if I could have made things easier for her to tolerate?"

"It wasn't until just recently that she let us know there was any type of problem. But, Gabby, I wouldn't go in there…"

Gabby tapped on the door three quick times, then turned the knob and stepped into the room—and froze. There was a man kneeling at Olivia's feet, his hands moving over her large, round belly, his face etched in deep concentration.

"What are you doing?" Gabby asked, completely startled. "Who are you? Olivia, what is going on?" Gabby was perplexed and flustered, trying to understand exactly what was happening. Why was this man touching her patient, her *prima*, or cousin, and why was Cade all right with that?

Slowly he stood, and Gabby began to notice other things. The man was tall. Very tall. He was built large through the shoulders, and would be very intimidating if it weren't for the fact that she was determined to take care of Olivia, and give her the *proper* care she knew she needed. She certainly didn't need whatever care this man was trying to give her.

He pulled off his hat and took a half step back from her to give her space to breathe, and nodded to her. That's when she noticed his doctor bag set to the side. "I'm Doctor Luke Davenport. And you are…" He hesitated, giving her the chance to answer, giving her a slight smile, and Gabby momentarily forgot her own name.

To hide her sudden and unexplainable loss of speech, she turned, presenting him with her back, and placed her hands lightly on Olivia's arms. "Are you all right? He didn't hurt you, did he?"

"No, no," Olivia said softly, though she was slightly pale. "It's just the babe has been very…restless. Luke was just checking me. I wasn't expecting you here so quickly, though!" She wrapped her arms around Gabby, and Gabby heard a shuddering sigh from her cousin's lips. Olivia was far from fine.

"I'm here now, and I'll make sure everything is taken care of. Now, I want you to get off your feet. Just take a short nap, and I'll be in to check on you again in no time."

She turned back to the tall doctor who was no longer giving her a disarming grin, but was frowning at her. "I haven't finished my examination." His thick accent threw her off her mission to get rid of him for a moment, and the natural curiosity that coursed through her wanted to find out more about the unusual man. She glanced over at Olivia again, though, and stood firm.

"Oh, yes, you have. Your services are not needed here any longer. I am the family midwife and healer and have been taking care of them for years. Now that I'm here, I can assure you they have no need for you."

His eyebrows shot up. "Midwife and healer? I've heard stories of people with your certain, um, skills, but I've yet to meet one."

It was only a slight hesitation, but hesitation enough to make Gabby incredibly sensitive. And when he had stuttered over the word "skills," Gabby's fuse had been lit. It was her turn to look astonished. "What do you mean certain 'skills?' I don't think I like your tone."

"I mean no insult. But you haven't been through any real training to prepare you for all the things…"

"No real training? I have been treating the ill alongside my mother since I was a child. I know more about healing than any of those fancy training institutes."

"Ah, well, perhaps, then, it should be your mother in here right now…"

"She's dead." Gabby spoke in a hoarse whisper.

"My deepest sympathies," he said, looking truly contrite.

"Where exactly did you train? With some sawbones up East?"

"I received my certificate of training at London University."

"London? Good grief! What brought you all the way out here?"

His face became guarded. "What does that have to do with my credentials to treat your…your…how are you related to her again?"

"She is my *prima*, my cousin, though that also doesn't have anything to do with the subject of her care. Why are you even here?" She sounded harsh, even to her own ears, but this British doctor was about to earn a boot out the door if he didn't start saying things she needed to hear.

"Gabby!" Serena exclaimed from the doorway, then dashed in and wrapped her arms around her neck. Temporarily distracted from the doctor, Gabby held her cousin closely. "I'm so glad to see you!" Serena practically squealed.

Gabby held a finger to her lips, motioning for them all to leave the room and let Olivia rest and was shocked to find the remainder of the family hovering out in the hallway, listening intently to the discussion inside. It would have been comical had Gabby not felt like she was part of the joke.

"Let's go to the living room," Cade said firmly, and gestured everyone in that direction, pausing long enough to pop into the room and give his sleeping wife a sound kiss on the cheek before quietly closing the door and joining the rest of them.

Grandma and Grandpa were focused on Gabby, telling her she needed to eat more because she was too thin, but they were soon interrupted by two youngsters racing as fast as their short, chubby legs would carry them with Cade's oldest daughter, Annabelle, following behind them with a comical grin across her face.

Gabby snagged one of the children and lifted him high, wrapping him in a loving embrace. "Hello, precious!" she said in a silly voice. "I've missed you so much! It has been too long!"

"Gabba Gabba Gabba!" he cheered, sinking his hands into her hair.

"Okay, let's try to get everyone to take a breath for a moment," Cade said in his baritone voice, drawing everyone's attention.

Gabby instantly remembered that the intruder was still in their home, and he needed to leave. She turned disapproving eyes on him, and was shocked to see him studying her, watching her with what seemed like fascination.

Gabby had never been one to hold her tongue or, for that matter, to even think twice before she spoke. "Didn't anyone ever teach you it is poor manners to stare?" she blurted out and the entire room suddenly went completely silent. Serena's jaw dropped slightly, then she hastily covered her mouth, obviously trying to hide the smile that threatened to burst through her shocked demeanor.

"Gabby, we are all very happy to see you and Raphael here," Grandpa, *Abuelo*, said with kindness. "And I know you are very…bold…in your speech, but I ask for you to be respectful to our guest."

"What guest? We're all family, here, *Abuelo*, except for this man who shouldn't be allowed anywhere near Olivia," she said, her last words directed at Cade who was frowning deeply at her.

"That's just it, Gabby," Angie said.

"Gabba, Gabba, Gabba!" the toddler in her arms squealed again as Gabby tried to concentrate on what Angie was saying.

"Meet our special guest for the winter: Doctor Luke Davenport."

Chapter Two

G ABBY CAREFULLY UNPACKED her belongings, placing them on the table and shelf she would use as a make-shift armoire. She shivered slightly and rubbed her arms, glancing around at the small cellar that had played a role in their lives in so many different ways.

Years ago it had served as the place where her uncle and aunt—parents to Olivia, Angie, and Serena—had met to plan their actions as Federalists. It was the movement prior to the full-blown decision to stage a revolution against Mexico. With their deaths, Olivia, then Angie, and then Serena had made the choice to jump into the Texas Revolution. They had utilized the cellar as a place to hide food and items they took to the soldiers camped on the other side of the San Antonio River.

It was there in the cellar that Olivia and Angie had made plans with Lorenzo on how they could get as many supplies to the Texan Army as possible. None of them would have guessed that Lorenzo and Angie would fall madly in love with each other, and now they had a three-year-old boy who was just as much of a daredevil as both of them.

Then, as the Mexican Army was camped outside the

walls of the Alamo, Olivia had made the decision to rescue a man on the verge of death and save him from the Mexican Leaders hunting an escapee. She hadn't known it would change her life forever, and bring Cade into their family, along with his young daughter in desperate need of a mother—Annabelle, or Bella as they affectionately called her. Now they had a two-year-old son who enjoyed driving the entire family hysterical with his clownish ways, and their second child together on the way.

She was closest to Serena, who was the nearest to her age. But sometimes, Gabby felt that, having led her life as a midwife and healer with her mother, she was far older than her *prima*. But Serena had also found true love, and Gabby wondered if it was ever going to be something she would get to feel. Or would she be the eccentric *tía* that the family loved, but who never truly fit in anywhere?

"Is it really that terrible down here? Honestly, Gabby, why won't you let me move…"

Gabby spun quickly to the stairs and shook her head vigorously. "No, Serri, no. I'm fine down here. I prefer it, actually. The rest of you have to share your rooms with kids or *Abuela* and *Abuelo*, and the men are doubled up as well. This is the best place for me to be."

"You should have taken the room Luke offered you. We should have put him down here in the first place. We just weren't thinking with everything happening so fast and—"

"Serena, please…please. Listen to me. It is perfectly fine. And I wouldn't take anything from that pompous know-it-all no matter how kindly he offered. Honestly, what bothers me is that all of you were—are—all right with him treating Olivia. How many 'doctors' have we seen come through this town? And how much illness and disease do they leave in their wake?"

Serena sighed and descended the remainder of the stairs, holding two thick blankets to help keep Gabby warm overnight. She sat down with a huff, peering at Gabby over the blankets, drawing emphasis to her tiny size. "I know you have no respect for doctors. And I totally understand why. But this one seems different."

"Why? Because he has that funny accent?"

"No. Well, partly. He didn't study with doctors here. He approaches everything so very differently. He's all about the cleanliness of the environment for a healthy procedure, and isn't one who believes in cutting off a limb as soon as there's a problem. He knows real medicine. Even things involving plants."

"Hah!" Gabby sat down next to Serena. "Has he shown you any of this? Or has he been all talk?"

"Well, he hasn't needed to, yet, thank God."

Gabby sighed heavily. "Does he have to stay here?"

Serena laughed. "Give him time, Gabby. Just give him time. He's truly a nice man."

"Why do I feel like there should be some sort of follow-up to that statement? Such as, 'He's truly a nice man, but he can't see well close up, so pray he doesn't have to stitch you up?' Or, 'He's truly a nice man, but he forgets where your lungs are located sometimes?' Or—"

Serena was already trying to hold back her giggles, but

broke out into full-blown laughter. "Enough, Gabby! Enough!"

"Oh! Here's the best one yet. 'He's truly a nice man, but…'"

Their joined laughter mixed together and traveled up the stairs as they finished unpacking Gabby's belongings and rejoicing in being together once again.

⚕

GABBY HAD CHECKED on Olivia multiple times throughout the afternoon, and each time she was sleeping soundly. When she went in late afternoon, Olivia stirred and smiled at her. "So, is the doctor still alive?"

Gabby smiled at her and sat on the edge of the bed, smoothing Olivia's shiny black hair away from her face. "Yes, he's still alive. I wish I had known you were having a hard time with your pregnancy. Why didn't you send word to me?"

Olivia closed her eyes and sighed heavily, and her eyes were damp with tears when she opened them. "It has been hard. But I thought it was only because I'm running around behind Doyle and not being as careful as I was when I was pregnant with him."

"What's been happening?" Gabby asked, trying to hide her concern as she took Olivia's hand in hers and stroked it soothingly.

"The babe is very strong." Olivia laughed tearfully. "Cade is certain it is another boy because it kicks and punches me so hard. But I've told him that it is a little girl warrior inside me."

"Have you bled any?"

"Only a little yesterday. That's why I asked Luke…Doctor Davenport to check me. I knew you were already on your way. Honestly, Gabby, I would never try to ask for help without you—"

"Shh, shh." Gabby patted her hand, reassuringly. "So it has only been a little blood?"

"Yes. But it scared me."

"What did you tell this doctor?" She had tried to keep the sarcasm from her voice, but could tell it had oozed through by the frown on Olivia's face.

"He is a good doctor, Gabby. I think the two of you may actually enjoy sharing your knowledge with one another."

"That remains to be seen. So, now, what did you tell this good doctor, and how did he examine you?"

"I only told him the babe has been kicking very hard and that I was having some pain. He had only begun his examination when you came in."

"So you left out the most important piece of information, and you didn't let your husband know that another man was going to be examining you."

Olivia blushed. "Cade is the one who invited him to stay at our home and even commented that he could be a great help should something happen before you arrived."

Gabby stood and began to wash at the basin on the dresser. "Exactly why is he here in the first place? Doesn't the town doctor have his own living quarters?" She turned back to face Olivia, casually drying her hands on the towel.

"You wouldn't believe the storm we had only a few nights ago. His living quarters are right above his clinic, and an old tree branch broke under the weight of the ice that had accumulated, and it crashed through there and even into the clinic. Of course, you know how Cade is, taking his role as the Sheriff so seriously, he—wow!"

"I haven't hurt you, have I?"

"No, but your hands are ice! A little warning would have been nice."

"If I'd warned you, you wouldn't have been so relaxed. Now, take a deep breath, and keep telling me about what Cade did. I'm going to press on the babe, and you tell me if anything hurts at all."

Olivia nodded and drew a deep breath. "Cade insisted that he stay with us. He wouldn't let him stay at the hotel, as I would have suggested. Instead, he made sure Luke came to be with us, and he gave Luke—oh!"

"That hurt?" Gabby's attention was suddenly focused intently on Olivia's face.

"No, no. I just realized that we gave Luke your guest bedroom. Oh, no. Please tell me there wasn't any problem getting him to move out."

Gabby smiled at her and returned to sitting next to her on the bed. "There was no problem at all. Now, here's what is going on with your babe. You indeed have a feisty fighter in there, whether it is a boy or a girl. And I think your little fighter is trying to send you a message and it took a really good kick, literally, to tell you so. You need to rest, Olivia.

I'm here now, so I'll help with the kitchen."

"But, Gabby, you don't understand. We have so many things to do with Christmas so close!"

"*Las Posadas* starts on the sixteenth. It is only the fourteenth. What day do we host?"

"We host on the twenty-first. That's only a week to get ready, Gabby. And we haven't even started on the decorations. Business has been so busy, which is a blessing, but it hasn't given us the time to make the decorations or to start cooking the food or…"

Gabby caught Olivia's hands. "No more. We know what to do, and I'll bring some of the decorations to you so you can do the work, what little work you're allowed to, and you know *Abuela* will take care of everything so that the food is perfect. Don't worry about it."

Olivia sighed heavily and a small tear slid from the corner of her eye. "What would I do without you, Gabby?"

"You would let a know-it-all 'doctor' try to boss you around and only agitate you even more." Gabby smirked, before Olivia shooed her out of her room in faked annoyance, requesting her husband so she could ease his mind.

Gabby stepped out of the room and quietly closed the door then sighed heavily and hung her head. "Didn't go as you'd hoped?"

Her head snapped up and she was staring at the last face she wanted to see. "Why aren't you out torturing others in town? Isn't there someone else who believes in you and has some desire to have you practice your terrible tricks upon them?"

The doctor leaned a shoulder against a wall in the hall-way and crossed his ankles, his hands stuffed into his pockets. With his neatly pressed slacks, pressed shirtwaist with the sleeves rolled up to his elbows, and suspenders, he was the picture of what she imagined a scholar looked like. But the muscles in his forearms and the signs of exposure to the sun and other elements were a complete contrast to the pale and weak man she had imagined a doctor would be.

"What is it that you dislike so much about doctors?"

"The fact that you experiment on innocent people, butcher their lives both literally and figuratively. The fact that you promise cures for people when you don't know a single thing you could possibly do to help them. Those are just a few of the things that I dislike so much about doctors."

"You don't know me, madam, and yet you say such terrible things. Why don't you at least let me show you who I am as a doctor?"

"Trust me, I don't need, nor do I want, to see." She began to walk past him in the hall, but his arm snaked out suddenly, his strong hand gripping her upper arm with a surprising speed. Her gaze jerked to his and she suddenly noticed his eyes. They weren't a deep blue, but more of the blue she saw out in the churning sea waters, and at the moment, his didn't look very warm.

"What did you notice when you checked her?" he asked for the second time.

At first, Gabby was going to protest even telling him. But he seemed just as determined to get his answer. "The babe has yet to turn. That is why the kicks are so incredibly painful."

Luke nodded firmly. "And by the size of her belly and when she thought she became pregnant, that babe should be due any day. It must turn."

Gabby raised an eyebrow. "Did that fancy school in London teach you all of that? Spend a couple of months with me and you'll learn far more."

A rakish grin crossed his lips, and he winked at her. "I just might take you up on that offer, Miss Torres. I just might."

WHILE THE WOMEN prepared food inside, the men cooked outside, and Luke made it his personal mission to chop enough wood to last them the entire winter. It was the only thing he could do to take his mind off the petite firecracker who had burst into his world that morning.

He had been startled when she had come into the room, but the fierce protectiveness she had towards her cousin was even more startling to him. He had heard of such loyalty in families, but he had never imagined it truly existed.

It did indeed exist, and was strong within this family. He brought the axe down on another log, halfway splitting it, then raised it, log and all, and came back down for the final split in half. Yet, it wasn't just the strength of the loyalty within the family that he was amazed at. They shared everything, helped each other with everything, and rallied behind each other if it was ever needed.

He had only been with the family a couple of days, but it had shown him more about family dynamics than he had ever imagined. He used his sleeve to wipe the sweat off his brow and went back to the wood stack. But Miss Gabby Torres was the biggest—well—biggest in a small package, surprise he'd ever encountered.

He smiled to himself as he remembered the look of shocked indignation on her face when he had caught her arm in the hall. For some reason she had a very low opinion of doctors, and he was determined to find out why. But when he had agreed to her suggestion of him following her around for a couple of months, she had flushed a bright red and had eagerly stormed away from him.

"I'm glad to see that Gabby hasn't affected you too much," one of the men said as he approached him, bundled up tightly against the cold, biting wind. "She can be a bit strong at first, but she means well."

Luke paused in his chopping and wiped his hand on his trousers before extending it for a handshake. "Luke Davenport."

"Raphael Torres. The family speak very highly of you." Raphael took the axe from Luke and began to chop the wood, giving Luke a brief reprieve.

"I am grateful for all that your family has given me. I certainly wouldn't get this experience if I was living at the hotel."

Raphael chuckled. "No, you certainly would not. There aren't many people who would want this kind of experience, though. It is tough work and tough love in the Torres family."

Luke nodded, swallowing hard. If only they knew. But he couldn't let them know. He wouldn't let them know. Texas was exactly where he belonged. He was needed, and he had no doubt that, soon enough, he would have the family he'd always dreamed of but never thought possible.

Chapter Three

THE BREAKFAST RUSH had come and gone, and Gabby was ready to make some magic happen. At least, that's what she thought decorating was like—making magic. Overnight a hard frost had settled over the land, and anyone who could stay indoors was doing exactly that. But there was a lot of work to be done, and Gabby couldn't afford the luxury of resting by the fire before the busy lunch rush hit.

Bundled up in her cloak, scarf, hat, and gloves once again, Gabby headed out to the shed to grab the family wagon. She was concentrating so hard on fastening the harnesses she didn't hear the crunch on the frozen ground as footsteps approached.

"I wouldn't have thought you'd be one to run away so easily."

Gabby whirled, holding her revolver low at her hip, having barely had the time to unsheathe it from its place within her cloak. Luke froze in front of her, but she saw something flash across his face, something that both frightened and intrigued her.

"I knew you were dangerous, but I didn't think this dangerous." He lifted his eyes from the gun to her face and raised an eyebrow.

She frowned at him and turned as she put her gun back in place. "You really shouldn't sneak up on someone. Especially not in Texas. I don't know how it was back in London…"

"So are you leaving?"

Gabby shot a sideways glare at him for interrupting her. She finished the harness fastenings and the old mule snorted, shaking its head and stomping its feet against the cold. "The short answer, yes, I'm leaving. The long answer is I'm coming back so don't celebrate too soon."

She had snapped the reins on the mule's back when the doctor quickly hopped up onto the buckboard next to her. At first she was startled at his agility and his height. But then she was angry. "You could have hurt yourself, or worse, been maimed or killed! Do you know how many accidents with mules or horses and wagons kill people? And it is almost always because they do something foolish like you just did."

He laughed, a warm and rich sound, and Gabby felt her heart skip a beat. She licked her lips nervously. She would not like this man. She could not like this man. He was in a battle with her about the way to heal people, whether he knew it or not. She'd yet to meet an honest doctor, and she suspected Doctor Luke was hiding more than his fair share of secrets from her. An uneasy shiver ran down her spine as she was reminded of her own secret.

"If you knew the number of crazy things I did as a young bloke, you'd be astonished that I'm still alive at all."

He was smiling at her. And she had forgotten she was

driving the mule. He calmly took the reins from her as if she had passed them over and he urged the mule forward. She couldn't stop looking at him. He was very different than anyone she had ever known, and she didn't know if that was because he was from London, because he was a doctor, or a combination of all the other factors that seemed to be one giant puzzle that was this man.

"You know, a helpful young miss informed me yesterday that staring isn't polite," he said, his tone calm and casual and not accusatory in any way.

Gabby sat upright in the cart in a snap and stared down at her gloved hands for several long moments. Finally: "I suppose I was a bit harsh on you yesterday, and I understand it was your intention to help my *prima*. I suppose I should be grateful she felt she could trust you with her care."

"Yet you aren't."

Gabby kept her eyes fixed on her gloved hands as memories rushed back to her, memories she didn't want. "I was fifteen when the Texas Revolution ended at San Jacinto. My mother and I had already been following the path of Santa Anna to help the wounded. When we came to San Jacinto— it was horrifying. The death and the carnage were almost unbearable to witness. But then—then we meet the 'doctors' who were literally tearing limbs from these young men and barely even giving them a bandage before calling for the next victim."

"War is a terrible thing." Something in the tone of his voice had changed, and her eyes shot to his face. His expression was cold.

"Have you been to war, Doctor Davenport?"

"You might say that. Medicine in the field is far different than in the controlled environment you and your mother were used to."

"I agree completely. But half of those men didn't need to have their limbs removed. Easily half who died from gangrene could have been saved before it came to that. From what I could tell, these 'specially trained doctors' were nothing more than glorified butchers."

"It's a good thing I haven't been trained by the scholars in your country, wouldn't you agree?"

"Some of those doctors came from overseas. How do I know you aren't trained to do just the same?"

He squinted and when he turned to look at her, the blue eyes that had caught her breath before made her want to shiver from cold. He was a haunted man, and his ghosts floated in the sea storm of his eyes. "Then you should be grateful that you are here to take care of the family and they won't have need of me."

"Doctor Davenport, I—I know I come across, uh, a bit difficult. But I'm not trying to accuse you of things. I'm simply trying to make sure you're as dedicated to your craft as I am to mine."

"What exactly *is* your craft, Miss Torres?"

Gabby leaned back from him, slightly shocked by his question. "Healing, of course, the same as you."

"Hmm," he mused, turning his attention back towards their destination: the market at Main Plaza. "I suppose that remains to be seen."

GABRIELLA TORRES WAS dangerous. She knew how to ask just the right questions to get under his skin. She made him want to pick up and head out of San Antonio and even further West. But there would always be someone like her no matter where he went. Questioning him. Doubting him. Resenting him.

But at the moment, she was the most alluring thing he had ever seen. She seemed to practically be dancing through the market, picking out long stems of evergreens, oranges, apples, and spices. She was also getting enough beans, flour, sugar, and other vittles to feed a small army. He smiled and nodded as the people spoke to him, took the items, and loaded the wagon, only to turn around and go back for more. When he thought there was nothing left for her to purchase, he found her among a stand of flowers and potted poinsettias.

She turned at his approach, and her smile nearly stopped him in his path. *Good God, she's stunning.* The thought startled him. It was the last thing he had thought he would feel towards the woman who tested his patience and the discipline he had worked so hard to achieve. *It's just an observation. Nothing more.*

"Doctor Davenport?"

If it was just an observation, then why did you completely miss what she has been saying to you? "What was that again, Miss Torres?"

Her brow wrinkled in confusion and she shook her head,

then blinked and began again. "We'll need about twenty of the poinsettias, but they are kind enough to bring them to the *cocina* later today. I just need you to bring these flowers to the wagon, and we'll be finished."

Luke eyed the large stack of flowers with skepticism. This would be a daunting task, especially given how full the wagon was already. A soft, whimsical chuckle at his elbow drew his attention and Gabby was smiling up at him. "I'll help you. And don't worry, I'll carry a lot of the flowers up front with me. I'm sure the wagon has gotten a bit full."

"Oh, hardly. Are you sure you don't need barrels of beverages or anything else?" he quipped.

"Those will be delivered later. You must know your way around *fandangos*."

He couldn't tell if she was being serious or joking with him. *Barrels* of beverages? Were they planning to feed the entire town? They both grabbed large bushels of flowers and headed towards the wagon. He had to slow his gait to compensate for her shorter strides, and he was rewarded by another one of her smiles. She stood by as he carefully loaded the bundle of flowers he held into the back of the wagon, and then he helped her get seated comfortably on the buckboard, still holding a large number of the flowers.

"Are you certain you'll be comfortable like that?"

Gabby let out a soft sigh, and for the first time he saw weariness in her face. He hadn't bothered asking her how far she had traveled, how her journey had been, or anything that would truly teach him something about her. But she hadn't invited the pleasantries, either. If anything, she seemed to drive them away.

"I'm quite comfortable. And, besides, think of how many people will believe you are lavishing me with all of these wonderful flowers."

Luke urged the mule forward, praying that nothing he had loaded fell out, and caught himself about to wrap his arm around the small woman next to him. The action had been completely subconscious, and he didn't know where it had come from. But he had the strongest inclination she needed protecting, even though she was a total spitfire and could hold her own ground.

He was relieved when they arrived at the *cocina*, or the family kitchen, and lunch service had just picked up. He took the flowers from her and delicately balanced them on top of the other items in the wagon, then turned back to her.

He felt her catch her breath when his hands wrapped around her waist, and it was as if he had been struck hard in the chest. His eyes lifted to hers and he saw a swirl of colors that were extraordinary against her fair skin and dark hair. He felt as if she could see his soul with her eyes, and he was both afraid and tempted, dangerously tempted, to let her in.

Her hands settled on his shoulders and he remembered he was supposed to be helping her down and he lifted her, marveling at how small she was when she came across larger than life. He pivoted and set her on her feet, but couldn't let go of her. He had the sudden desire to wrap her in his arms, to ease her exhaustion and take the burden of her worries.

I'm going daft, he thought suddenly, and forced himself to tear his eyes away from hers, her mystical eyes that had been looking at him so curiously. His heart was pounding in his eardrums, and he wanted nothing more than to kiss her, to taste those soft, pink lips that were slightly parted, tempting him.

Her hands moved slowly across his shoulders and down to his biceps, then paused and went back up to his shoulders. "Th—thank you," she stuttered, but neither of them parted. Suddenly the back door burst open and the men came out, grumbling about having to cook the meat for the noon meal.

Luke and Gabby jumped apart quickly and Gabby turned towards the wagon, gathering up the bunches of flowers. The men froze when they saw the wagon. "Did you buy the entire market, Gabby?" Raphael asked, his voice incredulous.

Gabby turned back to them, but avoided eye contact with Luke. "Olivia deserves to have the absolutely best Christmas possible. And we're going to give it to her."

Raphael folded his arms across his chest and frowned. "You know what this means, right, gentlemen? This means Gabby is going to be working us to death over the next few days, and we have no say in the matter."

Gabby bared her teeth in the semblance of a smile at her brother, then looked over at Luke and her smile softened. "Will you help me get the items into the house?"

How could he possible say no to the little vixen? Yes, that's what she was. A vixen. She was using powers he had no idea about to make him want to be with her, to make him crave her smile and her touch. "Of course," he replied gathering up the remaining bundles of flowers and following her into the house while the other men continued to scowl at the number of items still left in the wagon.

"Gabriella, what have you done?" Angie asked in shock as they came into the house with all of the flowers.

"This is going to be an extra special Christmas. I'm going to make sure of it." She swept past Angie and into the living room where she placed the flowers on the long family dining table and Luke did the same.

"I need to help with lunch service now..." Gabby's voice trailed away, as if there was something more she wanted to say to Luke, but didn't know how.

"I'll finish bringing the items in. Don't fret about it."

She began to turn away from him, then turned back quickly. "This family is all I have. They are very important to me. So...I may be a bit overprotective at times."

He raised his eyebrows, surprised at what he was hearing.

"I may have made a harsh judgment far too fast with you. And you didn't deserve that. I'm sorry."

"You don't owe me an apology. I would give anything to have someone care as deeply for me as you care for your family." *Fool! You've said too much!*

She tilted her head and looked at him quizzically. "Don't you have a family that cares for you?"

He shook his head, finding it hard to speak. "My family is gone now. It is what made coming to San Antonio from London an easy choice."

"I'm sorry," she said softly. "I didn't mean to open a sore wound."

He was about to say it was no longer a sore wound. He

had come to terms with their deaths as a child. They had died when he was so young, he could barely remember his father. But he remembered his mother with great fondness. "I, too, may have judged you a bit harshly. I've heard terrible stories about healers, but you aren't fitting the picture I had in mind. I'm also sorry. Truce?"

He held out his hand to her and she slowly slid her small one inside his. His hand enveloped hers, and he could feel her pulse at the base of her wrist. It was racing. Was she scared? Nervous? Or excited and thrilled to be close, as he was? He released her hand reluctantly and turned for the kitchen.

Once again she turned back to him. "Thank you for today. You've been so very helpful."

"It has been my honor," he said, bowing slightly to her, and was rewarded by one of her wonderful smiles. And then she was gone, off to help her cousins with their noon lunch rush of customers seeking the delectable food they prepared every day.

And the room felt empty and dark the moment she left.

GABBY HAD A hard time focusing during lunch service. All she could think about was the feel of his hands around her waist and the way he had looked at her. No man had ever looked at her in such a way. If they had, she had never noticed. But she was also constantly surrounded by her big, burly brothers, so she doubted any man had been brave enough to even make eye contact with her.

But there was something different about the doctor. There was strength and determination, and it was obvious he had worked hard in his life, judging by the callouses on his hands. She tried to guess his age and estimated he was in his late twenties, if not already thirty. At nineteen, she was already considered an old maid by many.

She muddled her way through lunch service, then helped with the cleanup. But her mind was hardly on the task. It was on a man with dark brown hair and pale blue eyes that could be a raging storm or a block of ice.

"You seem incredibly distracted," Serena said with a slight grin, as if she knew something that no one else did.

"Oh, Serena, there's just so much that needs to be done for the *posada* and for Christmas. I think I'm going to put the doctor to work on decorations to help me some."

"It seems you and the doctor are getting along much better now. It's nice to see."

Gabby forced a smile to her face. "He is helpful and seems to be as kind as someone from overseas can be. So we tolerate each other."

"Hmm," was Serena's only response, though the smile remained on her face.

As soon as the kitchen was clean, and the men outside had finished cleaning the grill and preparing it for the next day, Gabby took advantage of the chance to grab Luke as he walked in. He smelled of the barbecue smoke, and she had never thought of it as an alluring smell, but on him, she found it very appealing. She wanted to slap herself.

"I need your help, Doc," she said, trying to keep her tone even so no one would know the turmoil running through her.

He immediately paused, his eyes roving over her with concern. "Are you hurt? Did something happen?"

Gabby's heart thudded in her ears. Was he really worried about her? Was he really ready to tend to her if she was in need? But she forced the thoughts to the side. He was a doctor, her enemy. *If she truly were in need of medical help, he would be the last person she would turn to…right?*

"I'm fine. I need you to help me with the decorations. Come join me in the family dining room—we have a lot of work to do."

The other men snickered and Gabby turned fierce eyes on them. "I'll need you to handle the poinsettias that are to be delivered this afternoon. As well as a few barrels of wine."

Their snickers turned to groans and Cade even tried to bargain with Luke to trade places. But Gabby stood firm in her decision and ended up grabbing Luke by the arm and pulling him along with her to the dining room.

Luke looked completely lost. He followed her blindly, but she saw the look of apprehension on his face. "Don't worry. Just think of the garland you made as a child. Then you'll be able to make this garland."

An odd expression crossed his face, one that looked extremely sad. She wanted to ask him what he was thinking about, but just as fast as the look crossed his face, it was gone. "Sounds easy enough," he said, though his voice was strained.

Gabby had already organized the flowers and bunches of greenery into a functional assembly line, but she saw concern on his face. "It's very simple. Just take the greenery and weave it together. I'll add the flowers as we go along."

He hesitantly began to move the greenery around, but his movements were awkward. Gabby watched him for a few moments, frowning slightly as the crease of confusion in her forehead grew with each moment. "You remember how to make garland, right?" she finally asked.

He fidgeted with the greenery a little longer, then looked up at her, a hopeless expression on his face. "I don't know how to make garland," he admitted; though, by his stance he was prepared for her to laugh at him.

Gabby had no intention of laughing at him, and she felt her face turn crimson with a blush. "Oh, I'm such a fool. You probably have people who do all of this for you in London. I'm sorry, Doctor—"

"Just call me Luke, please. I'm here as a visitor to your family, and that's all."

Gabby gave him a weak smile. "I really am sorry for assuming you would know how to make this garland. I'm sure in London there were people making it in massive quantities for all of the folks decorating their homes."

She moved around the table and stood next to him, gathering the strands of greenery and with quick and agile hands, began to bring the bright green and deep green pieces together, using wire she had placed at one end of the table to hold them together. She then grabbed some of the flowers that she had been working on while he fumbled around, and carefully placed them within the greenery, careful not to tear the small bag of water she had fashioned around each stem to keep them perky and alive for the next two weeks.

"That is amazing," Luke said, leaning over her to observe her work. He reached around her, pressing against her back, as his finger trailed over the delicate, intricate design she had just made.

Her heart began to pound so hard she thought it was going to beat through her chest. Surely he could hear it. His other hand draped over her shoulder, almost as if it was a natural position to take, leaning against her, holding her gently.

"It's beautiful. And you did it with such ease."

His voice was right against her ear and a slight shiver ran down her spine as his breath blew over her neck. "Luke…" she said softly, turning her head slightly and they were suddenly nearly nose to nose.

His eyes dropped to her face, and the hand that had been touching the greenery moved up and cupped her cheek, his thumb lightly brushing the delicate skin. She was finding it hard to breathe, and couldn't take her eyes off of his lips. They were accentuated by the light shadow of his whiskers, and she couldn't think clearly.

"Vixen," he whispered softly, his eyes searching hers. "You must be a vixen, because of the things you make me think."

Gabby suddenly wanted to know what she made him think. Did he wonder what it would be like to let their lips brush, to touch, taste each other? Because that was exactly what her mind was doing at the moment, and she was finding it incredibly disconcerting.

Slowly, cautiously, he pulled back, but not very far. Outside it had begun to grow dark, but neither of them had noticed. In the light of dusk, his face seemed to glow in the various hues of color, and she raised one of her hands to his cheek, just as he had one on hers.

"We shouldn't..." she whispered.

"We can't..."

She responded by turning more fully in his embrace and slid her other hand up his neck and into his hair, thrilled at the feel of his strong arms around her supporting her, protecting her, comforting her. And, yet, deep in her heart she knew it was wrong. She needed to step away from him. But her feet wouldn't allow her to move.

"You truly are a vixen," he mused.

"I'm not sure that I like that title. What should I call you?"

"A fool," he said softly and began to pull away from her. "I'm sorry, Gabby. I took advantage of you. I took advantage of the situation. You are an incredibly beautiful woman, and I—"

"Are you truly sorry for what just happened between us? A fleeting moment where a kind stranger offered his warmth and strength? Because I'm not sorry in the least. I enjoyed every moment of it. I don't know if that makes me a strumpet or not, but I did. Go ahead and feel sorry. But I will remember this moment fondly."

She turned her back on him and began to fumble around

to light the lanterns in the room so she could finish the decorations. She heard his boots as he exited the room and she hastily wiped away the lone tear that rolled down her cheek.

Chapter Four

THE HOUSE WAS silent. Everyone had already gone to bed except Gabby. She had to finish making the garland or they wouldn't get it out to decorate the house soon enough. The *posada* would begin the very next night, and their home had to look perfect, even though it wasn't hosting the first night of the festivities.

She was finishing an intricate wreath when overwhelming exhaustion fell upon her. Four days of hard travel had taken its toll on her, and then to run non-stop from the moment she had arrived was just too much for her to handle. But she would persevere. She always did.

Mentally shaking herself she turned her attention back to the wreath and realized it was complete. She looked around the table and realized she had made all of the garland and decorations that were needed for the men to put up immediately on the doors and windows. The hardest part of the decorating was over.

Her legs and arms and back protested as she stood and tried to stretch. She was so very tired. The cot in the basement seemed a luxury at the moment, and she couldn't wait to get to it.

"Why are you still awake?" The deep voice behind her startled her and she turned to see Luke, his jacket gone and in a thin shirt and pants she would never have imagined a doctor from London to wear. They reminded her of the buckskin pants that Serena had a fondness for. But he filled them out far better than Serena ever could.

Flustered, she turned away from him. "I've actually just finished and am about to go to bed. I'm sorry—did I wake you with the noise I was making in here?"

"No, my mind had enough to keep it preoccupied and me awake. One of those things that kept me awake is you."

Even in her exhausted state, her heart pounded harder. Was he still sorry for their innocent, though intimate, embrace earlier? Was he still regretting what he had done? She knew she was plain, and she knew there was a reason she was a nineteen-year-old unwed woman. Men simply didn't see any hope where she was concerned. She lacked beauty, was too stubborn, and could handle many of the things that men could, which made them feel worthless. She understood why he had turned from her. But she didn't need him to rub salt in the wound.

"If you are expecting forgiveness for the embrace, you've come to the wrong woman. I don't do anything that I don't want to do. And that means I wanted to touch you. Take your regret elsewhere. I won't tell anyone what happened, so you needn't feel obligated to me in any way."

She turned to blow out one of the lamps and the room spun briefly. She reached for the table for stability. Instead strong, warm, comforting masculine arms were around her, lifting her off of her feet and causing the room to spin even more.

"L—Luke, what are you doing?" she asked in a quivering voice as he lifted her in his arms, holding her tight against his chest.

"Taking care of you," he mumbled as he blew out the lamps in the room, then moved to the couch, where he settled her down, draping a blanket over her before he went to work on her shoes.

With both Angie and Serena staying for Christmas, the house was overflowing. That's why Gabby hadn't complained too much about the cellar. It would at least be quiet and semi-spacious. But she hadn't planned to sleep on the couch.

"Luke, what are you doing?" she asked again, though the cushions of the couch seemed to be absorbing her.

"I already answered that, if you remember. I'm taking care of you." He pulled each of her boots off and she sighed heavily as he rubbed her feet gently, warming them before sliding them back under the covers.

She was half asleep as she watched him settle in a chair nearby, pulling another blanket over him. Without thinking about it, she reached out her hand and grasped one of his, and he held her fingers gently, yet firmly, letting her know he was there with her and wasn't going anywhere.

"How long did you travel to get here?" he asked softly.

"It w-was about four days. We made r-really good t-time." She was beginning to shiver now that her body was no longer moving and the cold was causing her to stutter through her words.

He frowned and shifted, sitting beside her on the couch and vigorously rubbing her shoulders and her back, generating warmth. Gabby almost sighed contentedly at the feeling.

"Hmm." The sound reverberated against her and she smiled through her trembles, enjoying the moment. "Did you get much rest on the journey?"

"Some. It's always a little difficult sleeping out on the ground. You have to sleep with one eye open in case you're ambushed. It happens too often out here."

"I'm familiar with the feeling," he said, almost under his breath. Then: "Where were you coming from?"

"Corpus Christi."

"Where is that?"

She chuckled as she snuggled down deeper into the couch. "You need to study a map if you want to have any hope of living in Texas. Corpus is South of here. We are near the bay so we receive a lot of freight and goods to be sold all across Texas. Even to the States."

She felt more relaxed than she had in days. And she never wanted the slight embrace to end. She tilted her head back and looked into his mysterious blue eyes. "Why are you taking care of me?" Her shivers were starting to ease. "I'm the one who's supposed to take care of people. No one is supposed to take care of me."

"That doesn't sound very fair," he said softly, his hand reaching up to smooth her hair back from her face. It seemed to be a subconscious touch, and was completely harmless. But it created a flutter low in her stomach and made her breath catch in her throat.

"I'm the healer. That's how I'm supposed to be."

"Hmm. So the healer takes care of the health of everyone, spends hours in the market helping her family get ready for Christmas, and stays up until the oil is almost gone from the lantern working on decorations? That sounds like an awful lot to expect from a healer."

"Maybe I'm just a unique healer," she said, smiling slightly.

"You're unique, I'll give you that." His eyes roved over her face and there was a tenderness in his expression. "Get some sleep, Vixen. Get some sleep."

HE DIDN'T WANT the warmth to go away. Or the sweet smell of lilac and something woodsy. Oddly enough, the two aromas complemented each other and he felt like he was back home, walking the road to get away from all that haunted him. To escape for a few blissful hours and pretend he didn't have to return to the life that he had created for himself.

He felt comfort, and solace, and joy. And then that warmth began to move, and he felt something quite different. It was a woman he held in his arms, and her curves fit against him perfectly. Barely awake, his hands threaded through her hair and the scent of lilacs became even stronger.

"Luke," a feminine voice murmured sleepily. He was slowly beginning to wake up, a smile on his face. Until he opened his eyes and saw Gabby. He nearly fell off the couch. Somehow, during the night, he must have stretched out alongside her, and now they lay face to face, snuggled up together, keeping each other warm.

"Vixen, wake up," he whispered gently, pulling away from her, even though every fiber of his being wanted to be closer to her. He didn't understand the emotions running through him as he looked at the sweet slumbering woman, but didn't want to examine the feelings. Not while he held her close and warm to him.

"Hmm." She made the soft sound, seeking the warmth that had just left her, and her hands landed on his chest. Her eyes flew open. "Luke!"

"Shh! Are you daft? You're going to wake up your whole family!"

"As much as I adore your accent, it is very hard to understand you this early in the morning."

"You adore my accent?" He was momentarily distracted.

"Doctor Davenport, how did this happen? I don't remember—"

"You were exhausted and freezing last night. I simply meant to get you comfortable and warm. I wouldn't be much of a gentleman to leave you in such a condition."

"That doesn't quite explain how you ended up on this couch with me like this!" she whispered loudly.

He watched her for several seconds as he gnawed on his inner cheek, having trouble with the thoughts tumbling around in his mind. Having Gabby in his arms had chased away the demons that haunted him at night. He couldn't remember the last time he had slept so soundly.

"What is this?" *Abuelo's* voice suddenly cut through the air, and the expression on Gabby's face would have been comical if he, too, wasn't suddenly feeling apprehensive.

He looked up slowly and saw the glare of the lamplight first before the angry glare of Gabby's grandfather. Before he could gain his feet, Gabby turned, and the blankets yanked from underneath him, causing him to tumble disgracefully to the floor.

"Young man, what is the meaning of this?"

"*Abuelo*—"

"Gabby, let me—" Luke attempted to stop her.

"—it is completely innocent. We fell asleep after working on the decorations—"

"Gabriella, I didn't ask you."

Abuelo's eyes were still fixated on Luke, who had been wondering how to gently tell Gabby to keep her mouth shut and that he could defend them. "It was a poor choice, sir. My sincere apologies. I can assure you, though, there were no improprieties…"

Her grandfather's eye ticked. "Go freshen yourself, Gabby. Luke, I expect to see you outside shortly."

Luke extended a hand to Gabby, and her eyes searched his face with curiosity, and the hint of an apology. He helped her to her feet and even lifted the door to the cellar for her to climb down, all under the watchful eyes of her *abuelo*. Once he lowered the door he stood to face the old man.

"You freshen up, too. Then come meet me outside."

Luke did his best to keep his face calm. "Yes, sir." He

nodded. Only a couple of weeks in America and he may have just earned a death sentence.

RAPHAEL'S FACE WAS almost purple with fury when Luke finally went outside. He could tell that somehow *Abuelo* had revealed to him what had happened, and he was fighting mad about it. Even in the cold weather he had removed his jacket and was pacing back and forth in front of the pit while the other male family members tried to calm him down.

Luke wasn't worried about Raphael. He'd beaten men twice his size in London and only had a few bruises at the end of it all. But he didn't want to beat down Raphael. He was Gabby's brother, and it would hurt her to see or know such a thing had happened. But as he came down the steps, there was one thing he suddenly realized he needed to be very afraid of.

Gabby's grandfather sat in one of the chairs, polishing one of his shotguns. As Luke's feet hit the ground, he opened the chambers and loaded, then cocked it and kept it across his lap. Slowly his eyes lifted to Luke's. "Go get your horse, son. Mine, too. We need to do a bit of hunting this morning."

Raphael stopped in his tracks and glared at Luke as he passed by, clenching and unclenching his fists. But Luke ignored him and instead focused on going to get the horses saddled and ready. *Hunting? At this hour in the morning? Or is the old man just planning to kill me?*

In a shorter amount of time than Luke would have liked, the horses were ready and Grandpa Torres and he were riding away from town. Luke desperately wanted to ask what they were hunting for, but felt, at the moment, it was best for him to keep his mouth shut. He had just been found asleep on the couch with the man's granddaughter. And this man was as strict about following the rules of propriety and traditions as he was about his religion. Luke swallowed hard and tried to focus on their path in case he needed to crawl back later.

The only sound was the creaking of the cold leather and the groan of the icy tree limbs above them. Occasionally the sound of wind blowing through the branches and dry grass would whisper at his ear, but other than that, silence.

"The conditions are perfect."

Luke almost jumped out of the saddle when the old man spoke, and he tried to calm his nerves. "Perfect for what, sir?"

"A fresh kill."

Luke wanted to find a church. He wanted to confess all of his sins so he could go to heaven, given that he was about to die. He cleared his throat slightly and shifted in the saddle, but didn't say anything. "Ah. Sounds—invigorating. I don't have much experience with killi—I mean hunting."

The old man grunted. "Don't you hunt over in England? You must in order to have food."

Luke cleared his throat again. "I'm sure they do, sir. I lived in a large city. We didn't hunt there." At least not the type of hunting that involved an animal to feed a family. No, there was a far different kind of hunting that went on in the slums of London.

"You strike me as the type that would be quite a good hunter," the old man said, then casually pulled a pipe out of his coat pocket and prepared the tobacco in it.

"Won't the scent drive away the game you are trying to catch?" Luke asked, before realizing it would be best not to judge the expert, especially when the expert held a loaded gun across his lap and already had at least one reason to see him dead.

"See, I knew you would have a knack for it," he said as he carefully lit the pipe, drawing deep on it, and the sweet-sour smell filled the air around them. "But you see, son, we're downwind of any animal right now. They won't be able to smell us. That's your first lesson."

Lesson? Was this old man really going to teach him how to hunt? Or was he just leading him on until he was ready to finally get it over with? Luke tilted his head to the side and felt the muscles in his neck pop from stress. *God, help me.*

"What exactly is it that we are hunting today?" Luke asked hesitantly, watching the old man's face closely.

There was an odd sound, a raspy, almost wheezing sound and Luke suddenly realized it was the old man laughing. He turned and looked at Luke with eyes that had seen more and experienced more than Luke probably ever would. "You should have seen the look on your face when you saw me with my gun." He laughed a little harder, pulling his pipe out of his mouth momentarily, then putting it back so he could puff on it.

"I'm sorry, sir, but I don't quite understand…"

"Of course you don't understand!" He chuckled some more. "Now, son, I've got to be serious with you. I wasn't all that happy to find my granddaughter lying on a couch with you this morning. No, it didn't please me at all. But—" he paused for a long minute, taking several puffs on his pipe "—I trust my granddaughter. And when she tells us that it was innocent, I believe her."

Luke felt the vise on his heart begin to loosen slightly. But only slightly. Because the old man still held his gun across his lap and hadn't told him what they were hunting today.

"Today, young man, we're going to go hunting for some wisdom. It's not an easy thing to find, and it will take you years to get most of it figured out. But, you're new here. And it's going to take a lot of wisdom for you to survive Texas. So I think today is a good day to get started. What do you say?"

"Yes, sir, of course."

"And enough of that 'sir' crap. Makes me feel old. My name is Tomas. Remember it. Say it when you really need to talk to me. Otherwise, just give me food and good drink, and I'll be happy and I won't bother you."

"Sir—Tomas, why have you decided I'm worthy of your wisdom? I am very honored, but I'm not one of your children; I'm not part of your family."

"The term family isn't always about blood. You know that, don't you?"

Visions of London flashed through his mind and he pressed his eyes closed for several moments. His understanding of family was very different than what most people would think. Finally: "I've heard the term family used in many different ways before."

"You're too young to carry the burdens that you do. I see it haunt you in your eyes. And it will haunt you the rest of your days. It is like an illness that must be cut out, and you can only do that by sharing it with someone else."

"Tomas, you don't know me. You don't know the things I've done in my past. I'm not worthy of your time, and certainly not your wisdom."

"Ah, humility is a good characteristic. Now, Doctor Davenport, tell me how you would treat an illness that festers and feeds on someone."

Luke looked down at his hands that held the reins of his horse. "It isn't that simple," he said, unable to look up and make eye contact with Tomas. "If I could cut it out, I would. In a heartbeat. But they are memories, actions, things that cannot be undone. If I cannot forgive myself, how can I ever ask anyone else to do so?"

"Now there is a tidbit of wisdom. Something you should think about as you continue in Gabriella's life, if that's an idea you're entertaining. I believe you have touched the heart of my granddaughter, something I feared would never happen. But if you want to love fully, and be loved fully in return, there must be honesty between both of you. You cannot hide your past. It will always come back to haunt you. Do you want it to come back and haunt her as well?"

"No!" His reply was so sharp the horses startled and the old man nearly lost his grip on the shotgun. Once they had the horses under control again, the old man let out his raspy, wheezing laugh.

"You almost got what you thought was coming your way," he chuckled. "I almost shot you."

Both men laughed together, before finally catching their breath and enjoying the silence once again. "You know," Tomas began after several minutes, "I used to explore these woods up here when I was younger. I learned a lot from listening to the wind and the trees. I went up there when I was mad, or sad, or confused, or just needed to get away from it all. I think, if you are ready, we will find some wisdom there today."

Luke swallowed hard. Was he ready? What would he tell Tomas? There was so much that had happened in his life... But he didn't hesitate to urge his horse forward, and ride to the tree line with Tomas. It was time.

Chapter Five

G ABBY TOOK HER time running the brush through the luxuriously thick hair, marveling at the way it caught the light and shimmered. "You certainly received the gift of beautiful hair," she said softly.

Olivia sighed. "Thank you, Gabby. Let's hope the babe receives the same. Doyle certainly has the gift of some wonderful hair. And a frightful loud yell, too." She chuckled.

"With his yell we could have held off the Mexican Army for days." Gabby laughed in return.

Olivia sighed again. "I don't want to sound ungrateful, but you don't need to fuss over me. How long are you and the doctor going to keep me trapped in this bed, anyway? It's already going on the third day."

"As long as your body needs it," a male voice answered from the doorway, and Gabby looked up in excitement and surprise upon hearing Luke's voice. From the way her *abuelo* had been acting, she wasn't certain he would survive the morning.

But he had, and her heart beat faster as she looked at his tall frame, leaning against the doorjamb, his coat over one arm and his hands in his pockets. He looked so casual, so at ease, and she desperately wanted to go to him and brush away the lock of hair that had fallen forward on his forehead.

He had treated her with such kindness the night before. She couldn't remember the last time someone had taken care of her. But it had been incredible, and she couldn't help but imagine what it would be like to have someone to share her burdens with.

You want him. He just doesn't want you. Her subconscious hit her like a splash of cold water and she stood and turned to face Olivia, regretfully taking her eyes off the disarming doctor.

"You'll need to stay in bed for a while longer. This babe is determined to give you a tough go of it. I certainly hope its temperament changes once it lets loose the first cry." She smiled at her cousin and eased her back down on the bed. "Don't worry, Olivia. You'll be back on your feet in no time at all."

"You say that, but I'm wondering if I should trust either of you," Olivia grumbled, then sighed as she settled comfortably back in bed.

Gabby walked towards the doorway and Luke moved out of her way as she closed the door gently. "I doubt we'll be able to let her on her feet until the babe comes, or at least until it turns."

Luke nodded. "I agree. She doesn't have much longer to go. Let's hope that babe starts moving quickly."

Gabby nodded and they turned away from Olivia's room. She could feel Luke watching her, but she didn't want to look up at him. She was worried she would see disappointment in his eyes, disappointment that she hadn't tried harder to protect him from her grandfather.

"I certainly didn't expect to see you up and about this early," Angie's cheerful voice greeted them as they came out into the dining room. Angie's smile was bright, and welcoming.

Gabby couldn't help but smile in return. "You know I've never been one to sleep late." She glanced over at Luke who also had a smile on his face. "Besides, you need the help to get ready for the morning meal."

"What about you, Luke? What are you going to do today?"

"I need to go check the clinic and see how much progress they've made in the repairs."

Gabby's head whipped in his direction and she hoped the longing she felt didn't show on her face. She would love to go to his clinic, and see if he truly was different than the other doctors she'd met and heard about.

He glanced over at her but his expression was passive. She turned back to face Angie and began to walk towards the kitchen. "I suppose I'll start the tortillas." She could feel Luke's eyes boring into her back and she maintained a poised posture. She wouldn't let him know how badly she wanted to be with him. She didn't want to admit to herself how much she wanted to be with him.

❦

LUKE DECIDED TO help the men prepare the meat for the

morning meals, and found himself in charge of the large pit as Raphael and Lorenzo stood huddled together nearby, trying to stay warm. Cade and Trevor were both at the jail working. While Cade was officially the town Sheriff, Trevor liked to help whenever he came in to see the family. As a Texas Ranger, Trevor knew his fair share of Texas law.

"Does she really expect us to put up all of the Christmas decorations today?" Raphael asked, frustration in his voice.

"She spent nearly all night making them. I think that, at the very least, we should get those decorations up," Luke said, coming across a little harsher than he had intended.

Lorenzo and Raphael turned their attention on him. "We know she did, Luke. We'll put them up; it's just a real pain in the neck." Raphael frowned at him.

"She just seems so determined to make this a perfect Christmas," Luke said, lifting the lid to the pit and turning the meat.

Lorenzo and Raphael chuckled. "That's the way she is every Christmas. And every Christmas she goes to the market and spends her money on all the decorations, and then special little gifts for everyone. She refuses to let us pay for a thing. Why do you think we were so frustrated with her when she came home with that wagon loaded with food and decorating supplies yesterday?" Lorenzo asked.

Luke looked back at the now closed pit lid, frowning. *She spends her own money?* He had never known someone to be so generous. He looked to Raphael, who simply shrugged at him. "She earns the money throughout the year. It is only fair for her to spend it the way she wants."

"Christmas is extremely important to Gabby," Raphael continued, rubbing his hands over the warm smoke coming out of the pit. "Family is very important to her. So when it comes to this time of year, she can be very intense."

"Why? I've never celebrated Christmas. What can be so special about it?"

"You've never celebrated Christmas?" Gabby's incredulous voice at the back door drew their attention. "How is that even possible? I know they celebrate Christmas in England!"

Luke looked with trepidation at Gabby. He had never wanted her to know, for he had feared just such a reaction from her. She descended the steps to the pit and stood staring up at him. "And just how long were you going to wait before telling me such a thing?"

"I didn't think you needed to know. It's really not that important."

"It's very important. What do you mean you've never celebrated Christmas? Aren't you Christian?"

Luke regretted having said anything about Gabby's decorations, her role in the family Christmas celebrations, or anything about Christmas at all. "Of course I am. But I just never had exposure to Christmas, unfortunately."

"How do you not have exposure to Christmas? I don't understand." Gabby was watching him with intent and even sympathy, the last thing he wanted.

"Gabby, you have no reason to concern yourself with my experience of Christmas. I look forward to seeing it celebrated here in San Antonio."

She chewed on her lower lip as she stared up at him, then without another word, turned and headed back into the house. Luke wanted to curse out loud, but he couldn't forget that the rest of her family was still surrounding him, and he wouldn't embarrass himself...or her for that matter. It was the truth—he didn't understand why Christmas was so special to her. But, perhaps, if he had grown up in an environment where there was an emphasis on Christmas as a joy instead of a reminder of pain and loss, he would be just as excited as she.

She was disappointed—he could tell. She wanted him to be just as excited as she was, and she wanted to share her joy of Christmas. But he had thrown it back at her. And he'd felt like a heel as she'd walked away from him.

He turned back to the pit and realized the other men were watching him with curiosity. "It's a long story, and not one worth being told," he said, trying to put closure on the subject.

It was almost humorous as they lifted their eyebrows, then shrugged and returned to trying to warm themselves by the fire. "We'll get the decorations out today," Lorenzo said, his tone reserved.

Luke nodded. "I hope to be back soon enough to help. I'm going to the clinic today to see how much work has been completed."

Lorenzo cleared his throat. "Not as much as you'd like, I'm certain. They've been trying to get the area cleared up in their spare time, but with the holidays, everyone has been otherwise occupied."

Luke's grip on the tongs tightened in frustration. "Then I'll do what I can, as well."

"Just be careful. There's a lot of broken glass and wood blocks that are threatening to fall. None of it is structural, but it could be dangerous if any of it shifts unexpectedly."

Luke nodded, his eyes darting to the back door where he wished he could see Gabby. "I'll make do just fine," he said, and wished desperately he could find a way to make things right with Gabby once again.

MORNING SERVICE SEEMED to crawl by. Why wouldn't he have told her about never experiencing Christmas? It didn't make any sense. Surely he could tell how important Christmas was to her. Surely he could understand why she was so shocked by his comment. And, yet, he had told her it was nothing.

Gabby concentrated on keeping fresh tortillas coming out and delivering coffee and water refills to the patrons. She avoided any interaction with the men as they brought in the meat, not wanting to encounter Luke. She wondered what else about himself he was keeping hidden from her. She didn't truly know the man, but it certainly felt like she did.

The few short days they'd had together so far had come and gone with them working together closely, and she had been her true self with him. Well, almost her true self. If he was only hiding that he'd never experienced Christmas, he was keeping far fewer secrets than she was. By the time morning sup had ended, she was feeling very much like a hypocrite. She wanted to apologize to Luke, but she didn't know what she'd even say. *Sorry I'm so self-absorbed I can't understand how anyone could not love Christmas as much as I do.* What if someone he loved had died at Christmas? What if something terrible had happened to him around Christmas, and he just wanted to avoid the terrible memories? What if—

"I'm leaving for the clinic now. I was hop... I was wondering if you would like to go with me. It could prove profusely helpful to have someone knowledgeable in the basics of medicine to help me sort through the damage."

Gabby prayed that her face wasn't showing her excitement. "Of course. I'll be glad to assist in any way possible." She did her best to maintain a serious tone, but even she could hear the slight uptick in her voice. It was exactly what she had been hoping he would ask.

She dried her hands on the towel she had tossed over her shoulder, pleased she had at least finished washing the plates and mugs so they would be ready when lunch service began. "Just let me gather a few things and I'll be ready to leave."

He nodded, but avoided making eye contact with her. *Did I hurt his feelings earlier? Or did I probe into an old wound?* Regardless of his secret, it was none of her business. She needed to remember he was a guest for the time being, and her curiosity was not appropriate. Though it was driving her crazy with all the questions floating around in her mind.

She rushed down to the cellar and gathered her medical bag and her hat and gloves. After nearly freezing that morning when she had briefly stepped outside, she wasn't going out into the cold unprepared again. Donning her oversized cloak, she said goodbye to her cousins quickly, told Raphael not to worry about her, and nodded to Luke as he held the door open for her.

She began to turn to the small stables at the rear of the house to get their horses, but Luke caught her arm and began to lead her down the sidewalk. "The clinic isn't too far from here," he said lightly. "A good walk will warm us up and is also good for the health."

She lifted an eyebrow at him. "I've never met a doctor who encourages walking for health, though it is something I encourage frequently. Now, as far as warming us up..." a cold wind whipped around them and almost felt like it went through them "...I'm not sure we'll achieve that objective."

A smile broke out on his features, the first she had seen since earlier in the morning. Maybe he had forgiven her for probing into his lack of Christmas cheer. "You'd be just as cold, if not more so, sitting high on a horse. No, walking is ideal."

She nodded and wondered if he realized he still had his arm linked with hers. Even through the fabric of her cloak and the thickness of his jacket she could feel his muscles, and she was fascinated by the feel of them rippling and moving as they walked. All of her brothers were strong, but their muscles had never fascinated her.

"What-all do you know about the City of San Antonio?" he asked casually, in an awkward attempt at conversation.

Gabby looked down at her feet, trying not to smile at his

attempt. "I've lived in San Antonio most of my life. It wasn't until about five years ago that my father inherited a large cattle ranch in Corpus Christi. We moved out there right as the Revolution was getting off the ground. I suppose it was a blessing, though I didn't see it that way at the time. I hated leaving San Antonio."

"Because of all of your family here?"

"That's part of it. But I also had a lot of friends, and my mother was being recognized as a good healer and she was finally pulling in income. We didn't have much money to begin with, but every little bit helped."

His eyebrows lifted, but he didn't say anything, just let her keep talking. "But no matter how long I've been away— San Antonio is still home. It has changed so much now, though. It used to have tons of Mexican soldiers patrolling the streets and enforcing their version of the law. They once came to our house and tried to accuse my mother of being a witch because she was healing people. I thought they were going to kill her."

Luke looked down at her, his brow furrowed. "What did she do? How did she escape with her life?"

Gabby smiled, picturing her mother's face, hearing her mother's voice, feeling her kind and gentle touch guiding her as she learned the role of being a healer, too. "My mother was an incredible woman. She invited a few of the soldiers to come into our home and have some fresh tortillas and honey. Only three of the soldiers would fit in our small home, and those who didn't get to go inside seemed upset. I don't know if it was because they were missing out on the tortillas and honey or the possibility of seeing a real witch's lair." Gabby laughed softly. "It truly was a sight to see."

"So she convinced them with food that she wasn't a witch?" Luke asked, shocked.

"No, though that certainly helped warm them up to her. Once they were seated and eating, she brought out her books and showed them the pictures she had drawn of various plants and all of the notes she had taken over the years. Then she showed them her homemade medicines, and even pointed out that the honey they were eating was good for their throats and the cough that had been plaguing the soldiers over the last several weeks.

"When she took them out to the back of the house and showed them her small garden that had many of the plants they had seen drawn in her book, they seemed reassured. One of the soldiers even asked her for something for a poison ivy rash that was bothering him so much."

"Unbelievable! They were about to imprison her or harm her under the suspicion of being a witch, and she used honey and tortillas to change their minds."

Gabby laughed. "If that's how you choose to see it. I think that her ability to show them her research, and the actual plants that she used made it easier for them to understand what she was doing."

Luke smiled at her but shook his head. "I've heard so many stories, so many things about healers that I don't know what to think about all of it."

Gabby sighed. "I'm sure you've heard many of the scary stories and the ones that make you cringe thinking I'm one of those types of people. There are people who call themselves healers who do terrible things and are nothing better than con artists. All they want is the hard-earned money families have gathered, and then they sell them a concoction that usually only makes them more ill. Then they make more money and give them some other concoction. Those are the healers who make people like me struggle to find acceptance."

He watched her closely for several more moments, then turned his eyes back to the street. "Why does it bother you so much that I've never had a Christmas?"

Gabby's footsteps hesitated, then continued forward to match his long strides as best she could. "Christmas is a magical experience. It was when our savior was born, and we get to celebrate it in such amazing ways."

"Such as decorating the home to the point that you exhaust yourself and nearly collapse in the middle of the night?"

"Oh, that isn't unusual for me." She laughed, then drew a deep breath. "The unusual part was to have a handsome man whisk me off my feet and lull me to sleep. Usually I just stumble to the room on my own just fine."

"I—I shouldn't have. I just wanted…you take care of everyone around you. You help the family with their business, then with their health, then with their children, then with the decorating. Who takes care of you? Who makes sure you get a break and that you feel special and loved the way you make all of them feel?"

Gabby looked at him, knowing her eyes were wide. "Is

that truly how you see me?"

"Is that a bad thing?" His eyes were searching her face intently, watching her reaction to all that he had said.

"N-no. No. It's wonderful. I never thought of myself in that way. I just do what anyone in the family would do."

"You do far more. You do realize how much they treasure you, don't you?"

Gabby smiled and lowered her head, once again watching her feet. "I pray for such a thing. My whole life, all I've wanted is to be with my family. To be surrounded by their love and able to give all of mine."

An odd look crossed his face, and she could tell he was about to say something, but then drew himself up short. "We're here," he said, gesturing across the street to the clinic.

Even from where they stood, Gabby could see the place was in a terrible condition. The sign listing it as the doctor's office was hanging loose on one side. Two of the windows at the front of the building had been broken, and inside it was obviously cluttered and chaotic.

Luke shook his head. "I shouldn't have brought you. I didn't realize it would still be in such bad shape." He turned, as though to take her home, but she kept her feet firmly rooted to the spot.

"I'd say we have a lot of work to do, and not much time for you to walk me back home. Now, Doc, what do we tackle first?"

Chapter Six

H E WAS GETTING too close. But she was like a flame and he felt like the moth, destined to be lured by her tempting light. Why was she still a single woman? Why hadn't someone already claimed her as his wife?

The questions plagued him as they worked on cleaning the clinic. It appeared as if it hadn't been used in a very long time, and all of the equipment was either rusted, broken, or outdated. He was glad he had saved up a tiny nest egg for just such a time when he would need to purchase equipment. Now would be the time.

Gabby worked alongside him at first, sweeping up the broken glass and layers of dust on the floor. The room was cold with the windows busted open, and she found a couple of spare blankets that they pinned to the walls, covering the cold draft and allowing the room to warm slightly.

Though they were quiet as they worked, they seemed in synch with each other. As soon as he began to clear items off to the side so he could work on the fireplace, she went to nearby shops and convinced them to donate some wood and kindling for them to use. He had just finished cleaning out the fireplace when she arrived with some flint and extra kindling.

Together they built the fire and Luke struck the flint only a few times and the kindling caught. They sat back and smiled as the warm flames jumped to life, dancing within the fireplace. Luke wanted to pull Gabby closer to him, to have her head rest on his shoulder as they watched the flames. But he had learned many things that morning from her grandfather, and making impetuous decisions wasn't one of them.

Could this possibly be happening to him? He'd wished for it all of his life, but it had seemed out of his reach. To have a woman to hold, to have someone who cared for him, cared about him, and with it came an instant family large enough to make up for all the many lonely years he had struggled against...

"I hardly know you, and yet I feel as if you've been in my life forever. How can that be?" Gabby turned her face to look up at him, but he continued staring into the dancing flames.

After several long moments of silence, he spoke softly, keeping the intimate atmosphere they were in. "It is an odd feeling, isn't it? I know some things about you, but it is as if my soul has known you for a very, very long time." Should he reach for her? She was practically giving him permission.

Slowly he reached his arm around her, and she didn't pull back. He pulled her up close against his side and he smiled to himself at her contented sigh. He turned his head to look down at her, and her lips were too tempting to pass up. He lowered his head to hers and gently pressed his lips against hers, moving them slowly and gently. At first she seemed nervous and timid, but the longer his lips gently persisted, the more willing and pliant and eager she became.

He pulled back slightly and pressed his forehead against hers, his eyes closed. "You must truly be a vixen. You draw me to you in such a way…"

"It is the same for me," she said softly, then suddenly pulled away from him and stood. "We still have much work to do." There was a slight waver in her voice. *What had scared her away from him? What had he done?*

"You are the most perplexing woman I have ever met," he muttered, shaking his head. He had moved too quickly. The kiss had been too much, and he had frightened her. But he didn't regret it. He could still taste her on his lips.

"What have I done to you to make you so curt with me? Only a few moments ago we were enjoying a moment in front of the fire, and now you stand away from me, as if to touch me would curse you. Why? Why do you act so odd with me?" He couldn't resist asking her.

Tears brimmed in her eyes, but she shook her head, refusing to let them fall. "There can't be this…this between us." She gestured between the two of them. "You are charming, and smart, and…well, and handsome. I can't let this happen."

"Can't let what happen?"

"I can't have feelings for you. I mustn't. My brothers…the ranch…it's all just too much, don't you understand?"

He placed his hands on his hips and chewed on the inside of his cheek. *This woman is going to be the death of me.* "No. I don't understand. What are you scared of?"

She kept shaking her head. "Nothing. Nothing. I shouldn't have let this happen and it is my fault. You could have any woman in the world. Don't settle with me...you will regret it."

Luke ran his hands through his hair, dislodging his hat. "You are the most perplexing... I don't understand you. One moment you seem to be happy in my arms, the next, you spring away from me like I'm some sort of monster. And you've done nothing to adequately explain your actions."

She turned from him and began to move some of the debris around. "We don't have much time left in the day, and we must get your clinic clean. You'll have patients soon, and soon, more than you expected."

Luke slowly counted to ten. He didn't know why he was pursuing the matter with her so hard in the first place. He didn't want a woman to tie him down, and he knew that he couldn't give a woman the love she needed. And if they had children...God, if he had children with Gabby, they would be the most beautiful treasures on earth. But he wouldn't have anything to offer them. He was empty, devoid of anything that a father should have to give to his children.

If she knew the truth about his past—if she knew the things he had done, she would run from him even faster. It was for the best that she didn't want to be with him, though his heart railed against his mind. They were good together.

Are you? Are you truly good with her? Or do you simply enjoy kissing her and touching her and the comfort of a willing woman in your arms? Aren't you just using her to get what you want, what you need, for right now, and to hell with what happens later?

Luke turned his attention to cleaning up more of the mess that was to be his new clinic. He couldn't argue with her anymore, especially when he was already arguing with himself. In silence they worked until the sun dipped lower in the sky and the fire was small, burning embers. There was still so much that needed to be done, but he knew he would come back again the next day. This time, without Gabby as a distraction.

"Well, we accomplished a lot for one day," Gabby said with false cheerfulness in her voice, but he could tell she was hurting by the look in her eyes.

"Many thanks to you for helping me." He nodded to her, hoping that his eyes didn't reflect the same hurt.

"I think we'll have it up and running within the next couple of days. But I don't know about your living quarters. How badly is that area damaged?"

"Far worse than this. They'll need to replace part of the roof."

"Perhaps over the weekend the boys can help you with that project." She smiled at him, and it was one of her genuine, kind smiles—the type that always made him smile in return. Yet, this time, he couldn't bring himself to do so.

"Your family has already done more than enough for me. I cannot ask for anything more."

She tilted her head and looked at him with curious eyes, eyes that he feared could see his soul. "You aren't used to anyone helping you, are you?"

"No," he replied. "I'm used to people running away from

me." He hadn't meant the last comment as a barb at her, but by the look that crossed her face, he could tell she received it as such. What did she want from him? "It's late. We should get back home."

Home. He hadn't had a place to call home in his entire life. And now he was referring to the Torres family home as his own. It felt like what he imagined a home would feel like. It was warm, and inviting, and there was love and laughter everywhere. Maybe being in that environment was what had put the insane thought into his mind that he could actually have something with Gabby. He was feeling content, and peaceful, and joyful...all things he had only dreamed of. And he had dreamed of a wife like Gabby. But some dreams weren't meant to come true.

"Yes," she said softly, her voice thick with unshed tears, and her chin trembling with the effort not to cry. "Let's go home."

THE MEN HAD put up all of the decorations she had made, and the poinsettias had arrived. Obviously the men had no idea what to do with them as they were all piled to one side of the porch. Gabby paused outside the house, standing directly in front of it, and smiled.

With the glow of the lamplight inside the house, the decorations stood out beautifully in the semi-darkness. The cold in the air would keep the greenery fresh through Christmas, though she worried about the poinsettias. Having been grown in Mexico where it was always warmer, they could possibly struggle in their cooler Christmas.

She hadn't realized she had been standing in front of the house for so long until Luke touched her elbow lightly to draw her attention. "You don't plan on putting the poinsettias out today, do you?"

"Oh," Gabby said in surprise, realizing she had been thinking of doing just that and realized how foolish she was being. "No, no, of course not. I was just deciding where I'd put them and all of the many things still left to be done."

Luke nodded and began to turn from her before she caught his arm, turning him back to face her. "Luke..." She hesitated, trying to think of the right words to say.

"Don't," he said, shaking his head. "There is nothing to be said about today." But she could see the pain in his eyes, and knew she had caused it. And she needed to fix things.

"I'm sorry for this afternoon. I have been alone for a very long time. I've had very protective older brothers who made certain I was never around any man. You are the first man I've ever kissed...the first man I've ever held...the first man in my life who isn't a bossy older brother."

"You've never been kissed before?" he asked, his tone incredulous.

"No. Never. And you make me feel things I've never felt before. You make me feel beautiful and...well, and attractive. I never thought I'd get to feel those things, and for that I am very grateful."

"You are beautiful, Gabriella. More beautiful than you realize. And it isn't just your outer beauty. You've got the biggest heart—you always give so much of yourself and expect nothing in return." He took a step towards her, close enough that he could look down at her, and he smiled slightly as he tilted her hat on her head. "You make me dream of things I never thought possible."

"Why? Why don't you think it possible? You can have any woman you want. I know you are lonely now having just left London. But you can't just settle with me. There is someone far better for you—someone elegant and sophisticated. Being the doctor for the town means you need a certain level of prestige. You won't have that if you settle for me. Even if you settle for me for just a short while until the right person comes along."

"Do you think so little of me? Do you think that I would toy with your affections until another woman came into my life? The heart is a delicate thing to trifle with. And I could never trifle with yours."

She watched him closely and saw the sincerity across his face. "I know we won't have much time together. Your living quarters will be prepared soon enough, and I'm only here until Olivia has her baby. Will you let me teach you about Christmas? Will you let me share that joy with you?"

He drew a deep breath and then a slow smile spread across his face. "Yes, Vixen. Teach me about Christmas. Show me why it is as magical as you seem to think it is."

"DO YOU KNOW why poinsettias are the Christmas flower?"

Gabby's excitement and passion for everything Christmas was contagious, and Luke smiled as he continued arranging the poinsettias on the porch the way she instructed. "No. I've never even seen a poinsettia before. They are beautiful flowers."

Smiling broadly, Gabby picked up one of the poinsettias and brought it over to him. "Do you see the cluster of petals? Look at it closely."

Luke couldn't resist leaning over her and smelling her hair as he looked at the flower she held out for him to see. Being with her was what he would remember about Christmas.

"It almost looks like a star, right? We believe that the poinsettia represents the star that was above Jerusalem, guiding the shepherds to baby Jesus. Can you see it?"

Luke smiled down at her. "Yes, I can see it now. It is gorgeous."

Gabby continued smiling, then turned and went back to work positioning the poinsettias. "You'll learn that there is a story behind everything that we do. Some of the stories are merely traditions that have been passed down over the generations from our ancestors. Others are rooted in the teachings of the church and the Bible. But every single thing we do for Christmas has a special story behind it."

Stories. Luke had heard many stories in his life, and had a story to tell of his own one day. But not today. One day he would share with someone all that his life in London had been. And one day he would have someone embrace him for who he was, flaws and all.

"Luke? Luke? Are you all right?"

Luke snapped out of his memories and was immediately in the present with Gabby. "Apologies," he said quickly. "My mind just wandered."

"You were far away," she commented. She took the last poinsettia out of his hands and placed it in the space she had saved for it. The porch now had a walkway of red leading up to the front door, where her wreath and large swag of greenery were hung. She smiled with delight, and Luke couldn't take his eyes off her.

Is it just because it's Christmas or does she always glow like that? he wondered as he saw her excitement at having completed the decorations. Or so he had thought.

"The luminaries are the easiest of all the things to make and you'll love them when you see them lit. And given how cold it is, I'm thinking cutting out snowflake patterns will give it that special touch."

"You want to do *more* decorations?"

Gabby shook her head at him. "You have no idea what you are about to experience."

He wanted to touch her. He wanted to feel the warmth that was shining from within her. But he had to stop. At some point she would find out about the man he really was, and she'd be horrified. She deserved a man far better than he. He glanced to the sky and prayed silently. *Please, Lord, finish my living quarters soon. If not, I may not be able to control myself when it comes to this woman. Lord, help me!*

Chapter Seven

L UKE WAS MOVING quickly, carefully folding the white paper into the perfect box shape so the snowflake was displayed boldly. Gabby smiled to herself as she continued cutting out the snowflakes, enjoying the look of pride on Luke's face with each completed luminary. They were almost halfway complete—they only had about twenty more to go.

The house was already quiet since the family had retired to their bedrooms for the night. Olivia had even gotten up to come and see how the decorations were progressing, and both Gabby and Luke fussed over her as she stepped outside and out into the road to see the full effect.

"Oh, Gabby, you always make it so beautiful. I don't know what I would do without you."

Gabby had blushed deeply, then urged her back into the house where it was warm. Once they had her back in bed, Luke and Gabby examined her together—Luke checked the baby's size and position from her belly while Gabby examined her more intimate areas.

"It's so nice to see the two of you working together," Olivia had said as they finished their examinations. "You make a great team."

Luke had looked over at Gabby, a rakish smile on his face. "Yes, I suppose we do. The healer working with the doctor. Who would have ever thought?"

"I believe you have that backwards. It is more of the doctor working with the healer. Don't forget, I'm in charge of things for Olivia."

He had only continued smiling at her. After reassuring Olivia that all was fine with the baby, they had washed up and left the room to begin making the luminaries. Now that the house was silent, they were able to talk.

"The babe still hasn't turned," Luke said, momentarily pausing from the work he was doing to look at Gabby, a frown on his face.

Gabby hesitated as she was cutting, then resumed, trying not to let his comment upset her. "I know. And her body is already preparing for the birth of the child. It could be here before Christmas if she doesn't do as we've been telling her."

"You think she's been getting up and doing things without us knowing?"

"It wouldn't surprise me. I was gone all day with you yesterday—she could have been up and about without us to put her back to bed." Gabby was having a hard time focusing on her cutting.

"Don't you think Cade would have stopped her? He is just as worried as we are."

"You don't know the Torres family very well. We tend to be a very stubborn bunch and we don't take orders easily."

"I would have never guessed," he said sarcastically.

Gabby looked up from her work at him and crossed her

eyes. "You needn't be rude."

He chuckled as he finished folding another luminary. "Such a lovely face. You should do that more often."

"I have been told how beguiling I can be," she said with a smile, turning back to her work. "Though that is usually only when I have a bag over my head."

Luke shook his head. "Whatever made you think you aren't beautiful? Or *who* made you think that? I'll go and challenge him to a duel immediately."

"A duel? Do you still do such barbaric things in London?"

"A duel is far from barbaric. It is two gentlemen squaring off for the honor of a woman, or their family."

It was Gabby's turn to chuckle. "I had no idea that such a thing was taken so seriously still. I've read about it in some of my books, but I had no idea... See, Doc, I'm learning more from you than I thought I would."

"And you, Vixen, have taught me how to make luminaries! Though I still don't quite understand their purpose."

"We're almost done with them, and then I'll show you," she said, a teasing smile on her lips. But it faded slowly and she returned her attention to cutting out the paper. She shouldn't let him in. She shouldn't let him get so close to her that he made her heart race with excitement and made butterflies dance in her stomach.

All day she had been deprived of his presence. He had been busy with the men preparing all of the meat they would need over the next several days as the festivities really took off in grand fashion.

Now that he was back at her side, all she could think about were the wonderful few moments when she had been in his arms. But she couldn't think about those things. She just couldn't. She would never be able to enjoy his embrace the way she wanted. Instead, she had to fight her true feelings and face the fate that was already determined for her.

She had waited so long, though. A woman could be married as early as sixteen. Why hadn't he come for her, yet? Did he find her repulsive? Had he seen her in town and realized he could never be married to someone like her? The only thing she could think was that it was her appearance. She had never thought of herself as classically beautiful. But she had hoped she would be attractive enough that he would come for her. Now, she was nearly twenty years old and he had yet to come.

"Are snowflakes truly that taxing? I'd say you're going to scare off the paper before you're finished cutting it."

His voice broke into her melancholy and she focused on Luke, forcing a smile to her lips. "We're almost done. And then I'll show you what all of this work has been for."

He raised an eyebrow at her, clearly expecting an explanation from her about her change in mood, but he didn't press her for it. In silence they both finished their tasks, and they finally had all of the luminaries made.

Gabby was almost giddy with excitement. "We'll put them all out tomorrow, but I'll show you one tonight so you can see why it is so special."

She grabbed one of the luminaries, a candle, and a tin box of matches. She was in such a hurry that she grabbed

Luke's hand and forgot to grab her cloak. She hurried down the stairs and pulled Luke along behind her. A few feet away from the foot of the stairs, she set one of his carefully crafted bags on the ground, placed the candle in it, then carefully lit it.

As the light came to life, the image of the snowflake was projected onto the ground, bouncing with each flicker. She turned to look at Luke, knowing that her face was shining just as brightly, if not more so, than the candle she had lit.

He smiled as he stared at the dancing snowflake, and then looked at her. His smile broadened and he reached out to tuck a loose strand of hair behind her ear. "Beautiful," he said softly, and it was obvious he was talking about more than just the luminary.

Gabby could feel the heat of a blush rushing to her cheeks. "Thank you for helping me with all of this. Are you enjoying it? Are you enjoying Christmas?"

He chuckled softly. "With you around, it is hard not to."

Suddenly singing greeted their ears, and Gabby once again grabbed Luke's hand and they stepped out into the street. Several houses down a large group of town members stood outside someone's home, singing sweetly to the residents within.

"What is happening?" Luke asked in wonderment. "Why are they singing outside that home?"

"Tonight is the first night of *Las Posadas*. It is a reenactment of when Joseph and Mary were seeking shelter to give birth to the baby Jesus. The townspeople go to one house and seek shelter. The owner of the home will turn them away, but they will persist through song and prayer. Finally, the owner of the home opens his door and there is a large celebration, or *fandango*."

"To the entire town?"

Gabby looked back at him and laughed. "Why do you think we are preparing so much food and beverages and decorations?"

"The people of the town are going to come to your house? Tonight?"

He almost looked like he was going to be ill and she chuckled, though her teeth were beginning to chatter from the cold. "No, silly. They go to a different home every night. We are hosting on December twenty-first. We still have a few more days to finish all of the preparations."

"What more preparations could you possibly make? You've done everything but put up a Christmas tree."

Gabby tilted her head sideways and studied his face curiously. "A Christmas *tree*? What is such a thing?"

"You've never seen a Christmas tree? How—I mean, surely you've seen them, right? With all of the decorations on them and the candles to light them?"

"I've never even heard of such a thing. Decorating a tree? What if you don't have any trees in your yard?"

He chuckled at her and again reached out to touch her hair. "You find a tree you like and you bring it into your home. When I was in London, I would walk through the neighborhoods of some of the most affluent people and stare into their windows at their trees. They were decorated with ribbons and bows, special garland made out of cranberries and even popcorn, and they were all so stunning."

Gabby filed away in her mind what he had just said. *I would walk through the neighborhoods...* Why didn't he get to see a Christmas tree in his own house? But she knew he would withdraw from her if she tried to ask. So she focused on the other part that was confusing her. "What would they do with these trees? I don't think I quite understand."

"The Christmas celebration was held around the tree. They would open their presents and sing carols around the tree. It all depends on the family."

Gabby wrapped her arms around herself to try to control her shivers. "I've never heard of those customs. It sounds amazing, though."

He smiled down at her and caught her arms, gently turning her around to look back at the *posada* that was finally at the point where the townspeople were being invited into the home. Standing behind her, he wrapped his arms around her offering his own body heat to warm her.

"It's a beautiful thing to watch," he said softly, resting his chin on the top of her head, his arms hugging her tightly.

Gabby swallowed, trying to collect her thoughts. "You're beginning to experience a true Texas Christmas," she said, thrilling at the feel of his arms around her. She knew she should break the embrace and walk away. But she couldn't, not when his arms felt so good. She didn't know if she had the willpower to move.

"Let's get you inside before you shiver to death," he said, the sound of his voice rumbling against her back.

She smiled and pivoted in his arms, facing him with joy

in her heart. "Let's go inside," she agreed with him, and she led the way, pulling him along behind her as she had done earlier.

Once inside, Gabby quickly cleaned the area where they had been working and slowly turned to face him. "Well, I suppose this is where we say good night," she said, praying that the longing in her heart didn't come through in her voice. She didn't want to say good night. She wanted to fall asleep with him on the couch once more. She almost wanted to stand outside again, within the circle of his arms and feeling the warmth of his embrace.

"Today was…it was an incredible experience with you, Gabby. Thank you for sharing everything you love."

Gabby managed to force a smile to her face. "Thank you for letting me. I'm sure my eagerness and excitement can be a bit much to tolerate."

"There's a name for that, you know," he said, and his disarming grin had her falling into his eyes.

"What?" she whispered, not wanting their hushed conversation to end.

"Passion, Vixen. It's called passion. And something tells me you have an abundance of it."

Chapter Eight

MORNING DAWNED WITH fresh frost covering the ground, and many eager customers looking for something to warm them from the inside out. Gabby had lost count of the number of bowls of *menudo* she had brought out to the guests, and they had already gone through three coffee pots.

But even with all of the work, she couldn't contain her joy. Luke had asked her to go back with him to his clinic, to help him continue the repairs and restoration. She had done everything possible not to seem overly excited, but she knew by the look on his face, she hadn't been very successful.

Finally, morning service was complete, and Gabby couldn't get out of her apron fast enough. She tried to dress as meticulously as she could, carefully pulling tendrils of hair loose from her bun on top of her head so that they would frame her face perfectly. Then she donned her cloak, hat, and gloves, even though she knew she would still be chilled to the bone.

They walked the distance to the clinic again and she didn't think twice about linking her arm with his. In fact, she had been looking forward to it, and her heart skipped a beat as his arm moved lower around her waist to guide her across the street to the clinic.

The door creaked open as they stepped inside and they saw that their work from the previous day was largely untouched. One of the blankets covering the broken windows had come loose and cold air was billowing in. Together they worked to tack it back down, then turned to their meager pile of kindling and wood for a fire. It finally caught alight and they turned back to face the room.

"It's a good thing *Abuelo* didn't kill you the other day," Gabby said, casting him a smile from the corner. "Otherwise, who else would clean up this mess?" She kneeled down and began to pick up books that had fallen from an ornately carved bookshelf embedded in the wall. Whoever had built the clinic, had certainly never anticipated it disintegrating into this condition.

She carefully put back each book, dusting the shelf until it had back some of its original luster, then she went in search of a broom while Luke occupied himself with the equipment, hauling most of the rusted and broken items out into the back of the clinic. Included was an entire medical set of tools, a set that would cost a mint were it still in good condition.

Even the bed in the room was destroyed. The frame was so rusted it appeared it could collapse at any moment, and the mattress filling had obviously been, or still was, housing some critters. The stench was almost overbearing, but they managed to get the entire contraption out the back door.

When they turned back, the room was practically empty.

Only the bookcase and a weathered wood desk remained, but Gabby was certain they would be able to restore it easily enough. The floors were swept clean, but not polished, and dust clung to everything around them.

"How long has it been since there was a doctor here?" he asked as he stared around the room.

"I don't think they've had a regular one since before the Revolution. So nearly four years. And each year the doctor who would attempt to hang his shingle here soon left. Texas is usually just a bit too harsh for you city folk." She winked at him, delighted to see that he looked flustered by her action.

She looked around the room, mentally taking inventory. "Okay, then, are you ready to go?"

His head jerked up from where he had been examining the interior of the desk and a plume of dust fluttered up at his movement. His face was so perplexed it was comical. "I'm sorry, 'ready to go?' Exactly where are we going and how would I even know if I am ready?"

Gabby laughed, wrapping her arms around her waist, trying to control the laughter. "Are all people from London this—how would you say it—daft?"

Luke frowned at her. "I don't quite see how this is funny."

Gabby straightened up, barely containing her laughter, and tried to put on a serious face. "Join me, Doctor Davenport. I have mischief up my sleeve and need accompaniment."

An eyebrow shot up as he looked at her, but he walked to

her and formally offered her his arm. She took it with a bright smile on her face and he escorted her out of the clinic. Instantly they were hit with a cold blast of air and they both cringed.

"Are you certain this mischief that is irritatingly persistent must be addressed now?" Luke asked.

Gabby laughed again, and her laugh was caught on the wind and carried down the street. "Do you see how your accent and your speech become much more *English* when you are frustrated? It's your tell."

"My what?"

"Haven't you ever played poker before?"

Both of his eyebrows shot up. "I may have indulged a time or two, but it is certainly not a sport becoming of a woman."

"Oh, that's hogwash. A woman should be allowed to do anything a man does, that's my belief. A 'tell' is a sign of when you are exhibiting an emotion that could give you away in the game. So, if I was playing against you and your English became more pronounced, I would know you were agitated or stressed. That would make me want to bid against you."

"Honestly, you shock me every day that I am with you, Vixen. I can't tell when you are being serious with me or when you are merely playing a prank on me."

"Oh, I rarely tell fibs or play pranks. The truth is always far more fun."

He shook his head and allowed her to lead him to the General Store. It was a relief once they stepped inside, for they had a decent fire burning in the hearth and all of the windows were shut completely. The shutters were open only to allow the sunlight in, and even then, with the dark clouds overhead, they had set up lanterns at various spots throughout the small store.

"Good day, sir, madam," said the man behind the counter, nodding at them. He was of average height and appeared to only be in his forties at the most, but he was mostly bald.

"Hello, Mr. Kerrigan!" Gabby said enthusiastically, dragging Luke with her to meet the owner.

"By golly, is it really you, Miss Gabby? I haven't seen you in so long!" He stepped out from behind his counter and moved to embrace her, but then stopped when he saw Luke. "And you've finally gotten married! Ma, come out here. Miss Gabby is here with her new husband!"

"No, no," Gabby tried to quickly correct him, but Ma came out, wiping her hands on the apron that covered her gingham dress. She was thin, same as Mr. Kerrigan, and had a fierce look about her, but she smiled brightly when she saw Gabby.

"Oh, our sweet Gabby is finally married! We never thought the day would come."

She stepped forward and embraced Gabby, then stepped back, looking Luke up and down. "I must say, you've done a good job in picking one. He appears to be sturdy enough. So, young man, where do you come from, and how did you catch our lovely Gabriella?"

"Mrs. Kerrigan, he isn't my husband."

Both Mrs. Kerrigan and her husband looked startled,

then disappointed. "Oh. Dear child, you're getting older. When are you going to settle down and find a husband? Even your dear mother, God rest her soul, was able to slow down long enough to be caught by your sweet father, God rest his soul."

Luke extended his hand to her. "We haven't met yet," he said lightly. "I'm Doctor Luke Davenport. I just arrived several days ago to become the new town doctor."

"Oh! Doctor Davenport." She gave Gabby a sideways glance. "Are *you* married, Doctor Davenport?"

"No, madam, I am not. Though I have no doubt the right woman will come into my life soon enough." He extended his hand to Mr. Kerrigan and shook it as well.

"Ah-ha," said Mr. Kerrigan. "How are you liking San Antonio so far?"

Luke glanced down at Gabby and she prayed he couldn't see that she was on the verge of tears. She hated being reminded of her age and the fact she needed to find a man and settle down. If only they knew the truth of things—if only they knew her fate had been decided for her long before she ever knew, and that her betrothed had never come to claim her. Then they might have some sympathy for her.

"I love it," Luke said, his voice earnest. "We're working on getting my clinic ready to receive patients. Unfortunately, a storm did some heavy damage to the building, and there are many repairs to be made before we can move forward."

"Then you are staying at the hotel right now? Are they treating you well?"

"He's staying with us," Gabby spoke up, hoping that she,

too, could lighten the mood. "The children love him, and he's so wonderful with Olivia."

Ma Kerrigan looked at her with a strange expression. "But you are the healer. You are the midwife. I don't understand…"

"I'm helping her," Luke said instantly. "She is teaching me some of her healing methods."

"And I am learning some of his ways, as well," Gabby rushed to say.

The two looked at each other and shrugged. "A healer and a doctor working together. Will wonders never cease?" Ma pondered.

"Well, now, surely you've come here for more than just to gossip with us, though we do have so many questions. Doctor, I can tell you aren't from here by your accent—are you from the Northeast?"

Luke chuckled and shook his head. "No, I'm from London."

"All the way from across the pond. I'll be," Mr. Kerrigan pondered.

"All right, enough of all the fuss," Ma proclaimed, clapping her hands quickly. "What can we help you with? What supplies do you need?"

As they moved through the mercantile, Gabby pointed out multiple items that were needed for the clinic, as well as a few cleaning supplies. Then she ordered the new windows and also purchased some of the varnish they had on hand. Luke followed them through the store, his hands behind his back, watching Gabby closely, but his expression was unreadable.

When they came to the counter, Gabby told them to charge everything to the Sheriff's account. Luke began to protest but Gabby turned on him with the fire of determination in her eyes. "Cade promised they were going to take care of the repairs to the facility. He's simply going to charge it to the City. You have nothing to worry about."

Luke frowned deeply for several moments, then nodded in agreement. "I'll agree to it as long as Cade agrees. I'll pay him back any differences I owe."

The owner smiled at him. "A doctor with good ethics. You just may do well here, sir. You may be what we've needed."

"Of course he is," Gabby said with enthusiasm. "He studied at London University. He's one of the most qualified doctors we've ever had. We just need to be sure to keep him happy enough to stay."

"I'm sure a wife will help with that. And then to raise a few little ones… That will make him want to stay for sure." Mrs. Kerrigan was looking directly at Gabby.

Gabby could feel her face turning beet red and gathered a basket of their supplies while Luke gathered two more baskets. "We'll be back to see you soon," Gabby said cheerfully, though she wanted nothing more than to get out of the store before there was any more talk of marriage. She was already facing a destiny she loathed to think about. The last thing she wanted to talk about was marriage.

"THANK YOU," LUKE said softly as they walked back to the clinic in the frigid air.

Gabby looked up at him in surprise. "For what?"

"For praising me. For supporting me. I must admit for a moment there I thought you had come over to my way of thinking and truly believed doctors are good people."

She smiled and looked away from him. "I never said I thought doctors were bad people. I just believe some doctors have no idea how to really treat someone who is ill or injured other than to cut something off."

"But you don't believe that of me?"

"I don't know yet. But I've seen how you are with Olivia. Your hands are gentle, and your manners are soothing. That is something I've never seen in a doctor. And you don't come across as though you are smarter and superior to all the people around you. That's the way most doctors are."

"It would seem you've been around some of the worst of my profession. I've met some doctors like that, but we're not all that way."

She glanced at him sideways, smiling. "Obviously."

He chuckled and wanted nothing more than to press a kiss to her cold cheek. But he needed to slow down. He was moving far too fast with her. So fast that he was at risk of having his heart crushed. Gabby was a fine catch for any man, and he was an outsider. He had lived a life that she might frown upon, or look at it with disdain. He certainly wouldn't blame her. He looked at it that way himself.

They arrived at the clinic, and the first thing Gabby did was pull a can out of one of the baskets and apply oil to the hinges of the door. "We don't want your patients to be scared when they enter through a creaking old door to meet the mean doctor with all the needles and frightening tools."

He smiled at her. "Good thinking. Now, what else do you have planned for us in here?"

For the next hour they spent their time polishing the wood throughout the clinic. Gabby tenderly cared for the desk and it was back in its shining glory quickly. She took one of the baskets and emptied it, then went to her medical bag and began to carefully arrange gauze, medical tape, scissors, and wound packing.

"Gabby, that is yours. I cannot—"

"Yes, it is mine, and I'll do what I please with it. And that is to help set you up for your practice to open."

She finished arranging the basket and looked back at him with a bright smile on her face. "I do believe you are almost ready for patients. We have the bed and mattress on order, we have sheets and blankets already, and of course you'll need whatever odd concoctions of medication you use."

"Odd concoctions?" He shook his head at her. "So this is where we become divided. My belief in medication and your belief in herbal treatments—is that right?"

"Mostly."

"I'm fairly certain we could compare the benefits of the two and find that mine is slightly superior to yours."

"Hah!" Gabby laughed sarcastically. "You medicine simply makes a person numb to all the horrific things you do to them!"

Suddenly there was a pounding on the door. "Doctor? Is

there a doctor here?" came a desperate plea.

Luke and Gabby exchanged glances before he rushed to open the door. A man stood there, holding a boy who was only about eight years of age. At first Luke didn't see the problem. Then, as his eyes traveled down the boy's body, he saw the massive fracture to his arm, with the bone protruding from his forearm and blood dripping on the floor. He had his first patient.

Chapter Nine

G ABBY MOVED QUICKLY, grabbing the chair from behind the desk as well as one of the towels they had just purchased at the mercantile. "Bring him in, quickly," Luke said to the man. The boy looked terrified, but he also looked lethargic, telling Luke that the boy had already lost too much blood.

Gabby held the towel to his arm as they carried him in and set him in the chair. The boy whimpered, but didn't cry out in pain. "What's your name, sweetie?" Gabby asked smiling at the boy as Luke began to examine the injury.

"Elijah," he said softly. "Pa, please don't be mad at me. It was an accident, honest!"

"I know it was, son, I know it was. I'm not mad at you." The father kneeled down and looked at Luke in desperation. "How bad is it? Please tell me you can save his arm. Please."

Gabby's eyes collided with his and he stepped back slowly, showing Gabby the injury. Gabby searched around the wound, holding her breath. She let it out slowly, and Luke felt she had probably come to the same conclusion he had. She tilted her head and looked up at him, her eyes questioning what he was going to do.

"We need to set his arm," he said firmly, and he saw a spark of approval in her eyes.

She went to her medical bag quickly and pulled out a small vial with a milky substance in it. She tilted the bottle slightly and got a small drop on her finger. "Here, Elijah," she said gently, "open your mouth and take this." He obeyed her, and very quickly his eyes became droopy.

"What did you just give him?" Luke demanded, fighting back the irritated anger that was beginning to bubble within him.

"A small drop of milk of poppy. It will help him not feel anything."

"You should have asked me first."

"Isn't it what you would have given him?" she asked, her face surprised.

"I would have given him something, yes. And probably a derivative of the poppy seed." She was right. He didn't need to get angry with her—she was doing what was best for the patient.

"We must wash our hands before we touch his wound," he said softly to her, and again she flashed him the look of approval. He didn't like how good it made him feel to get her approval.

Fortunately, there was a basin of water that she had brought in earlier in the day and they washed their hands quickly and efficiently, before moving back to Elijah. The father was practically in tears.

"Why isn't he answering me? I know he bled a lot... Is he going to die?"

"No, no. We simply gave him something so that he won't feel the pain when we put his bones back in place. It would be quite difficult on him if he wasn't numbed to it. That's why he isn't responding," Gabby soothed the worried man.

"Together?" Luke looked at Gabby, hoping she would say yes. He wanted to work with her.

"Together," she agreed. She placed her hands on the top of the boy's arm, while Luke grabbed his forearm.

"Now," Luke said, and they both pulled at the same time. The boy moaned low as they carefully moved his arm, and there was the sickening sound of the bones shifting into place and muscles sliding around the bones. Luke focused intently on the wound and lining the boy's arm up as straight as possible.

Very slowly he released his arm and Gabby slid her arm under the boy's to hold it steady. Luke went to the old medicine cabinet and dug through it until coming out victorious with an arm brace. Gently he slid it under Elijah's arm and Gabby settled it on the chair.

"We need to stitch up the wound," Luke said softly and headed back to the medicine cabinet.

"He needs a poultice first," she replied just as softly.

"What kind of poultice?" he asked skeptically.

"It's a comfrey poultice, made as a paste. It helps—"

"Stop the bleeding," he said, nodding in approval. "And it should help the wound heal faster. Perfect."

"You know of comfrey poultice?" she asked, her face expressing startled surprise.

"Of course." He winked at her, then headed back to the cabinet to get needle and horse hair to stitch up the wound.

Gabby dug the jar of poultice out of her bag and pressed it against the wound. The boy stirred slightly as the poppy was beginning to wear off. "We might want to get through the stitches quickly, Lu—Doctor Davenport."

He approached quickly with the needle, but before he could thread it, Gabby grabbed and wiped it clean with a damp cloth, then handed it back to him. He smiled at her. "Stitches have never quite been my expertise."

She smiled back at him, and her expression made it obvious that she knew he was doing it for her benefit. She turned to the boy and quickly stitched him up in small, even stitches. As she snipped the horse thread loose, Luke began to wrap his arm tightly with the gauze Gabby had provided. They had just finished when the boy began to wake up and his eyes met Gabby's.

She smiled at him gently. "You're going to be just fine," she whispered to him.

His eyes darted over to Luke, who nodded at him, then to his father, and his eyes grew wide with fear. "Pa, I'm sorry. I was just trying to move the hay in the loft. I didn't know how close I was to the edge..."

The father shook his head and pulled the boy into his arms, careful not to touch the wrapped arm. "It's fine, son. It's fine. I'm so glad you're okay. Just be more careful next time, please?"

The boy hugged his father tightly. The father raised his eyes to Luke. "I can't thank you enough, Doctor. How much do I need to pay you? Is there a way for me to make payments over time? Or, I have livestock I can bring to you. Chickens? Eggs?"

Luke shook his head. "You don't owe me anything. Take your son home and bring him back in about a week so we can check his wound. And, young man," he said, directing his attention to the boy, "no more tossing hay for you for a little while."

The boy nodded, holding his arm delicately away from his side. "Thank you," he said softly, nodding to both Luke and Gabby. The boy and father left, pausing to give a quick wave goodbye.

As the door closed, Gabby turned to cleaning up the area they had worked in, picking up the bloody towel and taking the needle to the basin of water to clean it and replace it in the medicine cabinet. Luke watched her, his heart pounding hard in his chest. They had been the perfect team. It had been almost as if they had worked together for years.

As she came past him to put up her vials of medicine, he caught her around the waist and turned her towards him. "Luke, what—"

"Thank you," he whispered. "Thank you for believing in me. For trusting me. And for being here with me." He lowered his head and pressed a gentle kiss against her cheek, then released her and took a step back.

She looked flustered as she returned her medicine vials to her bag. "I don't think you need to thank me for anything. You did a terrific job. I believe I may have misjudged you, Doctor Davenport."

"I certainly misjudged you. We work quite well together, wouldn't you say?"

She was smiling when she turned back to him. "Yes. Very well together. And given that we still have a few hours of sunlight left, let's go take a look at your living quarters. I want to see what kind of disaster we have to work with up there."

"If it is as I remember, there isn't much to see."

"All the more opportunity to improve," she said as she turned to the stairs. Her hips swayed in front of him and he paused to count to ten. *God, give me strength. Because this woman is making me lose my mind.*

IT WAS EVEN worse than he had remembered. As soon as they reached the second floor they were struck by the cold wind blowing in from the gap in the roof where a tree limb had gone through it. Debris was everywhere in the humble living quarters. The porcelain pitcher that had been near the water basin was shattered on the floor. The bed had been knocked askew by the tree branch and was lying on its side in the corner.

The space was small, so there were few furnishings in the room. But it did have a large window that looked out onto Main Plaza. "Come look at your view!" Gabby said, reaching out for his hand.

He took her hand with a smile, enjoying her excitement. It seemed she could always look past the worst and find the positive somehow, someway. He'd never known anyone like her, and doubted he ever would again.

He stepped towards her, over the broken pitcher, and looked out the window. It was a terrific view. He could see everything that was going on in the Plaza, the Market, and even the nearby streets. He leaned closer and looked in other directions, and that was when he saw it—the Alamo.

"What was it like?" he asked solemnly, remembering the stories he had heard in London. "Was it truly a massacre as the stories have claimed?"

Gabby's eyes turned in the direction his were looking and a shudder rippled through her. "Yes. It was terrible. I wasn't here, then, but Angie told me all about it. She thought she had lost Lorenzo, because he was supposed to be fighting in the Alamo the morning of the attack. We all thought he was gone. But she held on to a small thread of hope. And he had gotten out before the battle to send a missive to General Houston. God must truly be watching over him."

Luke watched her face as she spoke, seeing the variety of emotions that went through her. "Was your family safe during the Revolution?"

Gabby turned and gave him a weak smile. "I lost my father in the Revolution. He died as a member of Fannin's troops that were executed on Santa Anna's orders. That man has a black heart. I feel haunted by him to this day. Not much later my mother became ill. She fought it, and she was a strong woman. But each day she grew weaker. I think she died of a broken heart."

"That isn't possible," Luke replied, his medical mind trying to process what she had said.

"Someday, Luke, I hope that you find a woman who you love so deeply, the thought of being without her would be as if someone had ripped your heart from your chest. That is true love. And that is what my parents had. It's what I pray to have some day as well. To not experience that feeling would truly be a miserable existence, I'm sure."

Luke watched her closely as she turned from the window and began to evaluate the room. To have that kind of love would require you to give all of yourself to the relationship. And he didn't think he could ever allow himself to be vulnerable like that.

"Of course, I do come from the Torres family, and my mother's side of the family, the Iglesiases, weren't very timid characters either. So she and I both followed the path of Santa Anna to aid the fallen and injured until we finally arrived at the Battle of San Jacinto. It was there that we were able to save Olivia's life."

"You couldn't have been more than a child! How could your mother take you...?"

"Ah, remember, I'm an old maid. I was already fifteen, almost sixteen when this happened. I was able to help my mother, and I also witnessed the brutality of those doctors."

"Oh, yes, of course. That's where your loathing for doctors developed."

She glanced over her shoulder at him. "'Loathing for doctors?' I'd say I've been pretty kind to you, wouldn't you agree?" There was the glimmer of a tease in her eyes.

"Yes, you've shown me some generosity," he said, the corner of his mouth lifting in a smile. She smiled at him in return, then refocused on the room.

"I wish we had checked up here before we left the mercantile. We need to get you a new pitcher, and I'm certain you'll need a new mattress as well. This mattress has become exposed to the elements, and who knows if it got wet or damaged somehow."

"I think you like spending your town's money."

"Hardly. But if we are going to have a talented doctor in San Antonio, it only makes sense that we do everything we can do to please him and make him want to stay."

Several things ran through Luke's mind in that moment, but all of it had to do with Gabby pleasing him, and nothing to do with the town. "It actually isn't that small of a space," Gabby said, looking around, completely oblivious to the way he watched her. "If we position the bed in the corner, we can bring in a night stand for you to place your lamp. And we can find you a nicer dresser than this wretched thing," she said, walking towards the short dresser that had only three small drawers and an empty space at the bottom for shoes.

"I don't need much, Gabby. You don't need to make this into some sort of luxurious home."

"No," she agreed, and he saw her eyelashes lower in the fractured mirror over the dresser. "No, a luxurious home is whatever you believe it to be and whomever you have to share it with."

"Do you have a luxurious home?" he asked, suddenly very curious about the lifestyle she led. She was a very confident woman, and conducted herself in a manner unlike anything he had ever witnessed.

"By society's terms, yes, I suppose I live in a luxurious home. But I am all alone most of the time. The boys are always out on the trail with the cattle, though it does feel wonderful when I have them all home with me. But other than those few times, the house is hollow and empty."

She drew a deep breath and turned to face him, a smile plastered on her face. "My family has done incredibly well in the cattle market. And because of that, we are more fortunate than most. That's why my other brothers wouldn't come with me to San Antonio. They are so invested in that ranch they won't even take a break for Christmas."

He could tell that she would be willing to give all of that up, and more, if it would allow her to see her family and be with them more often. He took a step towards her, but she backed away quickly. "Really, Luke, what are your thoughts about the room?"

"Gabby." He reached for her, but she took another step backwards…and slammed directly into the tree branch. She froze, her eyes growing wide in her face as the tree branch groaned loudly and the roof creaked ominously.

"Gabby, come to me, now!"

Nervously she took a half step forward and the large branch shook hard—and then crashed down, along with the roof.

Chapter Ten

"GABBY!" LUKE SHOUTED, trying to break through the frozen branches of the tree to reach her. Instead he slammed into the thick trunk of the branch. He couldn't see Gabby anywhere. All he could see was dust and rubble.

"Gabby, I'm coming for you, do you understand? Don't be scared."

With a growl that was part groan, he shoved the tree away from him, the thinner branches snapping as it rotated on the floor. He climbed over the trunk and frantically began to dig through all of the debris and roofing material that was piled where Gabby had been standing.

Suddenly a hand grabbed his and he held on to it with a strong grip, still pushing away at the rubble that covered her. Finally, he found her hair and released her hand to dig even faster to expose her mouth.

Her face burst free from the rubble and she gasped, then instantly coughed on the dust. He quickly brushed the dirt and dust off her face and searched her expression. "I'm going to pull you free of all of this. Just tell me if it hurts. Now…where is your other hand?"

"It's—it's over here…" She seemed to be struggling to

breathe, and he realized the weight was probably crushing her. "I'll try to push it out," she said, her voice choppy.

Even with the chill sweeping through the room they were both sweating by the time her other hand burst through the debris. He grabbed both of her hands and held them tightly, then began to pull, slow and steady, and gradually her body began to come out of the pile of rubble. She gasped loudly and he stopped, looking her intently in the eyes.

"Did I hurt you? Do we need to stop?"

"No. No, just keep pulling, please," she said, though her voice wasn't terribly convincing. By the time he had pulled her out far enough that her waist was exposed, she was able to start helping, by pushing down with her legs and climbing free of all the rubble.

Once free of all of it she stumbled into his arms and he held her tightly. "I'm so sorry, Gabby. Had I known how dangerous it was here I never would have brought you up."

She was shaking and pale and clammy, but she gave him a weak smile as she pulled back. "I'm fine, truly. Thank you for helping me."

"Let's get downstairs where you'll be warm and safe. I'm going to have to take your family's offer for help to rebuild this roof over the weekend."

She nodded at him, but he noticed there was an odd glaze to her eyes. "Gabby?" She didn't answer him, just continued staring right through him. "Gabby? Can you hear me?"

She squeezed his hand. "How is it that you can be so delicate with such large hands?" she asked softly, randomly, before her eyes rolled backwards and she fell limp in his arms.

"Bloody hell," he cursed as he swung her up into his arms and raced down the stairs as fast as he safely could. He lay her down on the freshly cleaned floor and began to search her for injuries. It quickly became apparent where the injury was when his hand came away from the top of her head bloodied.

He hurried to the basin and washed his hands, cringing as the water turned pink from her blood, then went outside and gathered a few of the small icicles hanging from the eaves. He wrapped them in a towel and went back to Gabby, lifting her in his arms once again and settled down near the fireplace, pressing the iced towel against the top of her head.

She was terribly pale, and he prayed her injury was nothing more than a bad bump on the head. Anything further would be unbearable to tolerate. "Talk to me, Vixen," he said, his voice gruff. "Tell me what I'm missing here. Tell me why you think doctors are terrible. Just talk to me, please."

She remained silent, and the towel already had plenty of blood on it. He shifted her slightly in his lap and realized her dress had blood on it. With his heart thudding loudly in his chest, he looked more closely at her dress and saw a deep tear, probably caused by a nail or a sharp limb piece.

Without hesitating he tore the dress open further and saw a deep, angry gash with a long scrape down to her hip bone. He had to treat her. The sooner he did it, the less likely she was to catch infection. But he didn't want to let go of her in case she woke up. Cursing himself and every tree he'd ever known, he set her down carefully and made her another compress for the deep gash.

He pressed it to her wound, all the while watching her face and hoping he would see a reaction. But she remained silent and still. Then he raided her medicine bag.

She had dried rose petals, one of the best items to use to staunch bleeding when fresh petals weren't available. He pulled out the delicate petals and pressed one to the wound on the top of her head. Then he used the comfrey paste on the wound on her side, and sealed it with a rose petal. He lightly dabbed the comfrey paste all the way down her side, then bandaged her.

The entire time she didn't move, but it appeared some color was returning to her face. Or maybe he was just wishfully hoping there was. He pulled her back into his arms and held her tightly, trying to remember all the prayers he had ever heard. When he had been younger and it was a particularly bitter cold morning, the priest at the church would let him in and allow him to sit in a pew far away from the other patrons of the church. They would sing so beautifully, and even their prayers were songs.

"Luke."

He had become so intent on his prayers that he had closed his eyes tightly and was hunched over her. Hearing her sweet, gentle voice say his name nearly brought tears to his eyes. But instead his eyes snapped open and searched her face, looking for signs of pain or further injury.

"What were those beautiful words you were saying? It was almost as if you were singing."

He smiled at her and gently smoothed some of her hair

off her forehead. "I was praying. The way the priests in London would pray."

She smiled weakly at him in return. "Our priest sings his prayers, also, but your voice is so much better."

He continued to hold her, unable to set her away from him, even though he knew he must at some point. "Do you remember what happened?"

She let her breath out slowly. "I remember us going up to your living quarters."

"Good, good," he said encouragingly.

"We looked out your window and you asked questions about what happened at the Alamo." He nodded. "And then...then..." She looked up at him with confusion and a hint of fear in her eyes. "I can't remember. Why can't I remember? Why am I in your lap? What happened Luke? What happened—oh!" She winced in pain as she tried to sit up, one hand flying to the top of her head and the other to her side.

"Don't move. Don't move. Just take it easy for right now."

"What happened, Luke? What?"

"You bumped into the tree limb coming through the roof and it came down on you. That and a large section of the roof. You've got a very nasty bump on your head, and a cut on your side, but I was able to dig through your medicine bag and find some good things to help you heal faster."

"*My* medical bag? How do you know what to use from *my* medical bag?"

"You would be surprised the things I studied on the long journey to Texas." He was still watching her closely, still holding the compress to her head.

"You continue to surprise me every day," she said softly. She reached up and touched his cheek. "I'm sorry I caused such a problem. I'm sure the boys will work on the roof and get all of it taken care of over the weekend."

"I need to get you home. You need to rest."

"I'm fine. Just…just help me stand."

Reluctantly, Luke moved her off of his lap and kneeled next to her, supporting her head as he brought her to a sitting position. She winced, but didn't complain, and nodded when he offered to help her to stand.

He held her steady, and saw the pain reflected in her eyes, but she gradually stood straight and smiled at him. "You've done a good job, Doc," she said, drawing a deep breath. "Thank you."

"I never should have taken you up there."

She shook her head, but winced at the movement. "I think it would be good to go home now. I'm very tired."

He nodded and guided her to the door. "How do you feel?"

"A bit dizzy, but I'd be surprised if I wasn't." She leaned into him.

He wrapped an arm around her, careful to avoid her wound, and they stepped out into the cold. *How was he going to explain this to her family?*

⚕

"A MISSIVE CAME for you today," Serena said after they had settled in. Luke was worried about Gabby, but she was feeling better after the walk home helped clear her head. She had changed into a fresh dress, a pale blue one that brought out the dark sheen of her hair and the myriad of colors in her eyes.

They were all seated around the dining room table, having just finished their dinner meal. Luke's eyebrow lifted in question. "A missive? For me?" *Who knows I'm even here?*

"Yes," Serena said with barely contained excitement. "It carries the President's seal on it."

The President? Why would he have any interest in me? Luke did his best to remain unsurprised, as if the President of the Republic of Texas was a friend, and receiving a note from him wasn't an unusual thing.

Serena jumped up and went to the side table, snatched a piece of parchment off of it and handed it to him eagerly. Then she sat back down and watched him expectantly. The entire family was watching him with eager eyes, before the grandfather cleared his throat. "We should clean up from dinner, now, shouldn't we?"

Everyone at the table appeared deflated and Angie stood and began to gather the plates. Serena and Gabby also stood, ordering Olivia to stay put and not help with anything, and gathered glasses and silverware. They had taken everything to the kitchen and had come back to grab some of the serving dishes.

"Don't any of you want to know what he's written to me?" Luke asked hesitantly, wondering if they really did want to be that much involved in his life. Did they really see him as a part of their family?

All of the women quickly sat back down and there was a chorus of "Yes" and "Of course!"

He smiled as he carefully broke the seal and opened the envelope, pulling out a thick piece of parchment. He glanced around the table and they all had their eyes glued to his hands, watching with eager anticipation.

He slid the parchment out and opened it, and stared at the ornate writing with perplexity. The more he read, the more confused he became.

"Well?" Serena finally blurted out.

"Serena! It's his letter. He doesn't have to share it with us if he doesn't want to," Olivia chided her.

"No, no. It's just, well, it's an invitation."

"An invitation from President Lamar? What does it say? An invitation to what?" Serena was practically bouncing out of her chair. Trevor was chuckling and laid a hand over hers. She looked over at him, smiled sheepishly, and tried to temper her overwhelming excitement.

"Take a look at it. I'm not exactly sure what to think of the thing."

"To the esteemed Doctor Davenport, you are hereby cordially invited to President Lamar's Annual Christmas Gala, to be held Saturday, December 19th, the year of our Lord 1840, at the President's home in Austin. We look forward to meeting you and your special guest at 7:00 P.M. May your Holidays be filled with peace and love. Sincerely, President Mirabeau Lamar."

"Oh my goodness! It is a Christmas Gala! Luke, can you imagine what this will be like?" It was Angie's turn to start gushing about the invitation.

"We need to be certain you have the finest attire. Do you have a nice suit?"

"Whatever do they do at a gala?" Cade chimed in. "I've heard of them, but I've never actually seen one."

"Neither have we," Olivia said, her eyes turning to Luke. "We may not be able to get you ready in the appropriate fashion."

Luke smiled at all of them. "I've been to galas before. And I have the appropriate suit to wear. You don't need to fret about me."

The women kept talking as they gathered up the remainder of the dishes on the table and went to clean the kitchen. Their chatter and laughter could be heard throughout the house. Luke sat at the table and felt defeated. He thought he had escaped being the focus of special attention. Now he was being invited to an exclusive Christmas Gala, where he would be forced to mix and mingle with people he didn't know, and whom he didn't really care about.

Abuelo suddenly reached across the table and caught his hand. Luke looked up, startled out of his self-pity. "Don't forget the wisdom you gained today," he said, his eyes smiling.

Luke felt a load taken off of him. Yes, he had wisdom on his side. He would allow the women to have their fun. But in the end, he would remain true to himself and his beliefs. He had no one to prove himself to...other than perhaps the young woman with the flaming spirit that made his heart pound through his chest.

Chapter Eleven

"WE'RE GOING TO have a *fandango*."

"You've used that word before. What does it mean?" Luke was sipping hot coffee, still trying to wake up when Gabby had come into the room, bringing with her the fresh smells of winter and making his heartbeat tick up.

"A *fandango*, silly. It's our word for a magnificent party."

"When? Why are you having a party?" He had the sneaking suspicion that the party had something to do with him going to the gala at the President's home in Austin.

"We were supposed to host the *posada* on the twenty-first. We don't want you to miss out on the experience. So we're going to have it tonight instead."

"Are you going to be able to pull off a party that fast?" he asked incredulously.

"We switched with one of the other families. Today is going to be very busy. You're going to be immersed in what we do to prepare for a true *fandango*."

She was smiling brightly as she sat down near him, rubbing her hands at the hearth to warm them. Her joy was contagious, and he felt a smile pulling at his lips, too.

"There are so many beautiful women in San Antonio,"

she said suddenly, the tone of her voice changing slightly. "I'm sure you'll find someone who is poised and sophisticated and perfect for you."

"What? What are you talking about?" His smile had vanished and was replaced by a furrowed brow. Why was she talking about finding someone poised and sophisticated, and perfect for *him*? He was worried about the men who would have their eyes set on Gabby.

"Oh, you'll see," she said, and her own smile slipped a little. "I'm sure there is someone perfect just waiting for you to come into her life," she said softly.

What if I have already found her? his mind yelled at him. Why try to find someone else, when the woman he craved was already within his reach? And, yet, she must not share the same feelings he did. Otherwise, she wouldn't be talking about how he was going to find a different person—a person suited to him.

"And what about you? I'm certain there will be many men eager to have a few minutes of your time," he said softly, his stomach churning at the thought. She belonged to him. He felt it with every fiber of his being. *Why is she pushing me away?*

"I'm already considered an old spinster," Gabby said, shaking her head. "I turn twenty next month. By society's standards, I am no longer a desirable catch." She chuckled to herself. "Truth be told, I don't know that I ever was."

Luke caught her hands in his and began to rub them, bringing warmth to them. "Any man who thinks you aren't a catch is a fool." *If only I were good enough for you, I'd never let you go.* "One day some man will win a treasure—if he is able to catch you, that is. Are you sure you want to be caught?"

Her eyes lifted to his and he suddenly saw it...the longing, the craving to be loved. But surely not from a man like him. She would have nothing if he took her as his bride. She would have to live at the clinic with him until he earned enough money for them to have a small house, and even that wasn't good enough for her. She deserved a fantastic life, and all he could offer her was his heart. If only that were enough.

⚚

"OLIVIA, WE'VE TALKED about this enough. You are not going to be on your feet today, no matter what. The babe is more important than the *posada*. I will not see you do something foolish."

"What is foolish is the way you continue to block me from getting anything accomplished. I'm not ill, Gabby, and neither is the babe. Trust me, he or she has been kicking up a storm all morning long."

Gabby didn't want her feelings to be expressed on her face as hope blossomed in her. Perhaps the babe was finally starting to turn. "Nonetheless, you will remain in bed. Tonight you can come out and join us for the *posada*, but merely as a participant, and *no* dancing."

Olivia sat on the edge of her bed, her arms crossed over the top of her large belly. "Gabby, you don't get to tell me what to do. Now, I'm grateful to you for your help, but—"

"Angel, you're going to listen to her. And I've brought

the doctor along to be sure you follow orders." Cade walked into the room with Luke immediately following. Luke glanced over at Gabby and flashed her a brief smile, before focusing on Olivia.

"We've all been trying to get you to understand how important it is for you to rest, Olivia. We're telling you this to protect you and the babe."

Olivia threw up her hands in frustration. "How many times do I have to say that the babe and I are just fine? We're both healthy."

"Good. And we want to keep it that way," Gabby said sternly.

With her lips pulled into a thin line, Olivia stood and began to head to the armoire for one of her dresses. "I'm tired of talking. And I'm tired of lying in bed day in and day out. This *posada* is important to me, too, Gabriella, and I will be a part of it."

Gabby moved quickly to stand in front of Olivia, blocking her from the armoire. "I won't let you, Olivia. You know how much I want you to join in the preparation. But I won't risk you or the babe, and you should keep that in mind."

"Oh, for the love of God, Gabby, get out of my way!" She shoved Gabby hard on her side, and much to the shock of everyone in the room, including Gabby, she gasped loudly.

"Gabby? I didn't hurt you, did I? I didn't mean to push you too hard..." Her voice trailed off as Gabby shook her head furiously.

"You didn't hurt me. You just...surprised me with your

strength. I'm fine."

With a dark frown on his face, Luke headed straight for Gabby, but she flinched away from him when he reached for her. "Gabby?" His tone was firm, but she backed away from him until she bumped into the armoire. She could feel tiny beads of sweat collecting on her forehead, even though she felt cold.

"What is going on, Gabby?" Olivia demanded.

"There was an accident at the clinic yesterday," Luke said, even though Gabby was adamantly shaking her head no. "Gabby was hurt when the roof caved in on her."

"Why didn't you tell us?" Cade demanded, stepping forward and pulling Olivia back to the bed without her realizing it.

Gabby shook her head. "It's only a scratch. I'm perfectly fine."

"Then let me examine you." Luke's eyes were locked on hers, and she felt trapped.

"We don't have time for this today, Luke," Gabby said with exasperation, and then tried to move past him. His arm shot out and caught her around the waist and she couldn't contain her small whimper of pain. He pulled his hand back and there was blood on his fingers.

Gabby blinked rapidly as she stared at his hand, and then the room went topsy-turvy as he swept her up into his arms and strode out the door, turning to his own small room. Distantly she could hear him talking to Cade, but she kept her face buried in his shoulder, embarrassment washing over her.

When he set her down on his bed she began to push away from him. "I can tend to it myself, Luke. Please. It isn't that severe."

"It's worse than I thought it was yesterday," he said, still frowning. "I should have checked on it last night. We've been so preoccupied telling Olivia to rest and take it easy that we haven't seen that you are working yourself into the ground. I'm sorry. This is all my fault."

"Seriously, I can take care of myself. And this isn't your fault in the least."

"So you continue to say." He glanced up when Serena entered the room, holding rags and a pitcher of warm water. "Now, we need to get you out of this dress."

⁂

SERENA AND ANGIE managed to undress Gabby for Luke while he gathered his supplies out of his medical bag. They had semi-wrapped her in a blanket for modesty and warmth when they told him he could turn around and finally treat her.

His heart ached as he looked at Gabby lying on the bed, her entire frame shivering. He moved forward and Angie and Serena stepped back, giving him some room, but just barely enough.

"Are you cold, Vixen?" he asked softly, so softly that the other two women couldn't hear.

"I—I don't know. I suppose so. That must be why I am shaking."

"Or you may be in shock from an infection settling into your wound. Or you could be nervous about me touching you—treating you."

She darted a glance at him, and he was once again captivated by the colors that swirled around in her eyes. How could she not see how beautiful she was? Who had misled her so completely? Just looking at her took his breath away, and he wished so much that he could be the man who would spend his life with her. But there were better things coming her way—he knew it.

"I suppose it could be a combination of all of those things," she said hesitantly, her eyes studying his face, and he wondered if she could read his thoughts.

He focused on her wound, trying to force his mind off of how alluring she looked, and ignore the temptation to gaze upon her with eyes that longed to see more of her smooth, creamy skin. The cut was angry. It was bright red all around the main puncture, and the scrape that went all the way to her hip bone was crusting with a clear fluid. At least it wasn't pus—yet.

He wanted to hang his head in frustration. But he was a doctor. This was what he did for a living. He couldn't change the fact that a woman he was coming to care for deeply was being impacted. If anything, that stirred him to care for her even more carefully.

"We'll need to clean the wound first," he said, hoping that talking it through with her would make it much easier on her. "From there, I'm going to need to give you some balm to ease the infection, and stitch up the main cut. It's much deeper than we realized initially."

"What's in the balm?" she demanded, her eyes narrowed at him.

"Gilead, olive oil, eucalyptus, and beeswax."

Her eyebrows lifted. "That is something I would use. Are you sure you didn't just accidently go through my medical bag instead of your own?"

"You made many assumptions about me, Vixen. Some were true, but I am not your typical doctor. I see the benefit of using the land around us to heal us. It is what God gave us, right?"

She gave him a weak smile. "Yes. You are right. About many things."

"Now, ladies," he said, speaking loud enough that Angie and Serena could finally hear him, "I'm going to need your help. You'll need to hold her still. This first part is going to be rather painful."

Chapter Twelve

S HE HAD CRIED. She had tried so hard not to, had tried so hard to be brave and strong. But nothing had stopped the tears from running down the sides of her face as he had cleaned her wound. She didn't make a sound, but the tears couldn't be stopped.

She wouldn't make eye contact with Luke, even though a part of her wanted to. A part of her wanted to know that he was with her, that he was there to give her some of his strength. But she couldn't let him know that she was so weak that she needed him. That she wanted him to need her, too.

The pain was intense as he used warm, damp towels to clean the wound. But when he poured the alcohol on the deepest part of her wound, she couldn't hold back her short cry of pain before blissfully succumbing to the black hole that opened up before her.

When she awoke, he was watching her closely, holding one of her hands in his. His face held many different emotions, but he smiled when he saw her eyes open, though the smile didn't quite reach his own eyes. "Hello, there, Vixen. You're all stitched up and ready to conquer the world."

That brought her awake much faster. "How long have I

been asleep?"

"Only an hour or two. They've just barely started serving breakfast."

She tried to scramble to a sitting position but groaned as pain shot through her side. "I must go help! There is too much that must be done today. I have a whole list of things we have to take care of, and there are only so many hours of daylight before the procession for the *posada* will be upon us."

Luke sighed heavily and slid an arm under her, carefully lifting her to a seated position. "I suppose you won't follow the doctor's orders to rest in bed for the remainder of the day and give your cut a chance to heal."

"You suppose correctly. Besides, you've already cleaned it, disinfected it, and stitched me up. There's nothing left for you to do."

"Very well," he said tensely, and helped her to her feet, holding her for several seconds as she got her balance. God, how good his arms felt around her. The strength and vitality coursing through him, the confidence, the feeling that she could be safe for the rest of her life if she stayed in his arms. She shook her head at herself. What she was wishing for could never happen. Her life had been determined for her a long time ago—and she was at the mercy of someone she barely even knew.

And yet, the man hadn't come to claim her. If he didn't come by her twentieth birthday, the agreement would be null. Was that what he was doing? Allowing their prearranged marriage deadline to expire so he wouldn't be forced to marry her? She didn't have any way of knowing. There was only a month left for him to claim what had been given to him, and she feared it would be the longest month of her life.

"Thank you for everything you've done, Luke," she said softly, not quite able to look at him.

"It's what friends are for," he replied, though the tone of his voice sounded off. He almost sounded angry.

Reluctantly she broke free from his hold and walked to the door. She couldn't stop herself from turning to glance at him, but his back was to her as he stared out the small window of the room. Drawing a deep breath, she closed the door behind her and plunged forward into her day, unwilling to let anything disrupt the joy of preparing for the *posada*.

THE ENTIRE HOUSE smelled of spices and cooking, to the point that the smells wafted out onto the streets. Customers began coming in and asking for whatever was cooking, and the family reminded them of the *posada* that was coming that night.

Luke had taken his time freshening up before coming out after Gabby had left his room. He kept telling himself that she didn't see him the same way he saw her. Hell, she didn't even see herself the same way he saw her. He didn't know why she thought she was so plain and ordinary.

Had her brothers tried to teach her that so she wouldn't fall for a man? Had her parents told her those things?

Neither of the options seemed plausible. Her family loved her and treasured her—they would never say anything to hurt her. But the fact remained that she doubted her own beauty and charm.

"Oh, Luke! I'm so glad you're finally here," Serena said as he walked into the dining room. She was working on something on the table, but he couldn't quite make it out.

She grabbed his hand and began to head towards the kitchen. "It's almost time to pull the hog up from the ground. We dug the pit yesterday and have had the hog cooking all night. It should be perfect by now. It's my favorite thing to eat at the *posada!*"

He had no idea what she was talking about. "Exactly what am I going to do?" he asked hesitantly.

She looked back at him with a perplexed face. "Help get the hog out," she said, as if it was a given that he should know.

"Ah," he replied, still feeling completely clueless.

As they were rushing through the kitchen, she swung around the corner, dragging him behind her, and he crashed directly into Gabby. The sweet smell of her hair greeted him and he instantly released Serena's hands so he could hold Gabby, pretending to steady her.

She looked up at him with her mesmerizing eyes and gave him a weak smile. "I'm sorry. I was in too much of a rush…"

"No, no…it was my fault. I wasn't paying attention. How do you feel? Your stitches…"

"I'm fine. You did a good job. I thought you said stitches

weren't something you are strong at doing." A teasing smile lifted the corner of her mouth. "So you're going to help them with the hog?" she asked, her eyes searching his face for something, but he didn't know what. A sign that he cared about her more than he let on? A glimpse into the feelings he had pounding at the surface of his heart?

"As far as I know, yes. That's what I'm supposed to be doing."

"And he's going to be late if we don't hurry up," Serena said, tapping her foot impatiently.

Gabby glanced over her shoulder, then back at Luke. "It would seem you have a schedule to keep, and an overeager assistant to get you there. Go. Have fun."

He wanted to kiss her. Just a small kiss to see the joy in her eyes, to see her happy again. But he knew it wouldn't be he who made her happy.

With a frustrated groan, Serena grabbed his hand and pulled him away from Gabby and back towards the rear door of the kitchen. Luke was about to ask about coats, and suddenly realized she had one, but his was still in his bedroom. But before he could ask to go back and get one, they plunged out into the cold weather and down the stairs to a massive square pit in the backyard.

Several men stood around it—men who looked old enough to be grandparents themselves. There were a few strapping younger men, and he was grateful for their presence and could only pray that they would be the ones helping him lift the few-hundred-pound hog.

Abuelo approached him, a large smile on his face. "Today

you join us in one of our most prized traditions," he said, clapping a hand onto Luke's shoulders. "Every year we roast a pig in the ground as a special treat for the *posada*. Once you've tasted this, you'll be anxious for Christmas to get here every year."

Luke doubted that. Christmas was never a joyful time of the year for him. It had only been in the last few years that he had been able to enjoy the comfort of being indoors during the cold, which had made the day bearable. But there was no gathering of family or friends. Not true friends at least. There were plenty who wanted him to attend their parties for a different reason, but he always declined.

But there was something different with this family. They were genuine and sincere, wanting him to be a part of the celebration and enjoy himself. His mind flashed to Gabby and the special moment they had shared out in the cold, watching the *posada*, his arms wrapped around her, his chin resting on her head.

"Are you paying attention, Doc?" Raphael asked, his tone still slightly aggressive towards Luke.

Luke looked him straight on and almost wished for a fight. He wanted to punch something. He wanted to feel the rush he used to feel when he… He forced the thoughts from his mind. "Yes, I understand. At your call we will all pull evenly on the rope to haul up the pig."

Raphael nodded, but said nothing more. The strapping men Luke had seen earlier grabbed ropes, as did some of the older gentlemen. He moved quickly to a spot and grabbed a rope. It was made of rough hemp, and he knew his hands would be sore after hauling up the massive pig. But he couldn't deny that the smells coming up from the ground were enough to make his mouth water.

"Ready, men…now!" Raphael called, and he, too, began to haul on the ropes, hiking the pig up slowly, slowly.

Luke felt a small sweat build on his forehead. Had they deliberately made sure he was on the side with all the weaker, older men? He glanced over at Raphael and saw Gabby's brother grinning at him and realized he had been set up.

He was so annoyed by the move that he began hauling harder on the rope, pulling the pig up faster. "Easy there, Doc, we've got to all move together."

"Then pick up the pace, gents! This pig is ready to come out."

Not to be outdone by the British doctor, the men began to haul harder on their ropes, and within minutes the pig was out and they were carefully hauling it to a large wooden table. Luke followed their lead and helped remove the wiring that had held the pig wrapped together, and then peeled off the burlap bags that had kept the pig moist.

The pig carcass wasn't the most pleasant thing to see, but it certainly smelled wonderful. Much to his surprise, a few of the men peeled back the skin of the pig and grabbed pieces of meat. Suddenly a piece of meat was being presented to him, and he looked up to see Raphael holding it.

"For a job well done," Raphael said, shrugging slightly, as if casting off past insults.

Luke nodded his head to him, then took the piece and tasted it hesitantly. The flavors that burst in his mouth made his cheeks ache momentarily and then salivate for more. He ate the rest of the meat he'd been handed eagerly. It wasn't until he'd finished it that he realized everyone around him was silent.

He looked up and saw they were all watching him. "It's delicious," he said with sincerity. "May I have some more?"

There was a roar of laughter as all the men went back for second pieces, teasing each other about who could make a better roasted pig, and who had done the best job in setting the pit, and Luke was loving every minute of it. He had heard of men from a large family getting together for parties and sharing jokes and jabs, teasing to express their love for each other. Now he knew what it felt like. It was absolutely marvelous.

Suddenly there was the loud banging of two pots together and all of the men fell silent and quickly backed away from the pig. Luke followed their example and looked to where the noise had come from.

"Every year!" *Abuela* yelled at them. "Every year I have to pull you vultures off that pig so there's enough left for the *posada*. Now go! Be gone with you! There's plenty more work to be done!"

The men scattered, leaving Luke standing alone, until, thankfully, Raphael glanced back, grabbed him by the arm, and pulled him away from the evidence of their assault on the pig.

GABBY IMMERSED HERSELF in everything they had to do for the *posada* in order to forget about the ache in her side and the equally painful ache in her heart. She had searched Luke's face to see if he longed for her the way she longed for him. And all she could see was a man who enjoyed her presence, but had no desire to pursue anything further.

Even though she was hurt, she was still determined to make this a wonderful first Christmas for him. He had been in hiding with Raphael for some time since the pig had come out of the ground, but he had finally returned, grinning like a schoolboy. Knowing Raphael, she could only imagine what the two of them had been up to.

Luke's cheeks were bright red from the cold wind and his hair was tossed about, leaving a piece falling down over his forehead, and she thought he had never looked more handsome than he did in that moment. She had to shake herself out of studying him and came over to him, as he wiped his hands with a wet towel.

At first he looked down at her with surprise, and she attempted to smile up at him. "It's time you learn how to make the next most important food for Christmas, other than the pig."

He arched an eyebrow. "And that is?"

"*Tamales*, of course!" She laughed lightly, enjoying how little he knew and the joy it brought her to teach him. She grasped his hand and led him into the living room, where she felt him hesitate slightly.

The dining room had been turned into a massive production facility, with their cousins and friends filling the room, each doing different steps in the process of making the *tamales*, from spreading the *masa*, to filling them, to wrapping them tightly and sending them off to be cooked.

"Ladies!" Gabby said loudly over the chatter of the women and they all hesitated and looked in her direction. "This is Doctor Luke Davenport. He is our new town doctor here in San Antonio. He has never experienced a Christmas, so it is time we introduce him to a true Texas Christmas!"

A cheer went up from the women, and before she could say anything else, all of her eligible cousins had surrounded him and were pulling him forward to help with making the *tamales*. Gabby felt a slight twinge of pain. Perhaps one of her cousins was sophisticated enough to go to the gala with him. Perhaps he would fall in love with her. And then she would enjoy his sweet kisses in the morning.

But it was as she was having these sobering thoughts that he turned to look back at her, a pained smile on his face, and winked. Joy burst through her, and she had to hold in the laugh that threatened to bubble forth. The wink was meant for her, and she would treasure it, especially as he went through the process of picking a date for the gala.

At first she had hoped he would ask her, but as soon as she realized he needed the perfect woman—sophisticated, elegant, beautiful—she had known she wouldn't receive the invitation. She could be sophisticated and elegant if she put her mind to it. After all, her mother had trained her how to be those things, especially as they were invited to so many events in Corpus Christi. But beautiful?

Throughout her schooling she was made fun of for having such odd eyes. And when she was older, boys avoided her as much as possible. Her mother told her it was because she was a healer and they were scared of what that meant, but Gabby knew they simply weren't attracted to her. She had come to terms a long time ago with the fact that she would never find true love. The very fact that her own arranged marriage was falling through because the man hadn't come forward to claim her was statement enough about how attractive she was. Now she knew beyond a doubt she would never find true love. Because there was no man who would ever make her feel the way Luke did. She knew it in her heart.

"You are very deep in thought. Is this process that difficult?"

Luke's voice behind her made her heart leap and she turned to smile up at him. "I thought my cousins had taken you prisoner," she said softly.

He leaned down close to her and whispered against her ear, "I escaped. Would you like to break free, too?"

She fought the shiver that ran down her spine at the warmth of his breath across her ear and the temptation to be taken away from it all. But she still had to show him so much. She scooted over on the bench, making room for him.

Slowly, almost reluctantly, he sat down next to her. "I thought we were about to make our great get-away. What happened?"

"You need to learn how to make *tamales*."

"I already know how to. Your cousins explained it in thorough detail."

"Ah, but there is a difference between being able to talk about it, and being able to really do it."

She placed a corn husk in his hand and then pointed to the bowl of *masa* in front of both of them. "Take the *masa* and spread it on the corn husk. This is what holds everything together."

Hesitantly, he reached for the *masa* and began attempting to spread it. His progress was slow, though, and Gabby had three finished by the time he held out the one that he was willing to present.

Gabby took one look at it and started laughing so hard tears formed at the corners of her eyes. "I said to spread it. Not lump it."

Luke cast her a slightly irritated and amused expression. "If it is so easy for you, why don't you just show me?" Her laughter had eased and she saw a smile on his lips. "You truly should laugh more often. It is a beautiful sound."

She could feel the heat of blood rushing to her cheeks and prayed that it passed as an after-effect of all her laughing. "I will show you how to spread the *masa*," she said softly, and caught hold of his hands. Using gentle motions she began to guide his hand up and down the corn husk, carefully spreading the *masa* on the delicate husk.

"See, it's that simple," she said when they had finished, turning a bright smile his direction. But her smile faded as she saw the look in his eyes as he watched her. His stormy blue eyes were full of questions, and held the same look they had held when he had kissed her what seemed weeks ago but was only a short time past. Was it desire she was seeing?

Surely not.

"Are you ready to get out of here, yet?"

Her heart spoke before her mind could stop her. "Yes."

Chapter Thirteen

S HE HAD STOLEN Serena's coat before sneaking out the front door with Luke, her small hand interlaced with his big one. He smiled down at her as they moved further away from the *cocina* and her heart danced hard against her chest. She didn't pause to analyze it, didn't hesitate to wonder what the feeling was, she just simply enjoyed it.

"Where are we going?" she asked in a hushed tone as they moved further and further away. "The *posada* starts as soon as the sun sets, you know."

"That should give us just enough time," he said light-heartedly. He continued leading her further into town until she suddenly realized they were headed to his clinic. Curious, she hurried her pace to match his.

This time the door didn't squeak as they walked inside, and he immediately turned towards the stairs. Gabby balked. "I—I don't know if I can go up there."

He stopped, his expression worried. "Have you remembered what happened now?"

"No. That's why I'm so afraid to go up there."

He stepped forward and took a wayward strand of hair and hooked it behind her ear. "That's why I'm here to protect you."

Gabby's heart skipped a beat then plunged forward rapidly. Nodding, they turned back towards the stairs and made it to the top. Luke steered a wide path around the tree and the gap in the ceiling, then cautiously opened the door leading out to the balcony. After checking to make sure it was safe, he escorted Gabby out onto the balcony and she smiled broadly.

"You can see nearly the whole town." Gabby laughed.

"You said that last time," Luke said softly, his lips twitching in a grin as he watched her face.

Gabby felt the heat of a blush rising once more to her cheeks. This man had an uncanny way of making her blush for no reason at all. "I suppose I told you before that this is one of the best views of the town I think I've ever seen?"

"Something like that. Though I must disagree."

She looked back at him, startled to find him still staring at her. "You've found another place with a better view? Where?"

"Every place and time I look at you."

Gabby swallowed hard. "Luke, please…"

"Why do you doubt your beauty, Gabby? Why? You are absolutely exquisite."

"Have you been dipping into some of your medicine, Doc?" She forced a laugh. "Because what you are saying right now is absolutely loony."

"It isn't, Gabby. You're beautiful. Hasn't anyone ever told you that? You're beautiful."

Gabby's eyes filled with tears. "I'm plain, Luke. As plain

as one of those old buckboard wagons. Please don't say otherwise. I know because of the things I was told growing up. And I know now, because you are the first man to even pay remote attention to me in a very long time, and that is only because you long for female companionship."

"Female companionship? What in the bloody hell are you talking about? I spent nearly my entire life alone on the streets of London. I don't seek companionship, female or otherwise!" His face was tense, and he abruptly turned his back on her.

Gabby was shocked, then confused. "How could you have possibly lived on the streets? Where were your parents? You must have had a home of some sort…"

He turned back to her with such speed she stepped back in surprise. "Do you really want to know all the terrible stories of my youth? Do you want me to drag up what it was like for me day in and day out while people as naïve as you walked right past me?"

"Luke, please, I didn't mean…"

"No, you deserve to know the truth of who I am. My father died fighting the war over here in 1814. I believe you all simply call it the War of 1812. Very creative. I was only a small lad then, and barely knew him. But it devastated my mum. She was a nurse, and a fine good one at that. She was more qualified than some of the doctors. But she caught sick not long after my father died and no one knew what to do for her. I was six when she died."

"Oh, Luke, I'm so sorry. Please, I didn't mean to offend you."

Luke continued talking as if Gabby wasn't there. "It is because of my mum that I wanted to become a doctor. But I lived on the streets of London. No one wanted me. I had to literally scrap and fight for everything I needed to survive. After several years of living like that, I ended up getting really good at fighting. A man noticed me and decided to have me begin fighting for pay. I saved every little bit I made."

He looked over at Gabby, his face expressionless. "What do you think of me now? I'm a fighter from London who grew up as a disgusting orphan. The only way I became a doctor was through a scholarship I earned from boxing matches. I beat up other people to become who I am today. And I came here to Texas for a fresh start. Where I wouldn't be recognized as a boxing champion. Where I wouldn't be pestered for being well-known. Where I could be a nobody once more and enjoy a new life, one where I could focus on being a doctor, and maybe one day...one day have a family. A real family. A family like yours."

Gabby felt tears burning her eyes and her throat nearly closed up. "Oh, Luke—"

"I don't want your pity, Vixen. That's the last thing I want from you."

"I don't pity you! I admire you!" she said more harshly than she had intended, and his expression changed from anger to confusion.

"You made it to where you are all by your own hard work. No one gave you anything; you didn't get any special privileges. It was by your own hard work that you earned that scholarship and were able to put yourself through schooling to become a doctor. A doctor! I can only imagine how hard that was. I admire your determination and tenacity. And more than anything I admire your dreams of the life you will have here in Texas. And you will have that life, Luke. I know you will. There is a woman who will give you the family you desire and more."

Luke shook his head and looked off into the distance. "I never wanted to tell anyone that story. I shouldn't have told you."

"Why? I'm honored that you shared it with me. Now I understand you so much better. I wish you had told me sooner."

"The sun is starting to set. We better hurry back to the house," he said softly.

Gabby felt her heart sink. She turned to leave the balcony, but was suddenly pulled back by Luke's hand on her arm. He pulled her into a tight embrace and pressed his lips to hers. She melted into him, having longed for his touch all day long.

His lips moved over hers gently, then more urgently as his hands moved up into her hair. Gabby met his intensity, sliding her arms around his broad shoulders, clinging to his strength and warmth.

It wasn't a mistake. There was no possible way something that felt so right could be a mistake. As his hands slid down her shoulders and to her back, she felt heat flush through her entire body, making her forget the chill in the air. And then his hands settled around her waist and lifted her against him, causing her to gasp in excitement and surprise.

"Gabby," he whispered against her lips. "You make me want to be a better man. You make me want to be the perfect man. And I'm afraid I can't be what you need. You deserve so much more than me."

Gabby pulled back, shaking her head. "How can you say that, Luke? How can you... Oh, no! The sun is setting! We have to get back now or we're going to miss it!"

She turned to head back into the quarters, but his arm tightened around her, pulling her up short. She looked back at him with startled eyes. "What if I don't care? What if I don't want to meet all of these women that you and your cousins want me to meet? What if I only want to spend time with you?"

Gabby's heart lodged in her throat and she could barely breathe. "Luke," she said softly. "You don't know what you're saying. You don't know what you are talking about. If only you knew. If only it was different..."

"If only I knew what? Tell me, Gabby. Tell me why it is so hard to get close to you. Tell me why you are pushing me away."

"I—I can't. Please, Luke. We can't miss the *posada*."

Shaking his head and frowning, he followed her back inside and they quickly made their way back to the *cocina*. The crowd was just beginning to form as they snuck in through the back door, but Olivia caught them.

"Where have you two been? I've been going crazy fretting over whether you would make it in time." She was frowning darkly at both of them.

"Do we still have time for me to show him?"

"Yes, but only a few minutes. The first call is going to happen any moment."

Gabby nodded, then glanced back at Luke, smiling slightly. "I had to prepare a surprise for you. I hope it does justice to what you saw back in London."

They walked into the dining room, and in the corner stood a cedar tree they had chopped down. It was covered in strands of popcorn that had a string running through it, wild berries that had also been strung together, and various decorations that had obviously been painstakingly made.

Gabby looked back at Luke and his expression was one of surprise and immense gratitude. "I never expected... Not in my wildest dreams did I think I would see a Christmas tree here in Texas."

"After you told me about it, I couldn't resist. We had to make Christmas special for you."

"You already have," he said softly, squeezing her hand. "In more ways than one."

Gabby swallowed hard, but was saved from responding by the first call outside their door. In Spanish, a man called to the "innkeepers" inside, asking for shelter for his wife who was about to give birth to a babe. From inside the house, Cade answered in a bellowing tone, "No, we have no room for you here!"

Then the people outside began to sing a song about the Blessed Mother, a beautiful, haunting song that always brought tears to Gabby's eyes. They joined the rest of the family hovered around the door.

Again the cry went out for sanctuary for the pregnant wife. And again, they denied from the inside of the house. A new song, the melody sweet and poignant, touched all of them. Finally, after following the standard ritual, the family welcomed in all who stood outside in the cold, and soon the room that had been cleared of all the tables was full of friends and family and neighbors from around town.

They migrated to the dining area where the dining room table was loaded down with food, and soon people had heaping plates full of *tamales* and pork and a wide variety of other delectable items that were making Gabby's mouth water.

Her eyes searched for Luke, as they had been separated when the people had filed into the home. It wasn't hard to find him, as he was nearly six inches taller than everyone else in the room. It took her forever to make her way towards him, though, as she was greeted by so many who hadn't seen her in a long time.

Finally, she reached his side and smiled up at him. "So, what do you think?" she asked loudly above the noise of everyone talking.

He leaned down so he could speak into her ear. "This is amazing!"

"It's time for you to enjoy some of the food we've been cooking for a week," she called back to him, and caught his hand, pulling him towards the table of food. She loaded a plate for him and handed it off to him with a bright smile on her face. "Enjoy."

He took a few hesitant bites of the food, then began to

eat it with greater enthusiasm. Gabby couldn't contain her laughter. "Now you know why we love the food at Christmas."

He only nodded in agreement, as his mouth was full of food. As she glanced around the room for her family, she noticed all the young women who were eyeing Luke, and she felt a pain in her heart. It had officially started. Luke's opportunity to find someone beautiful, sophisticated, and elegant to take to the gala had begun.

※

AT FIRST LUKE didn't want the evening to end. The singing and food and friendly people made him feel as if he was part of a special party, and he was actually welcome. But the beautiful night came crashing to a halt when Olivia tapped her glass and the room suddenly fell silent.

"My dear friends and family, we are honored to have you here with us tonight. As most of you are aware, we have an esteemed guest with us tonight. Doctor Luke Davenport is the new town doctor and we want to welcome him properly. He has been invited by the President to attend the annual Christmas Gala held at the Capital. He is looking for the right woman to take as his special guest. He wants one of you beautiful ladies to be his companion at the gala."

Luke wished the floor would open up and swallow him whole. All eyes were suddenly on him, a position he didn't want to be in. He raised the glass of cider he held and nodded to the crowd. "It is a pleasure to meet all of you," he said, his voice carrying throughout the space. His comment earned him smiles and nods, and even winks from some of the eligible women. He wanted to go stand outside in the cold and not face a single one of them.

He looked down to tell Gabby exactly that, but she was no longer there. She had faded away and he couldn't find her even though his eyes probed the room. Suddenly the room seemed to take a deep breath as everyone moved closer together and cleared the space in the main eating area where they usually served food.

Music filled the air as guitars were strummed and a group of men began singing. There were shouts of joy throughout the room, and man and woman paired up then jumped out on the newly created dance floor, their feet moving in rhythm to the beat.

Several people approached Luke at once, but one man and young lady managed to push forward in front of the others. A rather large, rotund man, he still held a plate of food he was eating. But with his other hand he pushed forward a young woman who smiled at him as if he were something to be eaten.

"*Hola*, I am Gustavo Garcia. This is my lovely daughter Desiree. It would be wonderful for the two of you to get to know each other through the first dance, don't you agree?"

Luke carefully set his cider down and smiled at Desiree. "It would be my honor."

The next several minutes he was assaulted by the mindless prattle of a young woman who had only known privilege her entire life and didn't know a thing about what a doctor did. She asked a couple of questions, but usually had finished his sentence before even he could. The next three women were the same, if not worse. One of the women couldn't stop giggling, and another one snorted through her nose when she laughed.

After having danced with four different women, Luke took a break away from them and went back for more cider, this time adding some special rum to the mix. He was going to need all the help he could get in order to make it through the night.

"Doctor Davenport, I'd like to introduce my niece…"

And so it continued, over and over until he had lost count of the number of women he had danced with. Several had been charming and sweet while others had self-righteous attitudes and a sense of entitlement. A flash of green twirling around the room caught his eye, but he couldn't see who it was.

He strained to look at the woman in green, but every time he could get a good view of her, someone would dance into his line of sight. The woman dancing with him attempted to draw his eyes back to her by asking him a few questions. Even though he tried to accommodate her and answer every question the best he could, he could tell she was getting annoyed.

Finally, the woman in the green dress swept past him and his eyes landed on a petite frame. Her eyes were shining in delight, and she was smiling brightly at the young man who twirled her around. At one point Gabby even threw her head back and laughed at something the man she danced with had said.

Maybe she had found her soul mate. She certainly looked happy. And his heart sunk. He had been a fool. He had opened his heart to her, he had become vulnerable, and somehow, she had stolen his heart. The realization should have been more shocking than it was. But over the last few days he had felt it—he had felt love.

The song finished and the woman he was dancing with flounced away from him after snorting at him in irritation. He couldn't blame her. He had been a terrible dance partner. But he knew what he had to do now. He only prayed he wasn't too late.

GABBY WAS OUT of breath from dancing so much. She knew the evening was coming to a close soon, and she dreaded hearing from Luke about the woman he had chosen to take with him to the Christmas Gala.

She had watched him dancing with many different women, and had seen him smiling, laughing, and dancing close to some of the women he held in his arms. If only those women knew the true treasure that held them so gently, they would never let him stop dancing with them. They would never let go of him.

With a heavy heart she moved away from the dance floor and towards the refreshments. She drank heavily of the punch, wishing it would numb her even further but it didn't happen. Suddenly she felt him. She knew he was with her just by the scent of the barbecue he had worked with, as well as the fresh, clean aroma a doctor must have.

"Gabby," he said softly, and she turned around slowly, trying desperately to calm her heart. "You look amazing."

Gabby looked down at the green cotton dress and almost laughed. It was far from the beautiful designs he would see on the women in Austin. "Thank you," she said, nodding her head towards him.

"May I have this dance?"

She nearly chocked on the punch, and set the cup down quickly. "Yes, of course," she said quickly. *Was it too quick? And what possessed her to agree to a dance with him anyway?*

Because your heart wants to.

She couldn't help but smile at him, though, knowing that he would hold her in his arms. He took her hand and goose bumps prickled her skin as she followed him out onto the dance floor. He took her into his arms, and even though he was a good seven or eight inches taller than her, they seemed to fit together perfectly.

His hand settled on her waist and a slight shiver ran down her spine. Suddenly all she could think about was the intimate kiss they had shared together at the clinic. She wanted to lay her head on his chest and sway with him to the music for the rest of her life.

Good God, I've fallen in love with this man! How could I have let this happen? I knew I was tempting fire with kisses, but I never anticipated falling in love with him!

She tilted her head back and looked up at his strong jaw and mesmerizing eyes. *How could you* not *fall in love with him?* "Have you enjoyed the party?" she asked, attempting to start a conversation that would take her mind off of a forbidden love.

"It's been amazing. I think the entire town is here."

"Almost. I know it has been a lot to take in." She smiled up at him, and he returned the smile.

"My favorite part up until now has been the food. But nothing could top dancing with you."

Her heart skipped a beat. "I have to agree—this is by far my favorite part of the night."

They twirled around the dance floor and she felt like she was floating. She knew that part of that was because Luke was lifting her on the spins, making them glide smoothly across the wooden floor. She couldn't stop smiling the entire time they danced and never wanted the song to end.

A man suddenly entered her peripheral vision and she glanced to the side and saw a gentleman dressed in ranch attire looking directly at her. She had the vague inkling that she knew him somehow, but she couldn't remember how. But when he began to walk across the dance floor, weaving in and out of the dancers, her heart began to race.

He finally reached them and tapped Luke on the shoulder. "May I cut in?" he asked, his voice low and deep.

Luke looked at the other man who was only slightly shorter than him and shook his head. "If you don't mind, sir, I'd like to complete this dance."

Before Luke could twirl her away, the man spoke again. "Actually, sir, I do mind. I would greatly enjoy being able to dance with my fiancée."

Chapter Fourteen

LUKE DIDN'T CAUSE a scene. He had stepped away from Gabby, though he still held her hand and looked her deep in the eyes. "Is this true?" he asked, his voice sounding odd.

Gabby felt tears building in her eyes. It was ruined. It was all ruined. The fantasy world she had been living in had come crashing down. "Luke, please let me explain…"

"Is it true?" he asked again, his voice slightly harsher.

Gabby couldn't control the tear that rolled down her cheek. "Yes. But if you'll only let me…"

Luke released her and turned to the rough-looking man who had come to claim Gabby. "Enjoy your dance. And enjoy your future wife." Without any further words, he disappeared into the crowd of people and Gabby couldn't see him anywhere. Finally, her eyes landed on the man who was ruining her life.

"Why are you here?" she demanded. "I barely even know you."

"That's the exact reason I'm here. I wanted to spend a little time getting to know my future wife before we are married in a month. Don't you want to get to know me?"

"Married in a month? Why now? You've had years to come and get me, and you've waited until the very last month!"

"The agreement was made that you would marry me no later than the beginning of the year of your twentieth birthday. You turn twenty in only a few weeks. So we will be married in January."

"You certainly seem to know a lot about our arrangement. Did you have a hand in crafting it?" Gabby lashed out, though she maintained a calm face and moved with him easily on the dance floor. He was quite good at dancing—she hated to admit.

"I was eighteen when this arrangement was crafted and I wanted nothing to do with it. But our parents made their arrangement, and here we are. I hadn't expected such a cold reception, though."

Gabby felt like crying again. "I don't know anything about you, though if my parents wanted me to marry you, they must have seen something good in you."

"Thank you, I think."

"I know I'm handling this all wrong. A woman should be eager to get to know her fiancé and excited to become a part of his world. And I'm sorry I'm not either of those things."

"Let's move past the awkward greeting and just make things work from here."

"That's just it…" She looked him straight in the eyes. "I don't want things to work from here."

"You're engaged? How can this be? Why didn't you tell us?" Serena was spouting off questions so fast, she could barely catch her breath.

"All of you, this is Dominic Esparza, my future husband. Our parents arranged our marriage just prior to my father being killed in the Revolution."

"How could you have kept this secret from us, Gabby? And you, Raphael!" Olivia demanded.

Raphael held his hands up. "It wasn't my place to say anything. Gabby doesn't need to be coddled. She'll figure things out. Might have a bruise or two afterwards, but she'll figure it out." He then turned and extended a hand to Dominic. "Raphael Torres. I'm pleased to meet you. Been wondering how long it would take for you to come around."

Dominic smiled, and Gabby hated him even more for being handsome. "I'm glad someone is happy to meet me."

"Just give her time. She'll come around." Raphael chuckled, then quickly hushed at the look Gabby gave him.

Abuela and *Abuelo* were watching Dominic closely. *Abuelo* finally spoke. "Why would our own son not tell us of an arranged marriage for his only daughter? Why?"

Dominic made a helpless gesture. "I don't know. I've known about it for a long time. But then again, so has Gabby."

"I had no say in the matter. Our family had water that your cattle desperately needed. If it wasn't for us, you wouldn't even have a ranch today."

"And the second half of that bargain was for you to marry me, so that you could partly lay claim to some land, such as if I die or something as permanent as that. Your brothers got the ranch you have now divided evenly. All you have is a lonely house you sit in all day long."

"How dare you try—" Her slap was caught in mid-swing by Cade. "Calm it down, Gabby. It's all going to turn out just fine," he said soothingly.

"I'm a healer, you idiot," she nearly spat at his feet. "I don't just sit around darning socks and waiting for the boys to come in off the ranch. I feed them, I make sure their weapons are always clean, I take care of the animals, and then I spend the rest of my free time serving as a healer to the townsfolk."

"A healer? Are you a damned witch?"

"Obviously these two know absolutely everything about each other," Angie said under her breath, making Serena snicker and then two soft "Ow!" cries came from them when *Abuelo* knocked them both under the table.

"If you weren't such an idiot, you would know I'm not a witch. A healer doesn't use magic or potions. A healer uses the gifts of nature that God has given us to heal a person's body, if possible. But if I could use magic—"

"If you insult me one more time, woman—"

"What? What more could you possibly do? You're en-slaving me to be your bride already as it is."

"You aren't the only one unhappy with this arrange-ment," he said low and under his breath so that only Gabby could hear him. "But I'm not making a scene out of it in front of my entire family. We need to talk in private."

Gabby felt the heat of a blush climbing up her face, and

hated to admit that he was right. "*Abuelo, Abuela*, may I be excused? I want to freshen up and then continue my conversation with Dominic in private."

Her grandparents nodded, and she quickly left the dining room, now devoid of all partygoers, and certainly devoid of any joy. Just as she turned down the hallway she saw the Christmas tree they had made for Luke and her heart ached painfully. She had to talk to him. She had to tell him that she wanted to be with him and no one else.

She stopped as soon as she stepped into his room, though, because he was placing his few belongings in a travel satchel. "You're not leaving, are you?"

He froze and she saw his back tense. After a moment he continued packing. "I've overextended my stay here already," he said, his tone indifferent.

"Don't leave because of me! Olivia might need you!"

"She has you now. You made it very clear that you will handle the birthing."

"Yes, but that was before I knew you, and before I knew your talents. I can see why she trusted your opinion." Gabby was grasping for anything to make him stay. If he left because of her, it would be a huge disappointment to her entire family.

"You can stop now, Gabby," he said firmly. He turned to face her and she nearly recoiled at the anger in his eyes. "Do you know what I hated the most about living on the streets? Do you? I always had to be on my guard. I always had to be aware that there could be someone who would do me harm. But now, I come to this family, to you, and I finally feel I have someone I can trust with everything."

Gabby's throat closed up with tears and she wanted to reach out to him, but the look on his face made it obvious he didn't want to have anything to do with her. She was the same as one of his enemies on the street, now.

"I still felt that way when I came to Texas. I was very guarded when Cade offered for me to stay at this home. But I was welcomed with joy and warmth and was made to feel like a part of the family. And I began to trust. And when this beautiful woman came into my life, kissing me so sweetly, I bared everything to her. Only to learn she has been betraying me all along." He began to walk towards her slowly.

"Luke, please, I never meant to betray you. I made a terrible mistake I know, but..." Her words trailed off as he came to a stop so close to her she could feel his warm breath across her cheek.

"I just wonder...were your kisses real, Vixen? Were those at least genuine? Or were you lying with your sweet lips in more way than one?" His mouth was hovering just above hers—tempting her to the point of madness. And then he turned and walked back to the bed, leaving her longing and craving his touch and feel.

On the verge of tears, she hurried past the dining room where everyone still sat, speaking quietly, and ran out the back door to the shed. She had a horse saddled quickly and took off in the dark, urging the animal to race faster and faster and faster, letting her hair whip behind her and relishing the sharp sting of the cold air on her cheeks.

She rode until the town was far in the distance behind

her, but she could still see the lights. And that was when the tears broke free as her heart fell to pieces. The injustice of all of it was unbelievable. Because Dominic's parents had wanted to be certain he married and produced strong children to continue his legacy, she had been the sacrificial lamb. Her parents had wanted to see Gabby wed, as well, and had dreamed of what their children would look like. But more important to them was that she would have land she could divide off to her children one day, something that wouldn't happen unless she was married to a man with land. Their parents would get everything they had put in their agreement, except the fact that Dominic and Gabby would probably resent each other for the rest of their lives.

Hot tears streamed down her cheeks, a sharp contrast to the cold air. She didn't know what to do anymore. She wanted to talk to Luke. She wanted his help, his clear thinking. But he wanted nothing to do with her. She shook her head, wishing to clear it of all the wrong she had done to him. She had let him believe there was a potential future with her. She had withheld the crippling information about her arranged marriage.

She had wanted Luke to have the best Christmas possible. Now she knew she had ruined it for him. But he was a strong, handsome man, and would find a woman deserving of his love very soon. And she would make do with her lot in life and carry on with what her parents' wishes were, no matter how much it hurt.

LUKE COULDN'T GET to the hotel fast enough. He couldn't get away from the Torres home fast enough. He couldn't escape fast enough.

He'd been duped. He'd been lied to and betrayed, and he should have seen it coming. But he had been so smitten with Gabby he had let his guard down. Hell, his guard had been down before he had even seen her. Being with the large Torres family and being a part of their everyday lives, he had begun to believe that the images he had only glimpsed through windows could be true. A happy, loving family could exist.

But it had all been a lie. Gabby had toyed with his heart, with his emotions, and there was nothing more he wanted than to be as far away from her as possible. In the morning he would gather what he needed and ride to Austin. He didn't intend on going fast, he would take his time and arrive at the gala just in time. If he arrived in Austin any sooner, he may go drown himself in the nearest bar he could find.

Chapter Fifteen

G ABBY ARRIVED HOME to find the house dark. She knew she had been gone for a long time, but was surprised that first, everyone had gone to bed, and, second, that Raphael or someone else in the family hadn't come searching for her.

She was actually relieved, because she didn't want to face any of them, least of all her brother who seemed very happy to meet Dominic. He couldn't have known that she was falling in love with Luke. They had actually tried to make it seem to everyone that they were merely becoming good friends.

Drawn to his room by habit, she opened the door and saw her things on top of the bed in the moonlight. So her husband-to-be had been given the glamorous quarters of the cellar. Sighing heavily, she walked over to the bed and pulled a pillow to her face. It still smelled of Luke. It felt as if he was in the very room with her.

She closed her eyes and could feel the warmth of his chest under her cheek, the rumble of his voice as he spoke to her, and then the soft, gentle kisses they had shared. Her hand went to the cut on her side and she felt the dressing he had put there. Dear God, she missed him so much it was as if there was a hole in her chest where her heart should be.

She lit a lamp in the room and carefully arranged putting up her things in the small space available. She didn't know what time it was, and she didn't care. Everything that had happened during the course of the night kept playing over in her head, and she felt ill to her stomach. She shouldn't have been as rude to Dominic as she had been. After all, he was the man she would be spending the rest of her life with.

She lay in bed, hugging Luke's pillow tightly to her chest until she could vaguely make out the first shimmer of daylight. She freshened up quickly and put on a new shirt-waist and skirt, after realizing that she still wore her green cotton gown.

Finally, drawing a deep breath, she headed out to face the family. Much to her surprise and frustration, Olivia stood in the kitchen, with one hand supporting her lower back as she prepared coffee to boil.

"Olivia," Gabby said in an irritated whisper. "What are you doing up? You're supposed to be in your bed!"

Olivia turned to look at her, a hesitant smile on her face. "I thought I could help with just a few things. Just a few things here and there. Won't that be fine? I promise I won't overexert myself."

"You're absolutely right. You won't overexert yourself because you're going straight back to bed. We've got this, Olivia. We'll take care of it."

"What about all of the cleaning? We were all so tired and confused after last night that the place is still a disaster. At least let me help clean."

"I'll hear no such thing. Don't worry so much. We're big girls. We know how to take care of things." Gabby took Olivia gently by the shoulders and began to guide her back towards her room. "All we care about is you and that babe," Gabby finished softly.

Olivia leaned forward around her large belly and kissed Gabby's cheek. "I'm sorry last night was so disappointing for you. I know you've come to care for Luke…but Gabby, how could you when you knew you were to be married to another man?"

Gabby smiled weakly. "I've been asking myself the same question all night long."

"I can tell," Olivia said, lightly brushing her fingers under Gabby's eyes, and Gabby was certain she looked like a total mess. But she would power through the day. And the next. And the one after that. For the rest of her life. And perhaps someday, somehow, she could come to care for Dominic.

After making sure Olivia was once more secure in bed, Gabby returned to the kitchen where she began to prepare the dough for *pan dulce* and *empanadas*. It didn't take long to make, as the kitchen was laid out so perfectly for the assembly of the items, and she was soon making the small round globes to be flattened into tortillas.

Angie came in next, her expression flustered. "I must admit," she said as she pulled on her apron, "I didn't know if you would be here this morning or not."

"Where else would I be?" Gabby asked in confusion.

"Either over at the hotel or halfway back to Corpus," Serena answered for Angie as she, too, entered the kitchen.

Gabby nearly choked on a piece of dough she had been nibbling on. "You think I would have gone to the hotel? Do you really think that little of me?"

"We just know how much he means to you," Angie said. "We knew you had become close friends. We just missed the signs that it was something far more than that."

"Speak for yourself," Serena said. "I could tell they were falling in love. It was obvious. They spent practically every moment of the day together. And the way she looked at him made it perfectly clear how she felt about him."

Gabby drew a deep breath. "There's no need to dwell on the past, now, is there? Yes, I cared for Luke, but I'd hardly say that it was anything more than that. I've come to respect him and his methods, and to my surprise, I see a doctor worthy of carrying the title."

"Oh, yes. That's what I saw in your eyes that whole time. Respect. How could I have possibly gotten that confused with love?"

"I don't love him!"

"Are you talking about me or the other guy?" came a deep voice from behind them. All three women whirled around and Dominic stood there, his eyes fixated on Gabby.

"The other guy," Gabby said instantly, then regretted acknowledging there was another guy at all. She wiped her hands on her apron and approached him. "We need to clean the dining space and prepare it for customers. Will you help me with that?"

He nodded curtly and stepped aside to let her pass. Even with him giving her the space to go by him, he was a large man, and she could feel his breath blow across her cheek as she passed. It reminded her of when Luke's breath had caressed her cheek, and she instantly felt remorse. She had made far too many mistakes. Mistakes that she needed to start repairing immediately.

The dining area was a disaster. There were mugs and plates scattered on windowsills and in every nook that could possibly balance something. There were even plates on the floor, obviously discarded as someone went to join a dance.

"One thing I now know, the people of San Antonio certainly know how to throw a *fandango*," Dominic said, shaking his head.

"It was our night to host the *posada*," Gabby said, smoothing her hand over her hair nervously. "It can become a bit, uh, overwhelming."

"Is that what happened between you and that other man? It became overwhelming?"

"I wasn't expecting you to question me about these things so early in our conversation today," Gabby said, irritated. "A gentleman should refrain from asking such things so abruptly."

"And a lady should honor her promises. This goes both ways. I can wait and ask you things later, giving you more time to justify in your mind why what you did was right. Or I can demand to know the truth now, and start fixing things."

"Fixing things?" Gabby began to move around the room,

picking up the plates and mugs, balancing them carefully on her arm. "What do you mean by that statement?"

He hesitated, holding several mugs by their handles in his giant fist. "I fix things. Broken things at the ranch. Broken equipment for a neighbor. I've even fixed fences with your brothers a time or two. It seems to be what I'm good at. So if I need to fix things between me and you, then that is exactly what I plan to do."

Gabby's heart ached. How could he possibly fix something that didn't even exist? "Don't you see? That's the biggest problem of them all. There isn't anything between us *to* fix."

"Then I'll just have to make sure there is something between the two of us. I'll be damned if I'm going to have you pining away for that foreigner who speaks so sweetly in your ear without having a shot at you myself."

Gabby shook her head in confusion. "I don't understand what you are saying…"

"You're a good woman. I've heard from your brothers how much you do. I didn't mean to insult you last night, and calling you a witch was a vicious thing for me to do, and I'm sorry for it. In my mind, for the last four years you've belonged to me. I had thought—I had prayed you would want to marry me sooner. There is nothing more that I want than to have some kids running underfoot every time I walk in the back door and to smell a homemade meal, and be met by some sweet lips. And I always imagined they would be yours."

Olivia closed her eyes tightly and tried to draw a deep

breath. "Dominic, our agreement—"

"Yes, our agreement guarantees I'll have some of those things. But not the sweet lips. Not willing lips attached to a woman who is just as hungry to see me as I'm hungry to see her. What I want is more than what our agreement guarantees."

"Dominic, I don't even know you. I'm so, so sorry that I've made a mess of things. But what if you hated me regardless? What if I'm not the right woman for you?"

"One thing you'll learn about me real fast is that I don't give up easily. I saw the most stunning woman in the room last night. And I knew immediately that she was mine, but she was smiling up into another man's face. If I have to prove to you that I am just as worthy, if not more so, than that man...give me that chance."

"What...what are you saying? Are you saying I have a choice in this in some weird, twisted way?"

He didn't comment right away as they deposited the dishes in the kitchen then returned to the dining area. He caught her arm as she tried to pass him and he placed his large hands on her shoulders. "Yes, Gabriella. That's exactly what I'm saying. Let me earn your respect. Let me earn your love as this other man had a chance to. Let me prove to you that I can be the man you want to have returning to your side every night."

"And if you can't?" she whispered.

"Then I'll agree to back out of the agreement. I'll step away and let you live the life you want. But that is only if you give me a fair shot. Only then."

Gabby's heart was racing. She had never imagined two men would pursue her. And after the previous night, Luke might not want to pursue her at all. But if what Dominic was offering her was true…if she had the chance to choose her own life, her own destiny…the possibilities were endless.

She looked up into Dominic's eyes and was surprised to see genuine intentions. She had yet to really look into his eyes, she realized, and she prayed they reflected his honest feelings. "I don't know how I'll be able to do this," she replied, matching his truth with her own.

"Just be honest with yourself. I trust the right answer will come to you." He winked at her. "At least I hope I can persuade you of that."

She couldn't resist her burst of laughter that bordered on tears. She wondered if she was possibly losing her mind. "You must be absolutely insane," she finally gasped out.

"Probably," he said softly, then touched her gently under the chin. "Don't look now, but we have an audience."

Gabby's head whipped around and she saw Serena and Angie standing in the doorway, their mouths agape, watching her in stunned silence. All Gabby could do was shake her head and shrug, then she tried to shoo them away.

"We'd best get working if you plan on feeding any folk in here today," Dominic called from behind her. "Like I said, San Antonio sure does know how to have a *fandango*."

LUKE WAS ON his way to Austin while the rest of the town

still slumbered. Or, at least most of the town. He couldn't stop his eyes from drifting over to the *cocina*, where he could see lamplight slipping through the shutters.

Had she fallen asleep in *his* arms the previous night? Had she allowed *him* to kiss her delicately on the lips and taste her sweet essence? Had she allowed *him* to hold her so she wouldn't get cold in the night chill?

He had been in shock when she had confirmed that she was the man's fiancée. Was this truly the innocent woman who had been with him the last several days, teaching him the joys of family and Christmas, and slowly chipping away at the stone he had built around his heart? Was this really the woman who seemed to crave his kisses as much as he craved kissing her? The betrayal had cut him deep, and he hadn't even been able to look at her as he had turned her over to her fiancé.

Her plea to let her explain herself to him was still ringing in his ears. She had looked just as shocked as he felt when the man had announced he was her intended. Did she think he had passed away and she was trying to move on with her life? Did she think the man had run out on her, never to return? Should he have stayed and heard her story?

With an angry shake of his head he turned his horse away from the *cocina* and away from town and urged him forward into the cold, misty morning. Never had his mind been so certain of his decision, and never had his heart doubted him more.

DOMINIC ASSUMED THE role the men all took—outside cooking. It was a very damp and cold day, and the customers were few, much to Gabby's disappointment. Because she wanted nothing more than to take her mind off of the challenge she now faced.

All she could think about was Luke. Had he already left for Austin? Was he cold? Who had he decided to take with him, and was he relieved to be free of her? Had there ever been anything between them, or had she just imagined a good, strong, handsome man would actually want her?

The questions swirled through her mind, and she had no good answers. All she knew was that she cared for Luke very much. It was what she thought love felt like. Could it be she had fallen in love with him? But Dominic was an incredible man from what she could tell, and he was willing to fight for her. Luke had left. Of course, he had been asked to see the President of the Republic. His hands were tied. If he had even considered wanting her in the first place.

"At some point you have to tell us what he said to you," Serena grumbled under her breath as she passed her with mugs of coffee for the few brave souls who were out in the miserable weather.

Gabby's eyes turned towards the back door as Dominic entered, trying to shake the wet drops from his hat and duster just outside the entry. When he glanced inside, their eyes met, and a half smile kicked up the corner of his mouth, and she saw for the first time that he had a dimple.

Had she met Dominic before Luke, there might not be any problems at all. But she hadn't, and in her mind, the storm raging behind Luke's eyes was far more appealing to stare into than the olive green mystery that stared back at her right then. But she had to be fair. She owed it to herself. She owed it to Dominic. And—more than anyone—she owed it to Luke.

"Your *abuelo* is killing the fire now. He said no more business for today."

Gabby smiled back at him. "He's too old for the cold."

"So he told me, though in a much more expletive way."

Gabby sighed. "That's *Abuelo* for you. He'll always tell you anything, especially what you don't want to hear."

Dominic stood in the doorway, stomping his feet and blowing on his hands as he watched her move about the kitchen. She glanced sideways at him and shook her head. "You need to realize that being a guest in this house is the same as being a family member. If you're seen doing that, Cade will likely ask you to go cut more firewood since you're already cold."

He raised his eyebrows at her and shrugged. "What else should I be doing?"

Gabby dried her hands on her apron and frowned at him. "Follow me," she said, and turned on her heel, not looking back to see if he was actually following her or not. She walked quickly to the hearth, then gestured for him to sit down. "This is where we come to warm up. It should help you thaw out some."

"We were watching icicles forming outside. It *is* freezing outside, you know."

She ignored him and once again gestured for him sit on

one of the benches pulled up in front of the hearth. "Now, stay here and, uh, thaw out a little. I'll make you a cup of warm coffee. That should help you."

She began to turn away, but he reached out and caught her hand, pulling her back. "Perhaps talking with you will help even more."

"We will talk, and soon. But let me get you that coffee first since your teeth are chattering too hard for you to talk anyway." She forced a smile to her face and gently squeezed his hand, then turned back towards the kitchen.

As she turned she looked up to see Raphael standing in the doorway, one eyebrow raised. She narrowed her eyes at him and moved around him back into the kitchen. "So should I plan to see you wrapped in his arms in a loving embrace next?"

Gabby whirled and slapped him across the face before she could even think about it. "Oh! Raphael! I'm sorry. I didn't mean—"

He held up his hand, stopping her words. "No, no, I had that coming. But even you must admit you've gotten past Luke quickly. Is it the dimple?"

"I haven't gotten past Luke, and you have no right to ask about my love life. What happens between me and Dominic is none of your business. Nor is it any of your business what happens between me and Luke."

"What do you mean? Luke is gone. He left once he heard you had a fiancé, and as far as I can tell, that still happens to be the case. So what does Luke have to do with any of this?"

"Nothing," Gabby shook her head and turned back to

the kitchen. "Why don't you go warm up with your old friend out there."

"Now look, Gabby, it isn't as if you didn't know this was coming. We've known about this arrangement for a long time. Don't play the victim here."

"Victim? Victim! Are you being forced into marriage, Raphael? As far as I can tell you've just been enjoying time with your new pal Trevor and now Dominic."

"Pa made the arrangement that he felt was best for you. Get that through your stubborn skull. The arrangement was for you to have land to hand down to your children one day. You know the land was already divided between the four of us boys."

"That doesn't mean anything to me. It never has. And Pa should have known me well enough to know I felt that way. I never wanted to get married in the first place."

"And Pa knew how foolish that was. And he knew how foolish you were being. This was in your best interest," Raphael pressed again.

"Thanks, Raphael. You really do know how to make a person feel better." Gabby attempted to turn on him, but he reached out and stopped her. "Don't be unrealistic about this, Gabby. You know what you have to do."

Gabby looked out towards the spot where she had left Dominic, then her gaze drifted to the place she had been dancing with Luke when her whole world had come crashing down around her. "Yes," she said firmly. "I know what I have to do."

Chapter Sixteen

"YOU'VE ALWAYS LIVED in Corpus?"

"As far as I can remember. My pa and your uncle were both awarded large land lots when they first began to entice settlers further into Texas. My pa actually met my ma there in Corpus, and they were wed quickly. I was born a year or so later, and then my mother became very ill. We lost her many years ago. I thought it would take Pa, too, but he was strong, and promised me everything was going to be okay. He died just two years ago in a cattle stampede."

"Oh, Dominic, I'm so sorry you grew up without a mother," Gabby said softly, watching the light hitting the different planes and angles of his face as it filtered through the windows. They had been sitting together for nearly an hour, sharing their family stories. Unfortunately for Dominic, the story was a short one because he had no siblings.

"It really wasn't that rough. My pa did the best he could, and as soon as I was sturdy enough to be out on the ranch with him, that's where I was. I loved every minute of it. It's a part of me."

Gabby looked at his face and hands, darkened from being in the sun, and could almost smell the fresh air of the open fields in Corpus coming from him. He was a man of the land, and was proud of it.

Something tickled the back of her memory, and she tried to recall it. "Didn't you…leave at some point? I can't remember the details, but I remember my brothers would trade off going to help your pa."

"Something I'm very grateful for. Pa thought it best for me to get a higher education. He knew I wanted to follow his footsteps and be a rancher, but he wanted me to be educated, too. I stopped going to school about the time you started. Pa just wasn't as strong as he used to be, and he needed my help on the ranch, even though I was little. So I knew how to read and write, but he insisted I learn more. I was gone for just two years before the stampede. If Pa hadn't been so stubborn…"

Gabby laid a hand over his. "It isn't your fault. He was determined to take care of that ranch, and no one could have known the cattle would stampede."

Dominic made an odd face, but nodded reluctantly. "It brought me home, and I've been working to make things right with the ranch ever since."

"What do you mean? I thought with my brothers' help the ranch was running smoothly."

"There are little problems that crop up now and then. Things your brothers probably don't tell you about because they don't want you to worry, and I don't want to put you through any worry, either."

"Seriously? Is there something about me that makes you all think I can't handle knowing what is happening on the ranch? I expect to be a part of that, whether we are together or not. I expect to know what is happening on either of the ranches. Because if we don't get married, I anticipate we will at least be good friends and I will worry about you."

He smiled at her, and she realized he had a dimple in each cheek. He could have any woman he wanted if he would just smile at her. But not her. No…the more she got to know him, the more she missed Luke. If he had ridden hard, he was drawing close to Austin. If he had taken a slow path, he was probably over halfway. The gala was the very next night. Who had he picked to grace his arm?

"I never should have started talking about the ranch. I know that isn't where your interest lies anyway. Do you plan to continue being a healer?"

Gabby was momentarily perplexed by the question. "Of course I do. Why wouldn't I?"

"Because you'll be married. You'll be having children of your own. With the responsibilities of wife and mother, being a healer will be difficult."

Gabby's eyes narrowed at him. "My mother had five children, took excellent care of my father, and still managed to be a healer. Do you see me unable to fulfill the same expectations?"

Dominic shrugged. "I simply thought you might not want to. I'm not questioning your ability at all. I've seen a little of what you are capable of, and I know you could do more if you wanted." He hesitated for several long moments, then finally: "Is that why you started to have feelings for this other man? Because he's a doctor? The two of you had something in common."

Gabby removed her hand from where it had still been covering his and sat back in her chair. "I don't know what it was that made me have feelings for him. But it was a joy when we were able to treat a patient together. It was as if we were thinking the same thing the entire time."

"I certainly hope that soon the look on your face will appear when you think of me. Otherwise, I'll know your decision very quickly."

"What do you expect of me, Dominic? We only just met, and that blame lies partially on your shoulders. And I had no idea I would even *like* Lu—the doctor. Healers and doctors do not have that much of a good working relationship."

Dominic's eyebrows lifted. "Why is that?"

"Because doctors usually want to use tonics and medicine they don't know the ingredients of, but that they believe will fix or temporarily relieve the problem. And they don't have any problem sawing off a leg or an arm instead of trying to heal it and make it whole again. Everything a healer does involves the earth and the tools God gave us. We don't try to force things unnaturally."

"Then how are you able to get along with this doctor?"

"He is different than any doctor I've ever known or met before. He knows how to use the plants of the earth to treat a patient, and is respectful of alternative suggestions and thoughts. He uses his medicine when he needs to, but he is very open to learning the way of the healer."

"I'm sure he is," Dominic said dryly.

"Please don't judge him. You don't know him and he

doesn't know you."

"He was trying to steal my fiancée away from me. I take issue with that."

"You can't. He didn't know, Dominic. I didn't tell him, and I really didn't think I was going to start falling for him. It was a total surprise to me, too."

"You should have told him. If he is any type of gentleman, he would have stopped pursuing you."

"Oh! This conversation is getting us nowhere." Gabby stood, scraping her chair back on the wood floor, and went to one of the few windows that wasn't shuttered and stared out into the bleak, wintry day. The weather fit her mood perfectly.

Suddenly, large, warm hands settled on her shoulders and she could feel him standing behind her. She waited for her heart to begin to race the way it did around Luke, or skip a beat, or in some way show her that there was a chance she could feel something for this man. But she only felt nervous and her palms began to sweat. She felt slightly ill, the way she always felt when she was going to lie, or had told a lie.

He wasn't the one.

She had already known, but hadn't wanted to admit it to herself. She had wanted to give him a fair chance the same as Luke, but there was no chance for him. Luke had already won her heart, and no matter how handsome, no matter how good of a man Dominic was, she needed Luke in her life.

"Don't give up on us just yet," Dominic said, as if reading her thoughts. "We've barely had a few minutes together, let alone the days you had with him. Please, Gabby, for the sake of what our parents wanted for us, if for nothing else."

Gabby turned to face him, staring up into his eyes, wishing she could love him, but knowing she couldn't. "Do you feel anything for me?" Gabby asked bluntly.

"I'm not sure I understand what you're asking," he said, his forehead furrowed in confusion.

"Do you feel happy to be around me? Do you look forward to and anticipate seeing me? Does your heart skip a beat when you get near me?"

He frowned darkly. "Is that the way it is for you around him?"

"Just answer my questions, please," she pleaded, her face searching his.

"I'm happy around you. There is something special and unique about you, and I recognize that you are a rare woman to find. I enjoy touching you, and seeing your smile."

"But is there anything more than that? Friends have the same feelings!"

"Dammit, woman, I don't know what you want from me!" A vein pulsed in his neck.

"I want...I want..." *I want Luke.* She swallowed hard. "I just want to know my decision is right when the time comes," she whispered.

"I've yet to meet a woman so difficult and frustrating..." He ran a hand through his hair, and sighed heavily. "Gabby, I'll respect your decision. But think of what you will have with this doctor, or if he'll even still take you. He didn't seem too focused on telling you goodbye when he left."

He had just voiced her greatest fear. What if Luke didn't

want her back? What if he was already moving forward with the woman he had taken to the gala? She shook her head. No, what they had was too special. He wouldn't give up on her. He might be angry with her, but it would all change when he came back.

"You agreed the decision would be mine. I may choose you, I may choose him, or I may choose neither and spend the rest of my days as a spinster. It is my decision to make."

"Don't let the fancy ways of that doctor go to your head. He is a man from another country, a man who has certainly been around a lot of women and knows how to treat them the way they want to be treated. Don't be naïve about this whole thing!"

"I'm going into this with both eyes wide open," she said fiercely. "I know what I am looking for."

"And what is that?"

"Love. Above all else, I will choose love."

❧

DINNER WAS A retelling of everything that had happened the evening before. Serena, Angie, and Olivia all had stories to share of the festivities, of the family members they had seen, and the latest gossip that was going around town.

Gabby enjoyed the stories and laughed along with everyone else, even when Dominic reached for her hand under the table. At first she had wanted to pull it back, but she reminded herself that she was going to give him a fair chance. But in her heart, she knew she would be lying to Dominic and herself if she chose to be with him. It was Luke she wanted. She only prayed he would want her.

The men sat back and enjoyed more conversation, with the scent of *Abuelo's* pipe filling the room, as the women cleaned up from the meal. Serena and Angie cornered Gabby in the kitchen where she couldn't escape and began interrogating her.

"What are you going to do? Do you think you can love him?" Angie asked first.

"Of course she can love him. Have you looked at him? Most of the women in San Antonio can love him." Serena wiggled her eyebrows dramatically.

"That's lust, Serena, not love," Angie chided her.

Serena sighed. "Well, there's nothing that can be done. It's an arranged marriage. You must honor the agreement that was created."

Gabby pumped water over the plates and began to clean them. "You don't understand," she said softly, feeling more torn and conflicted than she ever had her whole life.

"What is there to understand? You must be wed before you turn twenty. To Dominic. There isn't anything else to understand. Other than whether you've grown to like him some while you've been with him today."

Gabby began to vigorously dry off a plate. "He is a good man. A very good man. But he isn't Luke."

Angie and Serena exchanged glances. "You're in love with Luke, aren't you?" Angie asked gently.

Gabby fought the tears that burned in her eyes, but nothing she could do would stop them from falling. "It wasn't supposed to be like this. I knew what my destiny was—I reminded myself every day. Yet every day he was there, my protector, my friend, and eventually, yes, my love."

"You'll get over him eventually," Serena said reassuringly. "After you have a child or two with Dominic, you won't even think of Luke."

Gabby shook her head. "No. No, things have changed."

Angie began washing dishes after receiving a sharp look from *Abuela*. "What do you mean? What could have possibly changed?"

Gabby took a shuddering breath. "Dominic has asked for me to give him a fair shot to gain his love. If he fails, I may choose Luke or my own freedom, whichever suits me more. But I will ultimately have to choose."

Angie and Serena both stared at her in awe. "Are you absolutely certain he will forgo the agreement? He assured you of this?"

"Yes. But now I'm forced to make a decision that would have pleased my parents or one that pleases me. And I have no idea what to do. Even if I chose Luke, I don't know if he would have me."

"Couldn't you tell that he was madly in love with you?" Angie asked in shock.

"His whole day revolved around you."

"That's because I forced my way into his life. I don't know if he really wanted me around."

"Hah!" Serena laughed. "He would find ways to delay starting his day so he could have you with him. And the way he looked at you…reminds me of how Trevor looks at me sometimes."

"I just—I just have a lot to think about. Does that make sense? I need to decide whether I'm going to honor the wishes of my parents or go in a different direction altogether."

Angie shook her head. "No one can make that decision for you. But I can tell you this: no matter what, your parents wanted you happy. Use that as your compass for whatever decision you make."

With the dishes cleaned, they told each other good night and headed off to their own bedrooms. Gabby quickly changed into her nightgown and had just blown out her lantern when there was the strike of a match in the corner. Gabby gasped and reached under her pillow for her revolver, but her grandmother's face came into view just as the handle slid into her palm. She quickly released it and propped herself up in the bed.

"*Abuela*? What is it? Are you all right?"

"No. And neither are you."

Gabby sat up all the way in bed and was about to approach her when her grandmother held up her hand telling her to stop. "Stay in bed. For now. After I have my say, then you can decide whether you stay there or not."

"*Abuela*, you aren't making any sense... Should I get Angie? What is wrong?"

"Just because I'm old doesn't mean that I need constant attention and have everyone worried I'm on the verge of losing my mind. Though, after watching all of the *locura* around here this week, it is a wonder that I haven't lost my mind."

"What insanity? Yes, it has been a busy Christmas, but…"

"No! No 'but.' The word you should use is 'and.' *And* this week my young granddaughter tells me that she has an arranged marriage with a man other than the one she has been sharing all of her time with. *And*, that granddaughter lets the man she has been spending all of her time with leave and attempts to fall in love with a stranger she is being forced to marry. Now, if that isn't insanity, what is?"

"*Abuela*, I'm sorry I didn't tell you. I didn't want to. I think I was fooling myself. I didn't want it to be real. But it is, and I have to move forward."

"By making a decision, is what I've heard. You think I'm deaf now, too? You girls gossip loud enough to wake the dead. I like this man Dominic. And I would have thoroughly supported him to be your husband. But he isn't what you want. Your heart already made the decision for you, but you are fighting it. Fighting your heart is a dangerous game to play."

"He left, *Abuela*. He left and didn't even tell me good-bye. In his eyes I lied to him—betrayed him. How can I ever hope for him to care for me the way I care for him?"

"Bah. You children today—you get caught up in all of the problems and you never see the solutions staring you in the eyes."

"What solution? All I can do is wait for him to come back and beg him to forgive me."

"No! That is one thing the women of this family never

do. We never beg. At least…well, sometimes a little begging is necessary."

The hesitancy in her grandmother's voice made Gabby curious. "What aren't you telling me?"

"I want to tell you a story. It happened a long time ago. It is a story only between the two of us, and not to be shared with anyone, understand? Not even anyone else in this family. *Comprender?*"

"Yes, *Abuela*, I understand."

"Many, many years ago there was a beautiful young woman who lived in a small village. The men in her village tried to win her heart, but she withheld it, determined that she would wait for the absolute best man. She had her eyes and her heart set on a great military *Capitan* who was revered throughout the countryside. He was strong and handsome, and all of the women of the village wanted him as their husband. But this beautiful maiden knew that she could lure him—unlike the others. He was away on assignment one day when a military troop came through the small village and stayed to rest for a couple of days.

"There was a young leader among the group who was loud and boisterous and had the confidence of a crowing rooster. But he was also handsome, and kind, and when he saw the beautiful maiden, he fell madly in love with her. He attempted to woo her, and, at first, she would have nothing to do with him. But he helped her carry her purchases home from market one day, and she agreed to go for a walk with him after he gained permission from the girl's father. You see, things were proper back then. Proper!"

"*Abuela...*" Gabby groaned.

"Yah, yah, yah. You know it all. I understand. Never listen to the older and wiser ones who have lived a little more than you give us credit for. Now stop interrupting and let me tell the story."

Gabby fought the urge to roll her eyes and instead nodded primly to her grandmother, her hands folded in her lap, her feet beginning to get cold on the wooden floor.

"The maiden went for a walk with this soldier, and he made her laugh with his wit, and made her happy in her heart. And when he touched her hand—just her hand, mind you, nowhere else!—her heart skipped a beat. It was as if she had known him forever."

Gabby's heart began to pound. It reminded her of how she had felt with Luke. Just being near him made her heart skip a beat. His touch made her breathless.

"So the maiden continued to see him as often as she could while his troop stayed in the village. And when he finally kissed her, it was as if her eyes had suddenly been opened from a deep slumber and she could see all the colors of the world."

Grandma paused for several moments, a smile touching her lips that were wrinkled from years of smiling broadly. "It was after that kiss that the soldier knew he had met the woman he wanted to marry. And when he had received blessings from her father, he rushed to ask her. But that very same day, the *Capitan* had returned, and the beautiful maiden had caught his eye. Whether it be fate, poor timing, or a combination of both, the young leader of his troop came upon them just as the *Capitan* was bending to kiss the beautiful maiden.

"Feeling betrayed and deceived, he rounded up his troop, and they left that very night. But the maiden, to her shock, had been unmoved by the *Capitan's* advances, and knew that only the young man she had kissed would ever make her heart happy. When she learned he had left, she took one of their fastest horses in the middle of the night and raced through the countryside, until she finally came upon his troop. But he was still hurt, and didn't believe her when she said he was the only man she could ever want. She pleaded with him, and then kissed him, reminding him of the magic they shared together. It was only a few months later that they were married, and they spent many glorious years together."

Gabby's heart was racing. Was her grandmother really suggesting to her what she thought she was? "I've heard there is a beautiful gala in Austin tomorrow night," Grandma said softly, then pulled something out of her hair. "I can only imagine what it will be like." She slid the object across the dresser, then stood slowly.

"I know things seem hard now, *hijita*. But give it time and let your heart truly be the guide for your life." She walked over to Gabby and kissed her gently on the forehead. "Remember the story. Love finds a way—if you let it."

Her grandmother left the room silently and Gabby waited several seconds, holding her breath the entire time. Then finally she jumped up and lit the lamp, and her fingers trembled slightly as she looked at what her grandmother had given her. She was going to Austin.

Chapter Seventeen

LUKE HAD ALWAYS enjoyed nature. But the last day and a half riding through the Texas countryside had done little to improve his mood. All he could think about the entire time was the look on Gabby's face when the man calling himself her fiancé had stepped into the middle of their dance.

She had looked as shocked as he felt. But when the shock turned more towards embarrassment and horror, he had known the truth. She had betrayed him beyond words. And it hurt more than he had ever expected. He had thought it impossible to feel any pain because he had lost both his parents so long ago. He had fought for everything he ever wanted and never let the pain get to him, never let emotions get to him.

But she had found a way past his armor. She had found a way to touch his heart like no woman ever had before. And he knew no woman ever would again. Because he wouldn't ever let it happen again.

He adjusted his formal dinner jacket and cuff links, irritated by the stiff fabric. At first he thought he would find it difficult adjusting to the simple life of Texas. But their style and comfort with one another had reminded him of a better time and place in his young life. His later years had him participating in plenty of events and celebrations where he had been required to dress formally, but he had never enjoyed it much. He hated being paraded around as the school boxing champion.

He wondered why President Lamar had invited him to this Christmas Gala. Had he heard something about his background and had some sort of fascination with the sport? Surely not this far into the West—surely no one as far away as Texas had heard of him.

Perhaps it was just that the President was recognizing doctors and leaders of the Republic. Or, the most likely scenario, his name had ended up on the list by complete mistake. Regardless, he couldn't turn down an invitation to meet President Lamar.

He planned to ride home that night after the party was over and ride hard until he made it back to San Antonio. He had to settle things with Gabby. He knew there was the possibility that she would already be long gone with her fiancé, but that only meant he would ride to Corpus Christi or to the very ends of the earth if that was what it took to track her down.

She owed him an explanation. He deserved to know how she could be so warm and caring with him, how she could allow him to bare his heart and soul to her, if she planned to marry another man. More important than all the rest, had she pretended she really enjoyed his kisses and gentle touches? Or was she that way with every man she met?

The more he thought about Gabby, the more his anger and frustration increased. In an attempt to calm himself he went back to dressing for the gala, tying his dress shoes and adjusting his red tie. He had opted for the red to celebrate the holidays, though he felt nothing like celebrating. Christmas would remain as it always had for him—a bleak and miserable time of year.

THERE WAS A steady, cold drizzle the entire ride to Austin. It slowed Gabby down and made her long for a hearth with a raging fire, but she pressed on.

The sun had been up for nearly three hours, and she knew the family was aware that she was gone. She just hoped her grandmother was able to appease them enough that they didn't send out a search party for her. She would not be stopped on this mission.

Yet as she rode on, she realized she was going to get to the President's home close to the time of the gala, and would make quite the spectacle if she arrived looking like a half-drowned cat. She had heard there were servants' entrances into the grander homes of the South, and she would try that route first. She could ask someone to summon Luke for her, she hoped, and she wouldn't force him to be seen with her in the condition she was in.

As evening began to fall she rode into Austin and had to pause to take it in. The town was far more of a bustling city than she had imagined, and on several occasions she had to move quickly out of the way or risk being run over by a wagon full of supplies, or even coaches carrying passengers.

Her horse pranced madly in the mud, startled by all of the chaos around it. She patted the slick neck and soothed him, trying to calm him as she attempted to find out where she was going. It was then that she caught sight of the grand building atop a hill, and knew she was in the right place.

Darkness was closing in quickly as she nudged her horse towards the hill. She had precious little time left. She came around the back of the house and could hear the bustle of servants and their chatter as they prepared for the festivities to begin.

"May I take your horse, my lady?" A dark-skinned man approached her and reached for the reins of her horse. Startled, her horse reared up and pawed at the sky and she had to cling tightly to its mane to keep from falling off of him. Then finally it settled back down and pawed at the ground in frustration.

Quickly she slid off the back of her horse and gathered the reins. "Oh, no, sir. Thank you so very much. If you'll only tell me where to put him, I'll take care of it."

"But, madam...it is my job to take the horses. You shouldn't be on this side in the first place. The entrance for the guests is around the front. You don't have a carriage to take you in this terrible weather?"

"Oh, no, I'm not a guest. I mean...I was going to be, but there was a slight problem. I just need to visit with one of the guests..."

"Ah," he said hesitantly, then very carefully took the

reins from her hands. "Susie!" he called out loud, and a dark-skinned woman came out of the house briefly, her hands planted on her slender hips, her hair wrapped up in a bandana and her foot tapping in impatience.

"This young lady lost her way out here and came around the wrong way. Can you see her to the proper entrance?"

"Oh, no, please, sir, I only need to get a message to the guest..."

"Did she really just call you 'sir?' Now I know this woman is lost. Come with me, child, and we'll get you all cleaned up and ready for the party right away." The woman grabbed hold of her arm and pulled Gabby towards the house.

"Please, I just wanted to see someone briefly. I don't need to go to the party—"

"Don't fret now. I'm going to get Miss Rebecca Ann to take care of you. It's warm in here. Come on in now."

Hesitantly, Gabby let Susie pull her into the house and she was greeted by the heat coming off the cooking hearth and scents that made her mouth water. She suddenly realized she hadn't eaten since dinner the previous night, and her stomach rumbled in protest.

"Okay, child, hand me your cloak. We'll get you dry and you'll be ready to go to the party."

"Oh, but I don't think I should go to the party. I'm not dressed for it at all, and I only need to talk to a gentleman that is here. Please, ma'am, I just need to talk to Doctor Luke Davenport..."

"Sir and ma'am. Will wonders never cease! I met your doctor. He's mighty fine. I can understand why you want to look your best for him. Now let's have that cloak."

Reluctantly, Gabby shed her cloak and handed it to the nice woman helping her. But at the woman's tsking sound, she knew that Susie had discovered Gabby was indeed in poor shape to see the good Doctor Davenport.

"Child, you surely had a better dress. This...this, well, whatever you want to call it, is certainly not fitting for the party. Now you just sit here by the fire and try to warm up. Take your hair down so it can dry. I'm going to go find Miss Rebecca Ann for you right now."

Gabby reluctantly sat down next to the hearth and pulled her hair free of its bun, letting the long black locks fall down over her shoulders. She closed her eyes in pleasure at the warmth of the fire and felt the cold gradually leaving her. She glanced around at all of the women preparing food and placing them on beautiful silver trays that men in black suits with white gloves would come and take. It was a well-run kitchen, and she was very tempted to get up and join them so she could learn some of the things they were doing. It could be so helpful to the *cocina*.

It felt like it had only been a few minutes that Susie had been away, but when Gabby noticed her hair was dry, she knew she'd been waiting much longer. Maybe they had actually gone to get Luke. She didn't know who Rebecca Ann was, but she didn't want to bother her during the time of the party.

Just as she began considering taking her cloak and making a run for it, thinking the entire idea had been foolish, a young woman came sweeping into the room with Susie, and

Gabby's breath caught.

The woman was extremely beautiful, wearing a taffeta gown that had a giant skirt with tiny shimmering beads sewn across the bodice and sporadically over the full skirts. Gabby suddenly felt like a beggar next to this extraordinary young woman, and wished the floor would open up and swallow her whole.

"Oh, my dear, you traveled here without a carriage?" She approached Gabby but then hesitated when she saw her dress. "Who are you here with?"

"I'm…well, I'm here to see Doctor Luke Davenport. He was—is—a dear friend of mine. We parted on bad terms, and I had to come apologize to him. It seems silly now. Thank you for your hospitality, but I'll leave now."

"No, no, there's no need for that. Fortunately, Doctor Davenport didn't come with a date, and I believe you would be his perfect match."

Gabby shook her head. "I'm not dressed appropriately. I'll only embarrass him." Then she suddenly realized what Rebecca Ann had just said. Luke didn't have anyone with him. A small bud of hope blossomed in her chest.

Rebecca Ann shook her head, and the carefully coifed curls on top of her head bounced with the movement. "I have a solution for that. Come with me, dearest. We'll have you ready for the gala in no time. Susie, I'll need your help. This is going to be our special project for the night."

THE PARTY WAS just as Luke had expected. Many people with too much time on their hands, dressed immaculately, socializing and trying to rub elbows with the highest ranked person they could find. President Lamar was entertaining large groups of people at a time, and they laughed when it seemed appropriate, with all of the women fluttering their hands and batting their eyes at the men they were with—and some they weren't with.

He did not miss this type of activity at all. It was the same thing over and over, just different faces and different places, but it was still all about climbing the social ladder and gleaning whatever gossip they could to scatter about the following day. He had lived in the slums of society. But he could say he felt more comfortable there than around these people, whose only goal was to step on someone else to make it further up.

He stood to the corner of the room, watching everyone silently as he sipped from his cup of champagne. He was tempted to go ahead and leave, getting to Gabby as fast as he could. But he had yet to speak to President Lamar, and he felt obligated to do so before he left.

He started towards the group surrounding the President, but was intercepted by the Austin doctor whom he had met soon after arriving. "What do you think of our Capital, Doctor Davenport? How does it compare to your London?"

The man was the epitome of the doctors that Gabby loathed. He was pompous, overly confident despite poor medical knowledge, and bragged about the number of limbs he had to amputate during the Revolution. It seemed as if he was proud about the number of men he had disfigured for life.

"It is certainly rougher than London, that much I'll admit," Luke said casually.

The doctor nodded with a smug smile, then his expression gradually faded as he tried to process what Luke had actually said. "I'm not sure I understand exactly what you're saying. What is rougher?"

"The land. All of London is flat and already has become civilized. There is still an element of wild here. Believe me, it is encouraging to see the progress you've made so far." Luke was doing his best to insult the man without directly slapping him in the face. And given how arrogant the doctor was, he doubted any of his thinly veiled insults would even register with him.

"It is wild, that I'll agree. Takes real men to settle this place."

Luke bit his tongue before he got himself in any real trouble. "If you'll excuse me, I need to see to—"

"Who is *she?*"

Luke hesitated and his eyes drifted in the direction that the irritating doctor was looking. "I believe that is the President's daughter," Luke said, inwardly laughing at the man who thought he knew so much and was part of the innermost circles.

"Not her. The other woman. Who is she? I've never seen her here before."

That's when a flash of red caught his eye, a flash of a skirt on the other side of the President's daughter's beautiful green gown. And then they were descending the stairs together, side-by-side, and his heart stopped momentarily. It couldn't be.

Garbed in an elaborate red silk and lace gown, the bodice hugged her tiny waist, and the neckline revealed a little more than he wanted other men to see. The skirts were full and round, same as all the other gowns being worn that night. Her black hair had been carefully curled and brushed, and instead of being up in one of the ridiculous styles the other women wore, it hung loose down her back, save for a ruby comb lifting one section of curls up over her ear.

His heartbeat lurched back so hard it was nearly painful. Completely ignoring the doctor, he began to make his way towards her, but was suddenly blocked by nearly all of the partygoers as they pressed forward to greet the President's daughter and the beauty who was a mystery to them all.

He could see Gabby's eyes searching the crowd and he began to weave his way through, trying to press forward as politely as possible. He was a few steps from the staircase when her eyes landed on him, and she gave him a wobbly smile. There was joy in her face, but fear in her eyes.

He was just taking the last two steps to reach her when the President stepped right in front of him. "And who, my dear, are you?"

"Gabriella Torres," she replied softly, taking his extended hand and dipping into a curtsy in front of him.

"Oh, no, dear, there is no need for that, Ms. Torres." He brought her hand to his hips. "The honor is entirely mine. Now, where might your escort be, so that I can steal you away from him?"

"Right here, sir," Luke said, his eyes never leaving Gabby. *God, she's stunning.*

President Lamar turned to look over his shoulder and raised an eyebrow. "Ah, so you are. I don't believe we've had the pleasure of meeting just yet."

"Doctor Luke Davenport," Luke said, nodding to the President in respect. But he wasn't going to respect him much longer if he didn't hand over Gabby, and soon.

"Doctor Davenport! What a delight. You certainly are no disappointment, nor is your young lady friend. I can tell that San Antonio is treating you well."

Luke was surprised that the President remembered anything at all about him, let alone where he was assigned within the Republic. "Yes, sir. I've grown quite fond of San Antonio..." his eyes darted back up to Gabby "...and to the people."

"I'm glad to hear it. I couldn't have been more thrilled to have someone of your education joining our proud Republic." His daughter came up to his elbow and pulled gently. "Ah. My daughter is reminding me that I have a party to tend to. Enjoy yourselves, and I certainly hope to see you off before you leave." He winked at Gabby, nodded to Luke again, then turned to the group of people seeking his attention, as well as the attention of his lovely daughter.

Gabby moved towards Luke hesitantly, watching his face pensively. "Luke, I had to come find you. I never intended to disrupt—"

"Stop. Don't say anything right now. Just let

me…enjoy." He smiled at her, taking half a step backwards, his eyes roving over her, before settling again on her face. "When I left you, I never thought I would see you again."

Her smile faltered slightly. "I know. I know, Luke, and I handled that entire situation so poorly. Please forgive me…"

"Now's not the time for this conversation," he said, and began to guide her to the dance floor as the small orchestra started to play their music and couples made their way in the direction of the large ballroom floor. "Now is the time for me to finally have the dance with you that I wanted two days ago."

A blush touched her cheeks and she followed him out onto the dance floor, smoothly sliding into his arms as he guided her in the dance. "Have I told you how beautiful you are?" he whispered.

"Yes," she replied with her blush deepening. "And I don't think I've thoroughly explained to you how bad I think your eyesight must be."

He chuckled and shook his head, unable to take his eyes off of her. He had imagined how he would storm back to the *cocina* and demand to know the truth from her. To demand to know how she could have betrayed him so thoroughly. Never in his wildest dreams had he thought she would come to him. And it eased an ache in his heart that he had felt from the moment she had acknowledged the man who had interrupted their dance as her fiancé. But there were still so many questions to be answered. Yet, he didn't want to focus on that at the moment. Instead he wanted to enjoy having this extraordinary woman back in his arms again.

Chapter Eighteen

G ABBY COULDN'T STOP shaking, even though she was no longer cold. Far from it…she was warm from head to toe with Luke looking at her so intensely. She had felt his eyes the moment she had begun to descend the stairs with Rebecca Ann leading the way. She had searched the crowd for him, and when she saw his face looking back up at her, she had nearly stumbled and fallen.

He was just as handsome as she remembered. But she couldn't tell if the storm in his eyes was one of pleasure or one of anger. Perhaps he would send her back out into the cold and sleet, regardless of her dress, regardless of her need to explain everything to him. But he hadn't. Instead, he had claimed her as his, and she had felt as if she could breathe, if only a little, again.

"Why do you tremble, Vixen? Are you cold?"

"No. No. I just—I don't know what to expect right now. I don't know if you hate me or if you are willing to tolerate the mistakes of a foolish girl. I don't know if I can repair the damage that has been done."

They spun smoothly with the music, his eyes never leaving hers. "The mistakes of a foolish girl?"

"I should have told you so much more, and—"

"I don't want to talk about this now, Vixen, but we will talk about it. I want to know when you left to come here? Was it soon after I left?"

"No, no. It wasn't until after *Abuela* gave me this comb that I got my head straight and knew that I had to come to you."

Luke's eyes darted to the comb in her hair, then back to her. "This comb came from your grandmother?"

"Yes. Along with a story that I believe was actually the true story of her own love life. My grandparents have never been ones to talk about themselves or their courtship much. Instead, they talk about our parents, and then more recently they've been talking about Angie, Olivia, and Serena. But this story was so elaborate—it had to be personal. But don't tell her I figured it out."

He chuckled. "I won't. And I'm glad you've finally stopped shaking."

She realized it was true. In true Luke fashion, he had caused her to relax, and her mind was no longer occupied with the possible repercussions of her actions and betrayal to him earlier.

"So when did you leave? I'm sure it irritated a few people in the house."

"Grandma is the only one who knows I left. I took our fastest horse and left in the middle of the night last night."

"You did what?" he asked incredulously. "Do you realize how dangerous that was?"

"It was worth it. No matter what the outcome."

He sighed heavily and shook his head. "You take too many risks, Gabby. Far too many. I'm sure Raphael is livid."

Gabby shrugged. "Let him be livid. It is my life, and I should be allowed to do as I wish. I'm tired of everyone else making decisions for me."

Luke shook his head in frustration. "You must be the most difficult, most challenging woman I have ever met."

Gabby smiled. "I just know what I want and I go after it."

A slow, very male smile touched his lips. "Is that so?"

The music for the first dance ended and the couples started to leave the floor when the band began to play an up-tempo song, one that had Gabby's feet itching to dance. Luke grinned at her and swung her around and back into his arms, where they began to move to the fast beat, interchanging with other couples around them until they were back in each other's arms once again.

By the time the music stopped, Gabby was out of breath from both laughter and exertion. She was also beginning to sweat, and she wanted nothing more than to feel the cool air from outside on her skin.

Luke seemed to read her mind as he took her off the dance floor, one arm around her waist. She smiled at the feeling of having his arms holding her again, of feeling free and alive around him. But she still had to explain to Luke everything that had happened, and that sat in her stomach like a heavy rock.

President Lamar was also just coming off the dance floor with an attractive redhead, who beamed at everyone looking at her. But she didn't look that thrilled when the President kissed her hand, thanked her for the dance, and left her on the side of the dance floor. He noticed Luke and Gabby and smiled and headed in their direction.

"You two are accomplished dancers, I see. How long have you known each other?"

Gabby couldn't contain her laughter. "Less that a fortnight, sir."

His bushy eyebrows lifted in surprise. "From watching the two of you together, I'd have thought you had been together for years. You better hold on to this one, Doctor Davenport, or someone may try to steal her away from you."

Luke's grip on her waist tightened. "I don't intend on letting that happen, sir."

Gabby's heart skipped a beat. *What does he mean? He doesn't know that the terms of my arranged marriage have changed.*

The President nodded his approval and attempted to move on, but was stopped by a group of people coming to grab his attention. Gabby felt sorry for the man. He barely had room to breathe, and she didn't see how he could be enjoying his party. But he smiled and laughed, and then asked one of the women in the group to dance with him as the orchestra began playing another slow melody.

Gabby moved towards the doors that led out onto the magnificent porch that surrounded the house. "Are you sure you want to go outside?" Luke asked hesitantly, looking down at her.

"Yes. I never knew that women wore so many skirts and

undergarments to look like this. That and the dancing have made me very warm."

Luke chuckled. "You should see the way it is in London. Most of the women put a powder on their faces that makes them even more 'warm.' By the end of the evening, some of them have streak marks on their faces from where their sweat has run down."

"Oh, that sounds terrible!" Gabby shook her head, trying to picture such a thing.

"The women believe it makes them prettier."

"It sounds more like they are trying to hide their faces to me."

Luke threw back his head and laughed. "I think you may be onto something there."

One of the men wearing white gloves opened the doors for them and they were instantly greeted by a strong blast of cold air. He kept his arm around her waist, steering her to a corner of the porch where they would be out of the wind and it wasn't as cold. "Better?" he asked.

She tried to give him a brave smile. "Better." The entire time she had been riding to Austin, she had been thinking of the moment, imagining when she would have him to herself and she could explain everything. But suddenly, she was at a loss for words as she stared into his eyes.

"Gabby...I shouldn't have left you the way I did at the *fandango*. Not only was it unfair to you, but it was also unfair to the rest of your family for all they have done for me. I was just so...so angry and shocked I wasn't thinking straight. Is your family angry with me?"

"No! Of course not," Gabby said quickly. "But they are with me."

Luke shook his head in confusion, his brow furrowed. "Why? What are they upset with you about?"

"None of them knew about the arranged marriage," Gabby confessed quietly. She shook her head, trying to fight off the tears that burned behind her eyes. "I didn't want anyone to know. I think it was partly because I didn't want to believe it was true. I wanted it to magically go away. The terms of the agreement were going to end when I turned twenty, which is only a few weeks away. Since he hadn't come for me, I didn't think he was ever going to come, and the agreement would be null and void."

"How could your family not know about it, especially your grandparents? Didn't they make the arrangement for you?"

Now was the time for her to tell him the truth. He had certainly earned the right. She drew a deep, shuddering breath. "Dominic Esparza's family owned the largest ranch next to ours. We had to fight hard to keep our land when the Revolution was over, but President Houston agreed to it. The only problem was that the Esparza ranch had no natural source of water. Their cattle were struggling, and with that, their entire ranch was struggling.

"In January, 1835, before my father went to fight in the Revolution, Dominic's father came to my father and asked if there could be some arrangement made for them to have their cattle drink from the large water tank we have. My father was a very generous man. But he also wanted to make an arrangement. He knew that the ranch would be passed down to my brothers after his passing and would continue being a part of the family.

"But I was the problem. He wanted me to have some land to hand down to my children one day. So he offered the use of the water tank to Dominic's father—on the condition that Dominic marry me, ensuring that any of my children would have land handed down to them. Given that Dominic was their only son, there wasn't much discussion on the matter. The agreement was made and then we were told about it after the fact."

"How could you keep that from me? Why did you let me kiss you, hold you, and be with you the way a man pursuing you would be? You knew all this time, and you never told me anything." The frustration across his face was obvious, and a vein pulsed at the base of his neck.

Gabby closed her eyes tightly, trying not to cry, but a tear slid down her cheek anyway. "I never meant to hurt you," she whispered. "Never. I was too caught up in being with you, in the way you made me feel. I didn't want to even remember that I had a fiancé. I had never even met Dominic until the night of the *posada*!"

Luke pulled back in surprise. "You never met him? You lived on the ranch right next to his. How could you never meet him?"

"Our ranches are very large. And after my parents died, I didn't want to do anything unless it was with family. I stopped going to any of the *fandangos* in Corpus Christi, and I had my brothers to help get anything from town that we might need. So there really wasn't any opportunity for us to meet."

"And so why are you here now? Have you come to toy with my feelings some more? To draw me in to your tangled web that only seems to be getting more and more complex every time I see you?"

"No! No, Luke, please…please hear what I have to say. I know I've hurt you. I know I've caused you great pain. I would take it all away from you if I could. My heart is yours if you will have it. I cannot love another man—you are my one and only."

He was breathing deeply as he listened to her, and she had barely finished speaking before he took her face in his hands and pressed his lips to hers, urgent and hungry for her returned affection. And she didn't hold anything back. She slid her hands up into his hair, pulling him down tighter towards her as she raised herself on tiptoe, matching his urgency and hunger.

He slowly and reluctantly pulled his lips free, trailing them down her neck. "Sweet, sweet Gabby, I've been craving this from the moment I stormed away from your home. But how? How are we going to break this arranged marriage? You are betrothed to another man. And I cannot come between that."

"Dominic is a good man." Gabby managed to gasp out as Luke's kisses were driving her to near madness. But fortunately he pulled away from her and listened to what she was saying. "He gave me a choice. He asked that I give him a fair shot at love and that if he wasn't able to prove himself, then I was left to make my own decision. And I've made it. I choose you, Luke, if you'll still have me. I choose you."

"Gabby," he whispered, dropping his lips to hers again and a happy tear slid down her face. Her heart was racing, aching with the need to be held by him, to be loved by him as unconditionally as she loved him. Would he accept her now that he knew the truth? Would he believe everything she had told him was true?

Suddenly there were several loud cries from within the home, and a few women screamed. They broke apart startled and turned together, running hand in hand through the doors and into the house. Just as they entered a man was being tackled to the ground and another man was beating at his arm with his jacket.

Smoke filled the air, and suddenly Gabby realized what had happened. "Oh, dear God," she whispered, praying that the man wasn't severely burned. There was a hysterical woman standing nearby, either his wife or his guest, but obviously someone who cared deeply about him.

"He was just standing near the fire and a spark hit his jacket… Oh, please, tell me he's all right. Please!"

Gabby and Luke rushed forward. Gabby saw Susie hovering in the background, her face worried. Gabby released Luke's hand and raced to Susie and asked her to fetch her medicine bag. When she turned back around, she was startled to see Luke in a confrontation with a man she'd never met before.

"Keep your hands off of him," Luke growled. "I won't see him turned into another one of your casualties!"

"How dare you! Just because you think you are better than us—"

"I don't think I'm better than anyone other than you. Your way of practicing medicine is archaic at best. Stay out of my way."

The man's face turned beet red and he stumbled backwards, stunned by the comments Luke had just made. Luke and Gabby shoved their way through the crowd of people and found the man lying on his back, his face pinched in pain, his right arm smoldering and shaking violently.

The hysterical woman wasn't making things any easier. Gabby turned to a nearby older lady. "Would you mind soothing her at this moment? He is in distress and her cries are not going to help him. I'm sure your knowledge of staying calm through difficult times will help her." Gabby's attempt took root and the woman nodded solemnly, then corralled the younger woman and led her away from the scene.

Next, Gabby turned to one of the servants who was standing about nervously. "You, sir." Gabby gestured to him, and his eyes widened, but he approached her anyway. "Will you please go collect some ice from the edge of the roof and put it in a bucket with water? I need the coldest water you can get me." He nodded enthusiastically and took off quickly to do her bidding.

Luke had shed his coat and was already on his hands and knees next to the poor man when almost simultaneously their medicine bags were delivered to them. Luke raised an eyebrow at her, but said nothing as she joined him, kneeling next to the injured man.

"Scissors, please," Luke said, and Gabby quickly presented him with a pair, then held the fabric out and away from the man's skin as he began to cut through it. "Some of his jacket has melted to his skin," Luke said softly, so softly only she could hear.

"I'm hoping the cold water will help with that," Gabby replied softly.

He glanced at her out of the corner of his eye. "Good idea."

Gabby turned to her medicine bag and quickly pulled out her small jar of crushed poppy leaves and gently smoothed the paste-like substance inside his lower lip. Within minutes he wasn't groaning as much, and he didn't seem as mindful of the pain, though his arm was still shaking.

"Here you go, little Miss. I had a bucket of water outside earlier, and it nearly froze over, but not quite. Will that work?"

Gabby looked up at the servant and smiled at him. "Yes, that will work just fine. Thank you so much." Again, his eyes widened in surprise as he handed her the bucket of water. She dug a couple of fresh cloths out of her medicine bag and soaked them in the icy cold water, then carefully draped them over the burned arm.

The man sighed heavily and then, blissfully, passed out. Gabby and Luke worked together quickly to keep the man's arm moist and cool. Gradually the remainder of his jacket fell away from his skin and Luke focused on removing the man's entire sleeve.

Gabby gathered together her essential burn ingredients: lavender, chamomile, and witch hazel. She blended the ingredients into a thick paste, then, at Luke's nod, began to smooth it onto his arm carefully. He moaned a couple of times, but, fortunately for him, remained unconscious.

Finally, with the paste applied, Luke took the bandages out of his bag and Gabby helped him wrap the man's arm gently. He began to move around more, and Gabby nudged Luke. "He's beginning to wake up."

Luke nodded and drew a vial out of his bag and poured a small amount onto a spoon and tipped it into the man's mouth, and he reflexively swallowed. Gabby desperately wanted to ask Luke what it was, but he hadn't questioned her on anything she had done. She would have the same faith in him.

But he must have known, because as he closed up his case, he murmured to her, "It was morphine. Only a small dose. I'll send some home with the wife to keep him numb to the pain the first few days. Then he'll need to go through the healing process without the help of medication. Do you have a paste you can give her?"

Gabby wanted to kiss him right there in front of everyone. But she knew it would cause quite the scandal. Already there were questions circulating about who they were and if she was his assistant. She didn't mind the idea of being his assistant. A healer was a healer, no matter what title she went by.

The man stirred awake, though he was groggy. "My

arm…" he said thickly.

"Is going to hurt for a while, my good man. But you'll be fine in no time. Do you think you can stand?" Luke asked, offering a hand to help him up. Fortunately for the man, it had been his left arm that had been burned, not his right.

The man nodded and he took Luke's outstretched hand, then stood slowly, leaning briefly against Luke as he tried to gain his balance. "Have a seat here," Luke said, guiding him towards a couch and the crowd quickly cleared the way for him. "Let's sit and talk for a bit while you get your bearings. You've had a bit of a fright."

The man nodded, obviously still fuzzy on everything that had happened. Luke took the small vial of morphine and gave it to Gabby. "Would you mind talking to the wife? Then you can bring her back over here so she can see her husband is okay." Gabby nodded and took the vial and headed for the parlor where the woman had been escorted. But as she entered the parlor she was plagued by one thought. Luke hadn't said if he still wanted her or not.

Chapter Nineteen

"**Y**OU'LL ONLY WANT to give him a little bit of this at a time," Gabby said gently to the wife who was still suffering from hiccups. Her crying had dissolved as soon as Gabby had told her that her husband was okay, but hiccups lingered. "It is meant to treat the pain. The less you give him, the longer you can stretch out the medicine."

"But won't that mean he'll—hiccup—be in more pain? Shouldn't I just—hiccup—give him more?"

"You don't want to give him too much. More than just a tiny spoonful every four hours could kill him."

The wife went pale and looked like she was about to faint. "So," Gabby pressed again, "use this as little as possible." She pressed the vial into the woman's cold hands.

"Now, to treat his burns, here is some ointment. I've also added some painkiller to it that should numb his arm, making him ask for the other one far less often. Make sure his arm has a fresh layer of this paste on it every day. Don't be surprised if some of his skin comes off." Now she was certain the woman would faint. "But it won't be much, just the upper layer. We got to the burn fast enough to stop it from going deep into his skin. So he should be feeling good soon. Right now he just needs you to take care of him."

The woman nodded, dabbing at the last of her tears with a kerchief that she then stuffed down into her ample bosom. She stood and her circle of friends stood with her, walking with her back into the ballroom where her husband waited.

"That was incredibly brave of you." Rebecca Ann stepped forward and sat down next to Gabby. "The two of you make quite the pair. Were you able to resolve your differences?"

While Rebecca Ann had been making sure that Gabby looked her absolute best, Gabby had nervously confessed to her about everything that had happened. She confided her biggest fear was that she didn't even know if Luke would take her back.

"I don't know," Gabby said hesitantly. "I said everything that I needed to tell him. But I don't know if he still wants me. I may have ruined my only chance with him."

"I don't think that's possible. Father wants to speak with both of you, though. He is extremely grateful for what you did."

Gabby was trembling slightly as she stood and followed Rebecca Ann, wondering how women could survive being garbed in such a fashion. Her feet hurt, the dress was even more scratchy than her new cotton ones, and she had to constantly watch where she was going for fear of knocking over a table or lantern with her skirts.

But when she saw Luke, all thoughts of discomfort fled. She stood as straight as she could and smiled at him, pleased just to see his face. When he didn't immediately return her smile, her heart fell to her stomach. She knew it had been too much to hope for. She had lost him.

Much to her surprise, though, he held his hand out to her and pulled her close to his side. President Lamar looked at her and gave her a hesitant smile. "Thank you, so much, for all of your help. The man you aided is a dear friend of mine, and I would have hated for him not to be cared for by the very best. Which leads me to an odd question, my dear… What exactly is your profession? Are you a nurse or—or an assistant of some sort?"

Gabby let her breath out slowly. She wouldn't lie about who she was. She never had, nor had her mother. There was a sense of pride in being a healer, even if others didn't see it that way. She opened her mouth, but was cut off by Luke.

"She's a healer, sir. Or, at least, she was up until she arrived in San Antonio nearly two weeks ago. Since then she's been my assistant, though I think I am learning more from her than she is from me."

Gabby looked up at him to convey her gratitude, but he didn't look down at her. Something wasn't right. Her eyes returned to President Lamar.

"There's a young man here. He is quite adamant that you are his betrothed from Corpus Christi. He said you are a healer, but that Doctor Davenport lured you here. He will not leave without demanding satisfaction."

"Demanding satisfaction? What does that mean? This is absolutely insane!"

"I couldn't agree more," Luke said softly. "But he won't go. Not unless I fight him."

Gabby whirled to face Luke, squeezing his hand tightly. "No, Luke, you can't. You mustn't. It isn't the man you want to be anymore."

"Yes, Doctor Davenport has shared with me a bit about his unusual upbringing. Are you afraid for him, or are you afraid for your fiancé?"

Gabby turned back to face the President, feeling as if he had just stabbed her in the back. "You know nothing of my life, dear *sir*, so I kindly thank you for not making any assumptions about it," she said through gritted teeth.

"Very well, she isn't worried about the fiancé," the President said, smirking slightly. "Otherwise she would have begged me to stop this whole thing instead of trying to pick a battle with me."

Gabby squeezed her eyes shut at the laughter that rang out among the small crowd that had gathered around them. "I am so very sorry, President Lamar. I meant no ill will."

"Of course you did." He chuckled. "And I don't mind. You are ready to do whatever it takes to protect the man of your choice. I wish I could find a woman like that for myself. Now, what are we going to do about the man outside?"

Gabby's mind was racing and she said the first thing that came to mind. "Do you have another bottle of morphine? I could convince him it was a drink from the party and he'd be out for hours…" Again there was laughter from the crowd.

"Gabby…"

"Or perhaps I can just go out there and talk to him and explain everything. I'll let him know that I came here on my own."

"Gabby…"

"Can't you scare him away with some gunfire?" she asked President Lamar. The laughter was even louder this time.

"Gabby!" Luke's rough, firm tone grabbed her attention and her eyes shot to his face, then down to his hands where he was rolling up his sleeves. "I'm going to fight him."

"Oh, no, Luke, you can't. You're a doctor now. You're no longer a boxer or fighter or whatever you were called over there. You're meant to protect and save lives, not do them damage."

"Which is why I'm only going to shake him up a little, and then we can all have that talk you want." He began to move forward but she stepped in his path.

"Don't do this, Luke. Not for me."

"I'd do anything for you," he whispered against her cheek, then headed towards the door. She stood as though paralyzed, hearing tidbits of conversation as it passed her.

"Did she say 'boxer'?"

"…it can't be! I know he's…"

"Yeah, he's British, and he's got the right name."

"…Luke the Champion, here in Texas?"

"…best damn entertainment of the year."

Oh, dear God, her fears were coming true. She had to stop them!

❧

LUKE HADN'T BEEN nervous before a fight in years. But he was nervous this time. Because this time he wasn't fighting just for his life. He wasn't just fighting for a title or a scholarship. He was fighting for Gabby, and he couldn't lose her, not after what they had been through. He had left her when she needed him most, and he wasn't going to do it again.

"It's about time you came out. I wondered how long you were going to hide behind her skirts," Dominic growled. He was obviously drunk and furious. Usually the best kind of guy to fight. But also the most unpredictable.

"I was trying to convince her not to save you. She's all torn up that I'm going to mess up that beautiful face of yours." Luke took a deep breath. He knew what he had to do to stay true to himself and to protect Gabby. "Let's go."

"I'm putting my money on Luke!" someone yelled out.

"I'll take that bet," yelled another, and before they knew it there was a full-out betting process in play.

"I don't want to fight you, Dominic. She chose me. You're just taking it a little hard. You barely knew her. Go home and find another woman who will enjoy marrying you."

"I don't want another woman," Dominic said through gritted teeth. "I want Gabby."

Luke was finally standing near Dominic on the porch and glanced over. There were dead rose bushes, frozen on the other side of the porch, nearly ten feet below them. If he could just knock Dominic hard enough in the chest to go flying backwards…

Dominic suddenly lunged at him, a roar coming from his lips. But Luke was able to sidestep him and he crashed his shoulder into the column that framed the front of the house.

Luke was almost positive he heard the bones of the house groan in protest. He could only imagine how much his own bones would have groaned if it had been him.

"Do you plan on running away from me all night?" Dominic said slowly, his words slightly slurred as he turned to face Luke, and Luke suddenly realized he was in the bad spot, where he would get thrown off the porch if Dominic hit him just right.

"No, dear fellow, not all night. Just until you pass out."

GABBY WATCHED EVERYTHING going on around her in horror as bets continued to be made and people were cheering for either Luke or Dominic. She couldn't let them fight. She *had* to stop them.

She finally pushed her way through the crowd and saw that Luke didn't even have his fists up, though he was in a defensive stance. What was he thinking? Dominic could have him reduced to a pulp if he hit Luke the right way. She understood that Luke never wanted to fight again, but this was not where she expected to find things when she came outside.

Dominic made another lunge at Luke, which Luke smoothly sidestepped, and he shoved Dominic in the back as he went flying past him. The only thing Gabby could think of was that Dominic must have been rather intoxicated. He weaved as he regained his balance, then aimed for Luke again.

Gabby couldn't stand to watch the fight any longer, although, so far, there had been very little fighting. She was determined it wouldn't escalate beyond that. And she was so self-certain of her plan that she didn't expect either of the combatants to know what she was doing and she thought they would just stop fighting to listen to her.

So she didn't hesitate to make the run between them, right as Dominic's legs began pumping forward. She stopped directly in front of Luke and turned towards Dominic, yelling, "Stop!"

But unfortunately for her, his body was already in motion, along with his fist. She felt Luke try to grab her around the waist, but he wasn't fast enough. Dominic was moving at a very high speed for such a large man.

His fist collided squarely with her jawbone, and pain burst through her head. She heard Luke yell her name and suddenly felt the porch railing catching her at the base of all of her large skirts. She heard a faint scream, but it sounded far away and insignificant. She had to stop the fight between Luke and Dominic!

But suddenly her skin was on fire as she fell through the rose bushes and the icy ground below caught her in its hard, cold mitt. From a distance she heard both Dominic and Luke yelling for her. She could hear the sound of gasps and cries from women who had earlier been cheering on the fight. But then sound and light faded away and all she knew was darkness.

THE SOOTHING SOUND of a crackling fire was the first thing she heard. Then there was the soft voice of a woman, met by the low rumble of a man's voice in return. She felt as if she was floating, but memories were beginning to return.

Luke. She had to help Luke. She had to stop…something. She felt as if she were drifting on top of water, bobbing along with the current, and it was pulling away everything she was trying to concentrate on.

The fight! She came awake in a rush and instantly gasped as pain burst through her head. Following that was the tiny fires all over her skin. Luke's face appeared above her, and she sighed. "The fight," she said, then winced because it felt as if her jaw was going to break.

"Lie still and try not to talk," Luke said, lightly caressing her cheek. "You've had a rough night."

"What…" She stopped and squeezed her eyes shut. Finally, she opened them and looked at Luke, trying to convey her need for answers.

"I'll explain in a moment. I know you are in a lot of pain. I gave you some morphine already, but very little. Do you want some more?"

"No," she whispered, barely moving her mouth and was relieved that she wasn't overwhelmed by pain again.

He frowned but nodded. His fingers moved from her cheek to her hair, where he pulled the strands through lightly, fanning her hair out around her. "I need to check your head. You took a rather nasty fall."

She watched him with trepidation as he began to gently feel around her head, and all seemed fine until he touched the back of her head at the top. Pain burst forth and she winced, drawing in a deep breath to fight the tears of pain.

"Just bear with me," Luke said softly as his fingers continued to probe around the area that was so painful. Finally, he carefully laid her head back down on the pillow and felt along her neck, searching for any tender spots, and she was grateful when he didn't find any.

With a sigh he leaned back, looking slightly relieved. "Other than your jaw, you've got a nasty bump on the back of your head, but it, too, will heal with time." He hesitated before he continued, "I don't know how much you remember, so I'll begin from where I think you'll remember. It was after we had tended to that man with the burn on his arm. Dominic showed up and demanded a fight for you. He was rather drunk, and not quite in his right mind at the time. I do believe you broke the poor man's heart."

Gabby's heart sank. "But I never..." The pain came again and she closed her eyes, trying not to cry.

"I know you never told him otherwise. But in his mind you left him to be with me. And he couldn't process the fact that he could lose you so easily. He wanted to fight, but I did not. So I wasn't going to. I decided to let him wear himself out trying to fight me until he either gave up from exhaustion or just simply passed out.

"But then this petite woman, this little slip of a thing—you—had to come running into the middle of the fight. You tried to stop Dominic, but he was in a blind rage. He didn't see you until it was too late. He caught you square on the jaw, and you fell backwards. Those damned skirts of yours tripped you to the edge of the porch, and you fell over, through the dead rose bushes to the ground. You've been out for nearly three hours now. You've had me quite worried."

Gabby felt the heat of a blush creep into her cheeks. "All those people…"

"Yes, a lot of people saw what happened, and were about ready to lynch Dominic. I was able to save him, though, with a few quick words to President Lamar, and he is sleeping off his drunken rage down the hall." He shook his head at her. "I can't believe you did that. Who were you trying to save? You're half the size of either of us—you couldn't have stopped anything. Except, well, except by doing exactly what you did, I suppose."

Gabby swallowed and began thinking some of that morphine might have been a good idea after all. Her head was throbbing madly and she was beginning to feel the cuts and scrapes of the rose bushes, and it seemed each one was its own little fire in her flesh.

"I—I didn't want you to fight," Gabby said, wincing and trying to reach up to touch her jaw. Luke's hand stopped her.

"It will only hurt more if you touch it. Your jaw is very swollen right now, and it's going to take some time for it to go down."

Gabby drew a deep breath, bracing herself against the pain in her head and jaw. Was the bump on her head really that painful? Or was it that Dominic had punched her that intensely? "I knew you didn't want to fight. I couldn't let you ruin your promise to yourself to never fight again on account of me." She spoke slowly, but was able to get the words out.

He frowned, his fingers having returned to her cheek. "So all of this is because of me."

"You? How can you think that? This entire mess is my fault! Dominic...I should have told him I had chosen you, I should have..." She closed her eyes and allowed the tears of pain and remorse to slip down the sides of her face.

"You've had enough for one night." Luke held a cup out to her and she tentatively drank from it and realized he had put morphine in it. "You need your sleep, and you need to heal. I'm right across the hall. The President will let us stay however long we need to."

Gabby nodded her understanding, though she was quickly beginning to feel fuzzy. "I've missed you so much," she whispered.

"As I've missed you, Vixen. Now sleep. You need it."

He turned to leave and she caught his hand and held on to it, not wanting him to leave her yet. But then the morphine took over and she felt her fingers slowly relaxing their grip around his hand. And then she fell into the arms of sleep.

Chapter Twenty

LUKE WAS FEELING far from sleepy. He felt murderous. Dominic was fortunate that he was in a room down the hall and that Gabby didn't want him to fight anymore. Otherwise, he would have beaten Dominic to a bloody pile as soon as he had the chance.

He had tried to get Gabby out of harm's way the moment she had run forward on the porch. But Dominic was already on the move, and he couldn't grab her fast enough. He had heard the impact of Dominic's fist hitting her jaw and knew it was bad. But to make it even worse, those bloody skirts she was wearing had tripped her at the edge of the porch, and there was nothing he could do other than watch her fall, tumbling head over heels to the ground below.

He had shoved Dominic out of his way as well as any other guests who got in his path as he raced down the steps to her, slipping on the icy footing. The frost covering the ground had crunched beneath his knees as he dropped down next to her, and his heart had been pounding through his chest.

Dear God, she could have broken her neck. The thought

returned as he paced his room, reliving the terror he had felt as he'd found her unconscious and completely unresponsive to his voice or touch. The punch alone was sufficient to knock her out, but he knew the fall had done its fair share of damage as well. He wouldn't know how severely she was injured until she awoke.

Fortunately, the crowd had kept Dominic from coming down to check on her, though several of the men were ready to beat him the way Luke wanted to. But it was a foolish notion. The damage had been done. Dominic would punish himself far more for what he had done than any other person could. Yet that still didn't take away Luke's desire to make him hurt.

He had carefully lifted Gabby into his arms and climbed the stairs, and the gathered crowd parted for him quickly. President Lamar had immediately told him to take her to one of the bedrooms upstairs, and it was in that moment that Luke asked for Dominic to be spared and given a place to sleep off his drunken state. It brought a smile to Luke's face as he recalled them taking Dominic to the small, uncomfortable servant's room at the end of the hallway and telling him not to leave until morning or there was a chance the President himself might shoot him.

Luke had cared little about the party after that. His only focus had been Gabby, and one of the servants, a beautiful older woman named Susie, and Rebecca Ann had come in to help him. Carefully they had pulled her gown off of her and revealed the numerous cuts and scrapes that covered her from head to toe. As gently as possible they had pulled the thorns from her skin, wincing for her at the more stubborn ones.

When she had first begun to stir, she had moaned in pain and he gave her a small amount of morphine. But only a little. He had needed her to wake up so he could fully assess her injuries, so he could tell if she had suffered trauma to her head from the fall. Nearly an hour later—an hour of him holding her hand and staring at her face—she had awoken. It had been nearly three hours since he had brought her to the room, and with every passing moment he had grown more worried.

But she was all right. She was bruised and in pain, but she was all right. Luke looked at the bed that waited for him and continued to pace. He wanted to be with Gabby. He needed to be with her. He had been so terrified he was going to lose her...again. He had lost her once by not staying to demand to know how Dominic could be her fiancé and had tried to convince himself she was the same as all of the other women he had ever known.

But he had been wrong, and deep in his gut, he had known it. He should have trusted Gabby. He should have given her the chance to explain. But instead he had stormed away from her, his pride more bruised than anything.

He sat down on the edge of the bed and removed his shoes, and sighed with relief when he could finally wiggle his toes again. So much had happened in just one short night it seemed unreal. He shucked his shirt and attempted to lie back on the bed, but couldn't get comfortable. He needed Gabby.

With his mind set, he grabbed his lantern and headed out into the hallway, listening intently. The entire house was completely silent. Tiptoeing, he crossed the hall to Gabby's room and opened the door quietly, locking it behind him. Gabby appeared to be in a deep sleep, but her occasional restless movements told him she wasn't comfortable.

With the fire from the fireplace providing enough light, he blew out the lantern and approached her bed, slowly sliding between the sheets and blanket until he was against her and was able to slide an arm around her waist.

She stirred slightly and her eyes fluttered open. "Luke?" she asked groggily.

"If you ask me to leave, I won't. I'm staying with you until someone drags me away from you."

Her lips pulled back into a partial smile. "Sounds fair," she murmured, then snuggled up close to him.

And with Gabby finally in his arms, they both fell into a much-needed deep sleep.

)⚿⸎

LUKE LEFT GABBY'S room early in the morning, before any of the servants were up and about. He made a point to lie in his bed and jumble up the blankets to make it appear as if he had slept there all night. Lying with Gabby in his arms throughout the night had been well worth the risk of getting caught.

But now, as the faint light of dawn filtered through his window, his mind ran through everything that had happened the night before. He couldn't have imagined that he would have Gabby in his arms, dancing with her once again. He had prayed that there would be a way he could convince Dominic that Gabby really belonged with him.

But now that he knew the truth, it was a bit harder for him to come to terms with. What if it actually hurt Gabby instead of bringing her joy if she stayed with him? What if, in a few years, she came to regret her decision, realizing that her children would have no land to their names?

He shook his head in frustration and got out of the bed and began pacing the room, the same as he had the night before. What if Gabby was making the wrong choice? Then again, he thought of the drunken man he had encountered the previous night and wondered if that would be the type of man she should be with. Regardless, he needed to make the decision that was the best for Gabby and her future, and he wasn't sure she knew what that was.

As the rays of sunlight filled his room, he shrugged on his shirt and buttoned it and wished desperately for his belongings from the hotel so he could once again be comfortable. There was a light tapping at his door and he hurried to it, worried that something had happened to Gabby.

A servant stood at the door with his satchel of belongings from the hotel. "The President sent for your luggage from your hotel room, sir. Would you like me to unpack for you?"

"No, that isn't necessary. I can take care of myself. Thank you." He took the bag from the servant and nodded to him, then closed the door and quickly shed his stuffy clothes from the night before. Soon he was in the clothes he had grown accustomed to—a simple shirt and pants, with a day jacket that complemented his broad shoulders. His feet were also relieved not to squeeze back into his tight evening shoes but instead slipped into his boots comfortably.

Once he was finally dressed, he stepped out in the hall and silently entered Gabby's room. Much to his surprise, Susie looked up at him as he entered from where she was sitting next to Gabby's bedside. She stood quickly at his entrance and nodded to him. "Doctor," she said softly.

He nodded to her in return. "How long have you been with her?" he asked, wondering how long he had been away. It had felt like only minutes, but now as he saw the sunlight in the room he realized it had been easily an hour or more. He had been too lost in his own thoughts.

"Only an hour or so, sir. She was fussing a bit when I came in to check on her, and I just couldn't leave her. But she still hasn't woken up."

Luke came to her bedside and saw her face was tense with pain, but as Susie had said, she wasn't awake yet. "Thank you, Susie. I'll stay with her from here."

"The man—that man who did this to the little Miss left this morning."

Luke raised his eyebrows in surprise. "When? Did he say anything?"

"About the same time I came in to check on the little Miss. He was apologizing to President Lamar, and then he was gone. I don't know what all they discussed, but he sounded mighty pained for the problem he caused."

Luke nodded, then turned back to Gabby as Susie left

the room. Gabby whimpered and, in her sleep, tried to raise a hand to her jaw. Luke caught it and pulled it back down and watched her eyes flutter, but they didn't fully open.

He hated seeing her in this much pain. He reached into her medicine bag, which had been set next to his, and pulled out the poppy paste. He smeared a little on the inside of her lip, and within a few minutes her face gradually relaxed and the sharp look of pain gentled. He couldn't keep her asleep all day, but the more rest she got, the faster she would heal, and the less time she would actually feel the pain.

President Lamar came in to check on her progress in the middle of the morning, and at some point a tray of food was delivered to him, but he barely noticed. He was in the process of checking all of the cuts and abrasions on her arms and legs when her hand reached out and caught his sleeve.

He looked up in surprise and was startled to see her smiling at him, though it was a small smile. He would take any smile he could get. "How do you feel?" he asked softly.

"Like I was in one hell of a fight," she whispered.

He chuckled. "Well, you were. Between Dominic, the rose bushes, and the ground, I'd say you were severely disadvantaged."

She reached up and stroked his face and he caught her hand and pressed a kiss into the center of her palm. "I still can't believe what you did," he said, shaking his head at her. "You're lucky Dominic didn't hit you with his full power. He was able to check it right before he struck you."

Gabby's eyes widened slightly. "I think he would have killed me had he hit me with his full strength," she said, trying not to move her jaw much.

Luke's stomach clenched. She was right. More than likely a full punch from Dominic would have killed her. She was too tiny to take such a beating. He decided to change the mood. "The good news is that the swelling in your jaw has gone down significantly. You'll be feeling better very soon."

"And Dominic? What have they done to him?"

"Nothing." Luke shrugged. "He left first thing this morning, but whether it was to go to San Antonio or Corpus Christi, I don't know."

Gabby shook her head, wincing slightly. "No, he's headed to San Antonio. He won't let this go until he knows *Abuela* and *Abuelo* have given their approval to break the marriage contract."

"Do they have to give their approval? They didn't even know about the contract."

"*Abuelo* has to approve whoever I marry—you know that."

"Yes, but I don't see what that has to do with the contract. He can petition to marry you, as can I. Given your recent conversation with your *abuela*, I doubt there will be a problem."

"Dominic probably thinks similarly—for himself. He's going to try to convince them he is the right choice for me."

Luke shook his head and smiled down at her, though inside his stomach was in knots. Everything she was saying only reinforced his concern that he was not the right man for Gabby. She deserved so much. He could offer her a small room above a doctor's clinic as a home. In a few years he may be able to afford a home in San Antonio, but there was no guarantee, and his future in general was uncertain. He may not even become a decent doctor for San Antonio. He had no idea what to expect.

"Don't worry." She squeezed his hand. He had forgotten that he was still holding her hand; he had been so focused on the thoughts whirling through his head. "I've already made my decision, and that's all that matters."

"What actually matters right now, Vixen, is that you listen to your doctor and get some much-needed rest."

"I'm feeling better, honestly."

"I'm sure you are. When you can talk and move your jaw at the same time, then I'll agree. But while you continue speaking through clenched teeth, I disagree and think you just don't want to listen to me."

She squeezed her eyes shut and drew a deep breath. "*Abuela* only expected me to be gone for the gala. She'll begin to worry if I don't get home."

"I'll have a message carried to them. It will at least be three days before we can leave. You took a solid beating."

"Oh, Luke, we must be home for Christmas Eve. We simply must. I don't want you to miss out on the magic."

He could see the sparkle in her eye, even through the pain. "If you listen to me, that shouldn't be a problem."

"Whatever you say, Doc," she began to smile then winced and attempted to look away from him, but that only put pressure on her jaw and she gasped.

"Here," Luke said, helping to lift her head so she could drink some water.

"No, Luke, no more morphine." Her eyes pleaded with him.

"If you are sleeping, you are healing. It makes your recovery easier. Now drink."

She glared up at him, then reluctantly did as he said. He let her head settle back down into the soft pillow and caught her hand again. "How do your cuts feel? Are any of them very painful?"

"Compared to my jaw, nothing is bad. But my arms are burning, if you must know."

"That's where you have the most cuts. I'll keep a close eye on them."

"Luke?" she said softly, drowsily. "Before I can't feel anything, will you do something for me?"

"Anything," he said just as softly.

"Kiss me."

FOR TWO MORE nights, Luke snuck across the hallway to join her in her bed, where they would sleep peacefully, snuggled together, until early morning called him back to his own room. By then, Gabby was off of any medication, and she thoroughly enjoyed having the arms of the man she loved wrapped around her, protecting her, throughout the night.

Morning dawned on December twenty-second, and Gabby was sick of being treated like someone who was ill. With Susie's help, she slipped into one of Rebecca Ann's day dresses, and, even though it still felt foreign, it felt better than just lying in bed with her chemise on.

When Luke came into the room to check on her, he did a double take when he saw her. "What are you planning on doing?" he asked, the suspicion obvious in his voice.

"I plan on having you show me Austin. I haven't done any of my Christmas shopping, and we head home tomorrow. I have to get gifts…at minimum for the kids."

"Do you realize how hard it is going to be for you to travel home? You haven't fully recovered, and instead of resting today like I'm telling you to do, you're insisting on me taking you shopping? No. Absolutely not."

Thirty minutes later the carriage pulled around and Luke helped Gabby climb up the steps. "For the record," he said, "I already stated this is a bad idea. If you're uncomfortable tomorrow, that's all your fault."

"We're taking two days to get back there. Are you planning to crawl back?" Gabby teased him.

"That's the last time I make sure you are comfortable," he grumbled.

Gabby leaned across the carriage and kissed him, pressing her lips to his tenderly. "You worry too much," she whispered.

"When it comes to you, Vixen, all I can do is worry."

Gabby laughed as she settled back down in her seat, drawing a smile from Luke, who said, "It is good to hear you laugh. It has been too long."

"Well, I happen to know a talented doctor who took great care of me and has me feeling better than I have in days."

"Good. I'm actually thankful for the cold weather because it is keeping your bruise hidden by that scarf."

Gabby's hand subconsciously reached up to touch the space that was purple and blue, but when she saw Luke's raised eyebrow, she dropped her hand. "I know how terrible it looks. Can you imagine what *Abuela* and *Abuelo* are going to say when they see it?"

"I'm more worried about Raphael. If he finds out Dominic did this to you...we may have another fight on our hands."

Gabby shook her head. "No. I'm just going to say I fell. And that's the truth, just not all of it."

"Why are you going to protect him? After everything he did!"

"He's a good person inside. It was just the alcohol that night." Gabby fidgeted with her gloves as she spoke, before Luke's big hand covered hers.

"It's fairly obvious you were hit, Gabby. You won't be able to convince them with lies."

Gabby looked up at him and saw the expression on his face and forced a smile. "It will all turn out fine. I'm certain of it."

They rode in silence the rest of the way, both seemingly lost in their own thoughts until they came upon the market. When the driver stopped the carriage, Gabby looked enthusiastically out the window, excited to see what a market in the Capital city would look like. There were carts set up in rows between shops, and boards had been laid down over the mud, but they did little to control the oversaturated soil.

Luke was the first out of the carriage when the driver opened the door, then turned to help Gabby out. But instead of letting her step out onto the ground, he lifted her by the waist and spun around to set her on a wooden board.

She smiled at him as she huddled deeper into the thick jacket Rebecca Ann had given her to wear. "I can only imagine the things we will find here!"

"So far I smell mud and horse dung. Pardon me for not being overly zealous."

"Sometimes you are just too…too…British. Have a little fun with me today, won't you?"

"If you wanted to have fun, I can think of far better ways for us to go about it," he murmured, reaching for her waist again.

She laughed and stepped away from him. "Maybe we can explore those ideas later. But for now, good sir," she said, looking up at him and trying her best to look dignified, "we are in public. And we must conduct ourselves accordingly."

He smiled down at her. "You are bewitching when you smile, did you know that?"

"Good. Then my spell is working on you." She winked at him, then headed for the nearest cart and began to explore the wonders of a new market.

Nearly two hours later they made their way back to the carriage, their arms full of bags and boxes holding special gifts for the family. "You do know we are going to have to find a way to pack all of this tomorrow, right?"

"Maybe I should just ride with you the whole way home and we use our other horse to carry everything," Gabby proposed, glancing up at him, doing her best to maintain a straight face.

Luke's eyebrows rose. "If we do that, you may never get home, Vixen."

Gabby smiled and suddenly felt warm all over. She had seen her cousins in love and had wondered if she would ever experience such a feeling. Now that she had, she didn't want it to ever stop. She glanced over at Luke as he climbed into the carriage. But Luke had yet to say how he felt towards her, and it caused fingers of doubt to spread anxiety through her.

Her heart clenched painfully and she looked out the window. Out of everything she had been through over the past few weeks, she had never felt more uncertain about her future than she did when she looked into Luke's eyes. And that frightened her as nothing else could.

Chapter Twenty-One

THE JOURNEY HOME was rough. But Luke had expected it to be hard on Gabby, and had planned accordingly. He just hadn't planned on the continued wet weather. Much to his own surprise, he had decided Gabby's suggestion that she ride with him was probably the best to keep her as warm as possible. It had also helped to keep them both drier.

Gabby sat in his lap, her arms wrapped around his waist and her face buried against his chest, her large, slick poncho keeping them dry, along with the one that he wore. He wanted her to sleep most of the ride, but he could tell by her fidgeting that she wasn't resting. He stopped frequently so they could both stretch their cold limbs, but something wasn't on point with Gabby.

Ever since the previous afternoon she had been avoiding eye contact and had been hesitant with him. When he asked if her jaw was paining her more, she shook her head no and just said she was tired.

That night she had fallen asleep very quickly, so he assumed she was being truthful with him. But as they traveled and her behavior still seemed distant, he became worried. Had she realized that he wasn't sure if he was the right person for her? Had she realized that he doubted whether she should give her love to him and perhaps should reconsider the offer from Dominic?

He needed her to understand his thoughts behind it if she had somehow gleaned the idea that he was having misgivings. But he hadn't done anything that he could think of to reveal those thoughts to her.

Along the path home he had found an alcove sheltered by a rock outcrop, preventing them from getting wet from the non-stop drizzle and occasional sleet. He dismounted and reached up for Gabby, holding her in his arms longer than he needed to, until he slowly released her.

"Can you try to find enough dry kindling to start a fire? It appears there are a few large logs up under there. At least to keep us warm most of the night."

Gabby nodded and began in that direction. But at the last second he grabbed her hand and pulled her back to him, hugging her in a tight embrace and bringing his lips down on hers hard and urgent, needing to feel her passionate response.

And she didn't hold back. She slanted her mouth under his and stood on tiptoe, matching his intensity. He groaned his approval and ran his hands up and down her back, eager to feel her passion. He needed this...he needed *her*.

When he released her they were both breathing heavily, and she flashed him one of her dazzling smiles. He felt his heart race, and he wanted to pull her back again, to get lost in her kisses, her caresses, her love. Her *love*. Had he ever been loved before?

The thought stunned him and he watched her walk up to the alcove with an odd feeling in the pit of his stomach. Was that why he was considering pushing her away? He had never been loved before—or at least, not since his parents had passed away. Would he know how to reciprocate her love? Would he know how to show her every day that she meant more to him than his very next breath?

By the time he had the horses unloaded and their sleeping area prepared, she had started a nice, smoldering fire that gave them a small amount of heat to warm their feet and hands. She was even able to use one of the pans to cook them a small serving of beans, and to that she added bacon and jerky that Rebecca Ann had provided them with prior to their departure.

Luke had tried to find a way to compensate the President for putting them up and tolerating them for as long as he did, but he wouldn't accept any compensation, other than Luke promising to attend the annual gala for as long as President Lamar was in office. Luke hadn't known what to expect when he had headed for the gala several days ago, but had been certain of his future. Now he knew the President of the Republic well enough to call him a friend, and he had no idea where his future was about to lead him.

They ate dinner in a comfortable silence. As soon as Gabby had put up the pot she had washed out with rainwater, she came back to his side and nestled in comfortably as he wrapped his arm tightly around her. They sat in silence for a long time as they watched the rain mixed with a little sleet fall around them, warm and safe under their rock outcrop.

"Gabby…" Luke began hesitantly, unsure of what he was going to say to her, and unsure if he even wanted to say anything to her. He didn't want to lose her. But he had to know that she had thought of everything before she made any decisions that would change her life forever.

She looked up at him and he temporarily lost his train of thought. God, she was so beautiful, and she was his if he wanted her. And he wanted her so badly he was afraid he would make a decision they would both regret years later.

The clouds parted briefly, though the cold air still blew sharp and cold. The light of a full moon peeked through the clouds and Gabby shivered. "We call it a Comanche Moon," she said softly, burrowing closer against him. "It used to be that the Comanche seemed to always attack when the moon was full."

Luke's arm tightened around her. "Were you ever—did you ever witness an attack?"

Gabby shook her head. "No, but I treated plenty after they'd been hurt by the Comanche. Including Serena."

"Serena was taken by the Comanche?"

"Yes, but Trevor saved her. He loved her so very much. Love is a powerful thing, don't you think?"

Luke shifted uncomfortably. "Gabby, have you really thought all of this through? I mean everything, every single aspect."

"Of what?" Her brow furrowed in confusion.

"Me. Choosing me. Have you really thought it through?"

"I love you, Luke. There can be no other man for me

than you. What else should I think about?"

"I'm a new doctor, Gabby. I don't have much that I can offer you. I can't even offer you a home right now, other than a small room above the clinic. What kind of home is that?"

"I'm not picking you for a home, Luke. Our home could be right here for all I care. I'm picking you for the man you are. The man I love."

Luke squeezed his eyes shut. He would never grow tired of hearing her say those words. "But what will we have to offer our children, Gabby? Your parents made that arrangement for you to be able to pass on a heritage to your children, for them to have land of their own someday. What are we going to pass down to our children?"

"What if I'm unable to have children? Or what if I only have girls? It is tradition that land is only handed down to the men of the family. What then? We will have our love to pass down to our children if we are blessed with them. We will have our knowledge to pass down to them. And in my opinion, both of those things are far more valuable than land."

Luke looked back out at the rain and ran a hand through his damp hair. Was she making the right decision? Her answers sounded perfect, but he wanted to hear those answers from her. He wanted to know that she had thought through the idea of marrying him and was ready for any concern her grandparents might throw her way.

"Why are you asking me all of this?" Gabby asked, then pushed away from him slightly, turning so she could look at him straight on. "What is this? Do you wish I had picked Dominic instead? Do you not want...I mean, was I wrong to think..." Her voice trailed off as her eyes searched his face, waiting for an answer, but he couldn't find the right words to tell her to respond to her questions. "My God, you don't love me."

"No! Gabby, no, that isn't it at all."

"Then what is it, Luke? What? Why are you trying to get me to rethink my decision? Why!" Her voice had risen an octave and he could tell she was on the verge of crying.

"Gabby, please, I don't know how to explain it—"

"You don't need to. I don't need any type of excuse. But I'm not going to marry Dominic. That isn't going to happen. I made my choice. It was either going to be you, Dominic, or nothing. If I can't have you, I choose nothing."

She whirled away from him and moved to the bedding, wrapping herself in the blanket tightly and keeping her back to him. "Gabby, don't do this."

She didn't respond to him. *Damn it!* He'd known he would mess up the conversation. He ran his hand through his now dry hair. *What do I do? How do I fix this? How do I tell this woman that I don't know if I am capable of loving her the way she deserves to be loved?* She wouldn't understand him. Either that, or she would think it was another excuse.

God, I can't go through life without her. Was that what love felt like? Is that what he needed to tell her? He looked over at Gabby's back. *How do you tell a woman you don't know what love feels like? How do you tell a woman you aren't worthy of her? You just tell her.*

Luke turned his head back and stared at the flames. Somehow he doubted that would change Gabby's mind. She was hurt. And he had hurt her. And he was going to have to find a way to fix things, or he would be miserable for the rest of his life.

SAN ANTONIO WAS relatively quiet as they arrived near dusk Christmas Eve. Even riding the rest of the way with him, her back against his chest, Gabby hadn't spoken a single word. She looked exhausted, and he had no doubt he looked the same. Neither one of them had slept well the night before.

In all fairness, he had said very little to her, either. He didn't know what to say. Most of the night he had mulled over how to convince her that he was only worried about her future, and the future of her children. But the idea of having children with her had temporarily derailed his speech for forgiveness as he had daydreamed about a life with her, and seeing her hold their child in her arms.

But then they certainly wouldn't be able to live above the clinic any longer. There were things he was going to need to provide for her, and he didn't know when or if he would ever have those things. Which took him back to his original fear—was she making the right choice?

They rode up to the house and a delightful plume of smoke rose above it, and he was eager to get inside to the warmth. But when he saw Dominic's horse in the corral, he wasn't as eager. He didn't know what he would say to the man, and still wanted to hurt him for what he did to Gabby.

He helped Gabby down from the horse and looked down at her, searching his mind for the words he wanted to say— words he needed to say to her. But instead she caught him by surprise and stood on tiptoe, pulling his head down to hers and her lips meshed with his, moving gently, caressing his lips.

"Gabby," he breathed against her lips when she pulled away. He tried to say more, but she turned before he could and headed for the back door of the house.

She looked back at him from the small porch. "Don't be long. I need you with me. I—I want you with me."

His heartbeat doubled. *Say something, you fool!* But she was already through the door. He quickly unsaddled the horses and gathered up their purchases and headed for the house. He was surprised when Trevor met him at the door to help him with the bundles.

"It's good to see you again, Luke," he said with sincerity.

Luke nodded. "Same here."

"Are you going to be able to sort out for us what happened with Gabby?"

"I wasn't aware there were any questions," Luke replied, perplexed.

Before Trevor could answer him, *Abuelo* and *Abuela*, both working in the kitchen, welcomed him home with warmth. Serena and Angie also greeted him, though they were more hesitant in the way they acted.

Trevor led him into the dining room where the Christmas tree still stood with a few carefully wrapped brown paper packages under it. They added the ones that he and Gabby had bought, and then Luke noticed Dominic and Lorenzo outside, their conversation appearing heated.

Luke nodded towards the window when Trevor had turned to face him. "What's that all about?"

"Lorenzo is a bit disturbed by the way Gabby looks. We are all a little confused about what went on over the last several days. That's what I'm hoping you can shed light on."

"We're not having any discussions until we eat our dinner. I've looked forward to this all year long, and we're not putting it off no matter what," Olivia said, entering the room from the hallway, rubbing her large, rounded stomach with Cade right on her heels.

"Trust me, fellows, you don't want to get between a pregnant lady and food," he quipped.

Luke looked at Olivia and raised an eyebrow. The babe had dropped lower in her belly. The baby could come any day now. They were all about to experience sleepless nights. All except him, he reminded himself. He was no longer staying in their home.

The table was crowded with nearly all of them huddled over it. Serena and Trevor had volunteered to eat with the children in the other room and were entertaining the rambunctious group, much to the relief of everyone else. The parents finally got some peaceful time to eat, and all of the adults present were thankful food wasn't being used as toys at the table.

But Luke had been placed across the table from Dominic, and they exchanged equally heated glares, and either everyone at the table was pretending they didn't notice, or they truly were oblivious. Luke wondered what they thought about the gradually fading bruise on Gabby's chin and jaw. Had they realized she had been punched, and viciously?

"So, Gabby, you must tell us about the Capital," Olivia said, excitement in her voice.

"It was magnificent! The town is large, though not terribly so. San Antonio is far larger. But there is much traffic that goes through there, so the market was magnificent, with things I've never seen before. I never went to the Capital Building itself...just to the President's home. It was stunning. And President Lamar and his daughter were wonderful to both of us." She glanced over at Luke and he wished he could convey everything he felt for her in that one look. He had to make things right. After dinner.

"So you spent time with President Lamar?" Angie asked. "What is he like?"

"Luke spent more time with him than I did. He was a gentleman, and very gracious. He made Sam look a bit rough around the edges."

"That's because Sam is a bit rough around the edges," said Olivia with a laugh, referring to their previous President, Sam Houston.

"Ah, Sam's just a bit unrefined. He likes his drink. Who doesn't?" Cade chuckled, half-heartedly attempting to defend his old friend.

Gabby smiled at them. "Well, I like them both. Oh, and, Luke, did you see the Christmas tree in their home?" At Luke's nod, she turned back to addressing the whole group.

"It was simply breath-taking. The tree was twice the size of the one we have, and it had brightly colored decorations all over it. Some of them appeared to be made of glass. It was extraordinary!"

"I'd prefer a poinsettia to a tree any day," Dominic said, and Luke took his eyes off Gabby to look at the man he wanted to strangle.

"I'm sure you enjoy the way it changes colors as the petals die, don't you? Going from red, to purple, to yellow, almost like Gabby's jaw, don't you think?"

Dominic tightened his grip on the glass he held, his knuckles visibly turning white, but Luke refused to look away and matched him glare for glare. If the family didn't know the truth, they soon would if he had anything to do with it.

"Dominic came back to us early. The day after the party. He also said the President is very gracious," Olivia said, obviously trying to relieve the tension.

"I'm sure he did," Luke said. "What else did he share about his journey?"

"*Abuela*, you are still the best cook in all of San Antonio, and further I'd wager. I cannot wait for some of your cake and pie later tonight." It was obvious Olivia didn't want certain subjects brought up, and she was going to make sure her role as the delightful hostess was not compromised by anything—or anyone.

"I don't see how you will have the room. That baby is taking up so much space." *Abuelo* laughed to himself.

"Yes, *Abuelo*, I'm very aware just how pregnant I am. It

won't be much longer."

"Not much longer is an understatement," Gabby said, smiling at her cousin. "I think if you stand for more than five minutes you'll go into labor."

Olivia rolled her eyes. "It isn't that soon. Remember, I've already had one child. I know a little about what to expect."

"The second child is always different," *Abuela* said firmly. "Always. Even if you think you are prepared...every birth is different."

That led the mothers of the family to begin talking about their pregnancies, and how their husbands had responded each time, and soon the entire table was laughing—at the expense of the husbands. But they were laughing along with everyone else.

Darkness enveloped the house and the oil in the lamps was beginning to run out by the time they finished dinner. The women, excluding Olivia, cleaned the table and plates, making quick work of the task, while the men moved the furniture around in the dining room.

"Exactly what are we doing again?" Luke asked as they rearranged chairs and brought in a rocking chair for Olivia.

"Opening our gifts, of course," Olivia said, as if he should have known. He smiled at her as though he actually did know, but in reality was absolutely clueless. He needed Gabby. *I will always need Gabby.* The realization was startling at first, then brought about a warm calm. He knew what he needed to do now. He just had to wait for the right time.

Chapter Twenty-Two

THE REST OF the family came in and gathered around the tree in chairs, and Luke was relieved when Gabby came and sat next to him, even though he could feel the daggers being aimed his way from Dominic. At some point he would have a conversation with *Abuelo* and *Abuela*, explaining why he wanted to marry Gabby and why he was the right man for her. But that would have to wait a little longer.

"So are you going to tell me how you got that bruise?" Raphael said in a firm tone to Gabby when she had barely walked into the room, and Luke turned quickly, wanting to protect her, but also wanting to keep peace for Olivia's sake.

"It was my fault," Dominic said, setting down the rocking chair he had just moved to make room for all of the chairs.

A silence fell upon the room and the tension was so thick it was palpable. "Do you want to tell me exactly what happened?" Raphael asked, his words clipped. "Because if I'm looking at her right, I'd say she was hit. By someone, not something."

"Raphael—" Gabby began but was quickly cut off by her brother holding up his hand for her silence, his eyes fixated on Dominic.

"She was hit. By me. I didn't mean to—"

"You son of a bitch!" Raphael charged forward and both Cade and Lorenzo tried to stop him. But Luke was in the best position to put up a solid wall between Raphael and Dominic, and he did just that.

"Get out of my way, doctor. You don't need to be involved in this conversation."

"It doesn't look like it is going to be much of a conversation. And with you two bulls going at it, all you are going to do is tear each other apart. Give him the chance to explain, Raphael. I was there. Let him explain." Luke recognized the rage in Raphael's eyes, because it was the same rage he felt towards Dominic. But he couldn't let them fight in front of the women. Later, out back, it might be a different situation altogether.

"He hit Gabby and you're going to try and protect him?" Raphael demanded, incredulous.

"I don't like it any better than you do, believe me. But now is not the time or place for a fight." *Please offer to go outside. Please. Please just suggest stepping outside...*

"I'm not invisible, you know," Gabby said roughly, and all eyes suddenly turned towards her. "And I certainly won't be silent. Dominic probably doesn't even remember what really happened. He was too drunk." Eyes darted back to Dominic, who had folded his arms over his chest and was watching Gabby intently.

Gabby shook her head. "If there's anyone to blame, it's me. I didn't tell Dominic that I had chosen...that I went to be with Luke. He arrived at the President's house that night demanding to fight with Luke. He felt, and probably still feels, that Luke persuaded me to go to the gala. Which he didn't," she said, staring directly at Dominic. "Regardless, Dominic had more to drink than he should have and showed up and demanded Luke fight him. I—I, well, I wanted to stop the fight, and I jumped in the middle of it. Right when Dominic was taking a swing. So I took the punch before he even knew I was there."

"I appreciate what you are trying to do, Gabby," Dominic said, "but I take full responsibility for my mistake. Yes, I had too much to drink. And I didn't realize you had stepped between us until it was too late. My actions hurt you, and badly, and for that I will forever be sorry."

"You mean—this—this is why she's been gone all this time? Good God, how hard did he hit you?" Lorenzo demanded, trying to examine her bruise in the lamplight.

"Her subsequent fall off the high porch and through the rose bushes didn't help her recovery," Dominic muttered to himself, and Luke winced, knowing that would only add fuel to the fire.

"That's it," Raphael growled and tried to lunge around Luke, who blocked him one way, and then the next. "How can you stand there and protect him? Isn't she your girl? Don't you care what he did to her?"

Gabby's eyes clashed with Luke's and she seemed to be waiting breathlessly for his reaction. "Yes," Luke said softly, but in the silent room only punctuated by the crack of embers in the fire, his voice could be heard by all. "Yes, she's my girl." He turned his focus back on Raphael. "But I made a vow to myself not to ever fight again when I left London. And it isn't worth breaking that vow over something stupid he did when he was too far in the bottle."

"What do you mean to never fight again?" Trevor asked, his eyes suddenly narrowing in suspicion.

"I have a past that I've only shared with Gabby, but you all deserve to know. I grew up an orphan fighting for my life on the streets of London. I was actually fairly good at it, or so I was told, and soon people were paying to see me fight. Then one day a man arrived and offered me a scholarship if I'd come fight for their school. I couldn't pass up the opportunity."

He looked around at all of them and they all had shocked expressions on their faces. "That's one of the reasons I wanted to leave London. Everywhere I went, people saw me as the fighter, not as a doctor. No one wanted me to stop fighting. So I jumped at the chance to come to Texas. I never imagined I would be welcomed in by a family like this. I've never had a family."

"Luke Davenport. *The* Luke Davenport," Trevor said, grinning at him. "I've heard stories that made me wonder if you were just a fabrication of London's imagination machine. Is it true that you once—"

"So who were you really protecting, Gabby? Me, or him?" Dominic demanded, suddenly frustrated.

"I didn't want him to be forced to fight and break his personal vow because of me. It would have been foolish!"

"So your concern was entirely for him. I'm flattered,"

Dominic said sarcastically.

"I didn't want to see you pummeled to death, either," she said with irritation.

"Glad to know you think so highly of me," Dominic replied through gritted teeth. He looked back at Raphael. "It's true. I was drunk. I never should have gone there. But Gabby is mine by our arrangement, and I needed to remind her of that. I never planned to hurt her. I hadn't even planned to fight Luke. But by the time I got there, I was furious with him, and couldn't think clearly."

"I'm not yours anymore, Dominic. You gave me the option—"

"And you haven't even attempted to meet my request!"

"This conversation can wait. We have Christmas Eve to celebrate, and I would like for us to do so. Now. I don't want to hear any more of this tonight." Olivia stood with her hands on her hips, the picture of a frustrated mother trying to rein in her wild brood.

The family looked at her with shamed faces, and each one gradually made it to their chair. Again, Gabby sat next to Luke and he had to fight the impulse to pull her hand into his own. But she looked up at him, her eyes watching him closely. "Did you mean it? Am I really your girl?"

He trailed his fingers lightly down her cheek. "Now and forever, if you'll have me," he whispered.

Dominic jumped from his chair, his face deep red, and a vein pulsing in his neck. "You have no right to touch her. She is mine, do you understand me? She belongs to me!"

Gabby stood in response, her face just as furious. "I belong to no one! You don't own me. And you gave me the option. I don't love you, Dominic. I tried. I tried to have feelings towards you, but I don't love you."

"You didn't even give us a chance!" he roared, his voice reverberating off of the walls.

"Yes I did, Dominic. I really did try. But my heart belongs to Luke. And if I can't have him, I want no one. That is what you agreed to, Dominic."

"I agreed to that on the condition that you would give me a fair chance at gaining your love. You barely gave me a day! And then that very night you race off to be with *him*."

"You aren't being logical, Dominic. You don't love me, so how can you demand that I fall in love with you? We even talked about it—you don't feel that spark of excitement when you look at me or touch me. We just aren't meant to be together."

"We could feel those things if only—"

Luke stood and put his arm around Gabby's waist. "You've had plenty of time. You've had years if you really want to be honest about it. So man up to the fact that she's made her decision, and it isn't you."

"Bastard!" Dominic took a menacing step towards Luke. "And you." He laid his eyes on Gabby. "You had an agreement your parents made. And you've disgraced them."

Luke felt Gabby trembling and knew she was close to losing her composure. "Did you or did you not say you would break the agreement? Because Gabby was going to honor it completely. I knew it the moment she acknowledged you were her fiancé. So you either told her the agreement could be broken, or you're accusing her of lying. Which one is it?"

"That's enough!" Olivia's shout startled all of them. "It is Christmas Eve. It is almost time for midnight mass. I will not have you ruin Christmas Eve! This needs to stop—oh!" she cried out and her hand flew to her stomach and her face was pinched with pain.

Cade was instantly by her side. "What is it? Did the babe kick?"

"No, no. It's fine. I just—I just need to breathe." She opened her eyes and looked at the faces around the room. Her eyes finally landed on Gabby. "You of all people know how precious Christmas Eve is."

A tear slid down Gabby's cheek as she looked up at Luke. "I'm so sorry. I wanted this Christmas to be perfect for you, and all I've done is to create a massive problem." She shook her head with her eyes squeezed shut tightly. "I'm so sorry," she whispered.

"You haven't done anything wrong," he said, tightening his hold on her waist and wishing desperately that he could kiss her. Instead he looked at Olivia. "I'm sorry. I'll leave if you'd like. I don't want there to be any further trouble."

Olivia glanced over at Dominic who looked like a young boy who had just been chastised by his mother. "I, too, am sorry. This wasn't the right time for this conversation."

"Finally, common sense prevails," *Abuela* said from the corner where she sat with *Abuelo*. They had all forgotten they were there, and several faces around the room blushed in humiliation, including Raphael's and Lorenzo's.

"Good. Now that we have all of that sorted out, we can begin to open our presents," Olivia said, though her face was still tense. Slowly she sat back down in the rocking chair, a smile plastered on her face. Luke watched her closely. Either the babe had kicked her exceptionally hard, or something else was going on.

The children were called into the room and they entered with excited faces, staring eagerly at the large number of packages under the tree. Slowly Cade began to hand out the gifts, and the children eagerly tore into the packages, squealing with delight at the things Gabby and Luke had found for them in the market.

From special sweets for the boys, to a beautifully made little doll for Angie and Lorenzo's little girl, to a special drawing pad and charcoal for Bella, all of the children delighted in their gifts. *Abuelo* and *Abuela* exclaimed over the soft, woven blanket, and like two young people in love they held the blanket up so the rest of the family wouldn't see them kissing behind it.

Everyone laughed—everyone except Olivia. During the course of giving out the gifts, her expression had become more and more strained. Something wasn't right, and Luke knew it. But there was nothing he could do until she said something or acted in some way that allowed him to do something.

"Luke, this one is for you," Cade said, handing him the brown paper wrapped package. Luke tried to hide his excitement. A Christmas gift for him... He had never thought it would happen. He glanced over at Gabby and she was grinning broadly, not making any attempt to hide her joy. "When did you—how did you…"

"Oh, just hush and open it," she said, the lightness in her voice making him wish they were alone together. Soon enough he would get her alone. He was determined to so he could make sure she knew how much he loved her. He knew it now, finally. He knew it beyond any doubt.

No longer hiding his eagerness he tore into the paper and found a simple box that he quickly opened. Lying within the fluffy paper was a new stethoscope, the newest style available with the single earpiece and the rubber tube that led to the piece to place on a person's chest. He had wanted one for the longest time, and it was one of the first things he planned to order when he got all of his supplies for the clinic.

"How did you know? How did you… It's wonderful. Thank you."

Gabby smiled broadly, and, obviously without thinking, leaned forward and pressed a kiss to his lips. Dominic's chair scraped backwards and without a word he stormed outside. Gabby cringed. "I forgot," she confessed. "I was just so happy to see you happy."

"Gabby," Cade said, clearing his throat slightly and obviously trying not to laugh. "This one is for you."

Gabby looked at Luke with surprise, holding the box in her lap. Then, almost as eagerly as the kids had earlier, she tore into the paper and ripped open the box. At that point, though, she stopped with a gasp. "Luke," she breathed, "it's beautiful."

"Well show us what it is, Gabby. Don't keep us all waiting," Serena urged.

Gabby reached into the box and pulled out a brand new medicine bag, with her name scrolled carefully across the leather. It was a deep black with a thin board in the bottom to support the shape of the bag, and it closed with a shiny silver clasp.

"You both are completely hopeless," Angie said with a chuckle. "A medicine bag and whatever that thing was you got for him…I mean, couldn't it have been something more romantic or *normal?*"

"It is romantic to me," Gabby said, looking at Luke again, and he could tell she wanted to kiss him again. And he wanted her to.

"Oh!" Olivia's sudden cry drew their attention and they set aside their gifts and went to her side.

"What is it, Olivia?" Cade was already asking her, kneeling down on the ground and looking up at her with worried eyes.

Olivia was breathing rapidly through her mouth, her hand splayed across her stomach. After a couple of minutes, she finally opened her eyes and saw Cade, then Gabby and Luke. "It's the babe," she said softly, but the entire room could hear her. "I've been having pains since this morning."

"Why didn't you tell someone, Angel?" Cade asked, his eyes dropping to her stomach where he splayed his large hand.

"I didn't think it was time. The pains weren't very strong. And it is Christmas Eve."

"Christmas Eve or not, I think this baby has decided it's

time to meet everyone," Luke said gently.

"No, no. Not yet. It's almost time for midnight mass. We can make it to that—oh!" She grabbed Cade's shoulder and he winced as her fingernails dug in.

"I think you're right," Cade said. "Let's get her to the bedroom."

Gabby quickly began telling Angie and Serena about supplies to gather for them, and before Cade and Luke had even moved Olivia down the hallway, her room had been prepared, the bedding had been changed and towels had been placed down, and a stack of fresh towels waited for their use. Lanterns had been placed in several spots around the room, making it glow brightly. And Gabby stood waiting for them, wearing a fresh apron and holding a towel to dry Luke's hands after he washed them in the basin.

As usual he was impressed with her talent and knowledge. He only prayed he hadn't hurt her so much by his actions the previous night that she would choose to be alone rather than with him.

Olivia groaned low as they settled her onto the bed. Regardless of how Gabby felt at the moment, they needed each other to help Olivia. Because whether she wanted it or not, her baby was about to enter the world.

With Olivia as comfortable as possible on the bed, Luke quickly washed his hands and watched Gabby as she dried them. At first she was only looking at his hands, but she must have sensed his intense gaze, for her eyes looked up at him.

He smiled down at her, loving the beauty of the eyes that

stared back up at him. "Are you ready for this?" he asked so softly no one else could hear.

She smiled back at him. "I don't think I'm the one who needs to be ready. She still seems to be in denial."

He glanced over at Olivia who was telling Cade to make sure everyone made it to midnight mass. "No, it doesn't seem she's accepted it yet. But it's going to be a reality she's going to have to face quite quickly."

Gabby nodded. "I'm glad you are with me."

"There isn't any other place I'd rather be." God, he wanted to kiss her right then and there. He wanted to beg her to forgive him for being a fool the previous night and not declaring his love for her. And he wanted to ask her to spend the rest of her life at his side, completing him—making him whole.

Olivia moaned low and her hands grabbed her belly. Gabby turned to Cade and began to gently usher him out of the room. "I need to be with her. I need to help her," he argued.

Gabby sighed as she looked up at him. "It may be a while, and we need her to focus. When it is getting time for her to birth, I will call for you. Will that be okay?"

Cade hesitated, looking over at Olivia. But she waved her hand at him, essentially shooing him out of the room. He shook his head and looked back down at Gabby. "Take care of her for me, please."

"We will," Gabby answered, and gently closed the door behind him.

She and Luke immediately went into action. Luke began

to feel the abdomen while Gabby removed Olivia's under-garments and examined her. When she peered up from under Olivia's skirt her eyes met Luke's and he knew she had discovered the same as he.

"The babe is still facing the wrong way."

Chapter Twenty-Three

"WE HAVE TO turn the babe. We have to."

Luke looked incredulous. "Do you realize what you are talking about doing?"

Gabby was doing her best to remain calm for Olivia's sake. "Yes, I know what I'm talking about. I did it once with my mother and it saved the babe and the babe's mother. We must try it."

"It is going to be horribly painful for her."

"The alternatives are even worse," Gabby said with determination, rolling up the sleeves of her dress.

Finally, Luke nodded at her, and she went to Olivia's side, gently pushing her hair off her sweaty forehead. Gabby spoke quietly but firmly. "Olivia, I need you to focus on what I'm going to say."

Olivia was breathing heavily as she lifted her eyes up to Gabby's. "What is it, Gabby? You're scaring me."

"No, no. It is nothing to be afraid of. But the babe is facing the wrong direction. The feet are where the head should be. Now, we are going to try and turn the babe in your stomach. It is going to be painful, so I need you to be strong."

"How are you going to turn it?" Olivia asked, her eyes huge in her face.

"Don't worry about that part. Just stay strong for me. And resist the urge to push. I know that is what you feel like doing, but you must resist."

Gabby kissed her on the forehead, then turned back to Luke, doing her best not to show her own fear and worry. *Dear God, help us, please!*

Luke nodded to her and they leaned over Olivia's body and locked their arms together tightly around her belly. Holding as firmly as possible, they began to twist, moving their arms around her belly.

Olivia cried out initially, then held her breath as they continued to turn. When they stopped she gasped for breath, tears rolling down her cheeks. She was panting for air, watching both of them with fear in her eyes. "Did it work?"

Luke and Gabby looked at each other, a half smile on their lips. "The babe started to move," Gabby answered her. "We'll have to do it again a few more times, but we are making progress."

Olivia nodded, though the tears were still flowing down her cheeks. Together they locked arms again and began to turn and Olivia groaned low and deep, but to Gabby's joy she felt the babe turning slowly within their arms.

They had to lock their arms and turn the babe multiple times, and by the end, Olivia was crying loudly. But the babe was almost completely turned.

Suddenly Olivia gasped and grabbed Gabby's arm. "I think—I think something is happening."

Gabby quickly moved to look under the sheet she was using to give Olivia a feeling of modesty and saw that her water had broken. "It is nothing of concern. It is all part of the process. Don't you remember this from when you had Doyle?"

Olivia nodded slowly. "Yes, but that was two years ago. Everything feels new again!"

Gabby laughed softly and patted her hand, trying to soothe her. "Everything is in the right place for the babe now. I know it hurt. You are so incredibly brave."

"I don't feel very brave—oohhh…" she moaned low and squeezed her eyes tight. "Gabby," she gasped after a few moments had passed. "Gabby, I feel like I should push."

"May I?" Luke asked Gabby, asking her permission to check Olivia. Gabby's heart swelled. He was treating her as an equal, as someone he respected and trusted. They had come so far in just a few short weeks.

She nodded to him and he peered beneath the sheet then looked back up at Gabby. "She's ready."

Gabby went to the door to call for Cade, but he was already standing there, waiting. She laughed slightly at his worried expression. "It is all going to be just fine," she reassured him. "But she needs you now."

He hurried into the room and went to Olivia's side, grabbing her hand into his. She smiled at him. "You worry too much," she whispered.

He shook his head and kissed her cheek. "So what are you going to give me? Another boy? Or will it be a girl this time?"

"You're going to find out soon enough," she said through clenched teeth as a contraction gripped her.

"Okay, Olivia, the next time you feel that pain you need to push," Luke said, his tone calm but firm.

Olivia nodded, panting for air. "Try to breathe deeply," Gabby said encouragingly. "It will make it easier."

Olivia tried to breathe deeper, but was interrupted by a low moan. "Okay, now's the time to push," Gabby said, standing on the opposite side of the bed from Cade. "You need to bear down and push," she guided, supporting Olivia's shoulders and encouraging her to put her whole body into pushing.

Olivia drew a deep breath and very slowly released it, the entire time pushing down. When she had finished, she was once again gasping for air and covered in sweat. Gabby used one of the clean towels to wipe her forehead and neck.

"You're almost there, Olivia," Luke said, popping his head up from under the sheet. "I can see the head."

Olivia smiled amid tears of relief and joy until another contraction grabbed her. Gabby once again supported her shoulders with Cade's help and Olivia groaned low in her throat as she pushed.

"That's it, that's it…just a little bit more, Olivia, just a little bit more."

Olivia pushed with all of her strength, her eyes closed tightly and her face the picture of pain and concentration at the same time. Gasping, she fell back on the bed. "Is it out yet?" she asked, her voice wavering with fatigue.

"Almost. Gabby, will you come assist me?"

Gabby knew Luke well enough to know that something wasn't right. While his tone was calm and relaxed, she could hear the tension hidden in his voice. "Of course," she said lightly, and quickly moved to join him and instantly saw the problem.

The babe's head had made it through, but the cord was wrapped tightly around its neck, and the babe's entire face was blue. "Okay, Olivia, I need you to push again."

"I can't. I can't anymore."

Gabby stuck her head up above the sheet. "You can, and you will. Where's the stubborn woman I know and love?"

Groaning, Olivia bore down again, and one of the babe's shoulders came out, giving Gabby enough room to remove the cord. She instantly began rubbing the babe's back vigorously, trying to revive it.

Olivia moaned and pushed again. "Keep pushing, keep pushing," Luke encouraged her while he supported the babe as Gabby continued trying to rub life back into the lifeless form. With a loud groan, Olivia pushed hard and the babe came free into their arms.

Gabby took the baby and put her finger in the infant's mouth, trying to be sure it was clear and free of anything that would prevent it from breathing. There was nothing there. Luke leaned over and placed his mouth over the infant's nose and mouth and breathed into it. The babe's chest and stomach rose, but still there was nothing.

Gabby was beginning to feel desperate, but she knew she couldn't give up. Not yet. Not with Olivia's baby. She flipped the babe over onto its stomach and smacked its bottom hard. There was a pause, and then a faint cough, and then a wail that filled the room.

Luke and Gabby looked at each other, both with tears in their eyes, and without hesitation kissed each other over the squalling baby. "I love you," Gabby whispered, knowing there was nothing she could expect in return.

"And I love you," Luke said, staring into her eyes earnestly. "With all of my heart and soul."

"Is the baby all right?" Olivia asked, her voice trembling with fear and exhaustion.

"Yes, yes, and she's beautiful," Gabby managed to answer, tearing her eyes away from Luke.

"She? It's a girl! Angel, you gave me a baby girl!" Cade's enthusiasm was contagious, and they all laughed with joy.

Luke was still smiling at Gabby. Her heart skipped a beat just looking at him. "Why don't you clean up the new little princess and I'll finish here with Olivia."

Gabby couldn't resist leaning forward and kissing him again, then quickly stood and went to the table where she began to use the towels to wipe the baby clean and finally wrap it in a small, thick blanket. She turned and nearly squealed with surprise, as Cade was hovering right at her shoulder.

"Everything is good with her? She's healthy and has all her fingers and toes?"

Gabby laughed softly and held the infant out to him. "She's perfect, Cade. You two make some beautiful babies."

A happy tear rolled down his face as he turned to Olivia who was anxiously waiting to hold her little girl. Cade placed her in her arms and Olivia was overcome with tears. "I've been waiting to hold you," she cooed to the infant.

Gabby looked over at Luke and tried to imagine what their children would look like. She could only dream about what it would feel like to have their child placed in her arms after intense labor. She would probably feel similar to the way Olivia felt.

Luke had finished tending to Olivia and stood, a wide grin on his face as he watched Cade and Olivia coo and whisper to their newest member of the family. Gabby watched Luke's expression as Olivia looked up at Cade and whispered, "I love you," and they kissed tenderly. Luke's eyes turned to hers, and his smile broadened.

He walked to her and dipped his hands in the basin of water, cleaning them thoroughly, then holding them out for Gabby to dry them. As she did he caught her hands and pulled her against him, lowering his head to hers and kissing her passionately, his lips moving urgently and demanding a response.

She met it with eagerness, her hands tightening on his and pulling him even closer. She didn't want the kiss to ever stop. She had never been happier in her life. He loved her. He truly loved her.

Cade cleared his throat and they broke apart, and Gabby felt a blush heating her cheeks. "If you two love birds don't mind, I'd like to take our new daughter out to meet the family and would be honored to have you join me."

Luke and Gabby smiled at the same time and nodded, and Luke stepped forward to open the door while Cade walked out, holding their precious bundle carefully in his arms. Gabby dashed over to Olivia and kissed her cheek. "You were amazing," she said softly.

"As were you. I know this wasn't a simple birth. I owe so much to you and Luke."

Gabby shook her head, tears in her eyes. "You owe us nothing. We're just grateful you let us be a part of this incredible moment in your life."

Olivia smiled. "So it seems you may be staying in San Antonio. I may actually get to see you more often."

Gabby hadn't thought of that. Her heart leapt with joy. She would be moving back to San Antonio if she became Luke's wife. If. She just needed him to ask the question. She gave Olivia another kiss on the cheek and squeezed her hands, her cheeks hurting from the smile on her face. Then she dashed out the door to join Cade as he introduced the newest family member to the household.

§

DOMINIC HAD RETURNED. He sat quietly by the hearth as the family crowded around Cade to see his little girl. But when Gabby and Luke entered the room he stood and approached them slowly.

"May I speak to both of you in private?"

Luke could feel Gabby's gaze on him, but he didn't take his eyes off of Dominic. "Let's go to the front room," Luke said, gesturing for Dominic to lead the way.

The rest of the family was so caught up in the baby that

they didn't notice the three of them disappear into the other room, taking one of the lanterns with them. Luke watched Dominic cautiously. He didn't know what to expect from the man.

Once they were in the front room, Dominic turned to face them, his face expressionless. His eyes focused on Gabby first. "I didn't know you before, but after meeting you—I find you special and unique, and I doubt there is another woman in the world like you. But I don't love you. I don't know that I'll ever love a woman. I care for you, though, and I wish that would be enough for you, but I don't think it will be."

His eyes turned to Luke. "You've been good to Gabby. And to me. Do you love her?"

"Yes," Luke said tightly, wondering at the game Dominic was playing.

"Do you love him?" Dominic asked Gabby.

"With all my heart," Gabby said softly, looking over at Luke. Subconsciously, he reached out and took her hand into his.

Dominic closed his eyes briefly. When they opened, there was disappointment on his face, but it soon vanished into the same guarded look he had worn before. "I did give Gabby the option to choose what was best for her. I had hoped for more time, but her heart already belongs to you. I could have years with her and it would never change how she feels. I won't have a wife who longs for another man."

Gabby's hand tightened in Luke's hand. Dominic continued, "I've already spoken to *Abuelo*, and he agrees you would make a fitting husband for Gabby. If I must forfeit to someone, I am honored to forfeit to you."

Dominic held his hand out to Luke and Luke hesitated a moment before taking it in his and shaking it. "I wish the two of you the best of success," he said. "I need to get back to my ranch."

"Surely you can stay for Christmas," Gabby said, and Luke could tell she was trying to make him feel better about the decision he was making.

Dominic shook his head. "I've made things awkward enough as it is. The best thing is for me to leave."

Luke had noticed that he was already dressed in his long duster and held his hat in his hands. He had already known he was going to walk away from Gabby, but had needed to hear for himself that Gabby couldn't love him.

He nodded to both of them and took off through the back door, leaving only a blast of cold air in his wake. Gabby looked at Luke with a half smile on her lips. "I feel sorry for him," she said softly, "but I can't help but feel excited for us."

He smiled down at her and pulled her into an embrace. "What could you possibly be excited for, Vixen?"

"Oh, I don't know. I'm sure I'll think of a good reason." She smiled at him and he leaned down, tempted by the soft, pink lips that she had just licked. The kiss began gentle, then intensified as his hands roved over her back, pulling her closer and closer to him.

"Ahem." The sound of the male voice caused them to pull apart quickly, and whirl to face *Abuelo*. "I need to speak with this young man, Gabby. Go in the other room and enjoy Marisol. She is as precious as she is beautiful."

"Marisol? That's the name they chose? Oh, how beautiful!" She looked back at Luke and he squeezed her hand gently, then released her. Hesitantly, she walked away from him, pausing at the door where her grandfather stood and looking at him for several moments, then she moved on into the other room.

"It's obvious she loves you very much," her grandfather said, walking into the room further. He sat down at one of the tables, groaning softly as his knees and back popped and cracked at the movement. "It broke my heart when she moved to Corpus Christi with my son and his wife. She and Serena were the best of friends, and those two little girls lit up my world. Gabby was always the more level-headed of the two. Serena has always been our wild child. Still is." He chuckled slightly and fished out his pipe. His old hands fumbled with the tobacco and match, but soon he was puffing contentedly on his pipe.

"My Gabriella, though…she is quite extraordinary. She's a constant ray of sunshine, always able to find the good in everyone. I thought the two of you were going to be like oil and water when you first met. But you both had to prove me wrong."

"Sir, I've never meant any disrespect…"

Abuelo shook his head, waving his finger in the air. "No, no. You have never disrespected me. Or my wife. Or anyone in this family for that matter. Might explain why I like you. Do you remember our hunt the other day?"

Luke stopped talking altogether, nearly holding his breath with hope. *Does he know how much I love Gabby? Does he know that I will do anything and everything to protect her and give her a good life?*

Abuelo sat there, puffed on his pipe, and watched Luke closely. "Well, son, I've watched you, and you've put your newfound wisdom to use. Now, isn't there something you want to ask me?"

Chapter Twenty-Four

THE ROUNDS HAD been made. Everyone had held Marisol and cooed to her, and then, gradually, everyone went in to see Olivia and praise her on the beautiful baby girl she had given birth to. And one by one, they all began to drift to their rooms, as none of them had slept the entire night.

Gabby, however, seemed to be having a hard time winding down, as Luke found her in the kitchen, carefully wrapping all of the pies that they had never had the chance to taste to preserve them to be eaten later in the day. Morning wasn't far away, but fortunately it was Christmas Day, and they weren't open for business.

Luke snuck up behind her and slid his arms around her waist, pulling her back against him and resting his chin on the top of her head. "You should get some sleep, Vixen."

He could hear the smile in her voice as she replied. "Too many wonderful things have happened to be able to sleep." Her arms wrapped around his, holding him tightly. "Marisol is gorgeous. And she is a miracle. You saved her life, you know."

"If I remember correctly, she didn't start crying until you

gave her that smack on the backside."

"But you gave her the air from your breath—you literally breathed life into her."

He kissed the top of her head. "Then let us agree we saved her together."

She leaned her head back against his shoulder. "Luke…the other night…"

"Shh," he hushed her, then brought his lips down onto her neck. "I made a mistake," he murmured between kisses. "I didn't know what to say. Or at least, the right thing to say."

Slowly he turned her around to face him and his eyes searched hers. "Gabby, I can't remember what it is like to be loved. And to be honest with you, it scares me to death. But what frightened me even more was that I didn't know if I could love you in return. Especially love you the way you deserve to be loved."

"Luke, we'll learn together. We can make it through anything as long as we are together."

He smiled at her and took her face in his hands, dropping his head and capturing her lips in a tender kiss. He had to force himself to pull back before the kiss intensified to the passionate embrace he craved with her.

"I came to realize something very important," he said softly. Her eyes searched his face, and once again he thought of how he could get lost in her eyes. "I realized that I can't live without you. I can't even make it a day without you. I need you in my life, Gabby. I will always need you in my life."

"Oh, Luke," she whispered, tears brimming at the corners of her eyes.

"So…" he cleared his throat "…that leaves me in a difficult position. It is either live a very sad and lonely existence without you, or convince you to become my wife and stay with me forever."

Her face burst into a bright smile. "Oh, Luke!" She threw her arms around him and held him tightly. He chuckled and buried his face into her neck, breathing in her sweet aroma. "Yes. A thousand times, yes. I will be honored to be your wife."

Something caught Luke's eye out the window and he pulled free from her and grabbed her hand, pulling her to the back door. "Hurry," he said. "I don't want to miss this."

She looked at him quizzically but followed him out the door and into the backyard. The sun was just barely beginning to shine faint rays in the distance, but most of the land was still in the dark. But in the faint light the tiny white flakes could just barely be seen.

"It's snowing!" she gasped.

He grabbed her around the waist and twirled around with her, and she laughed out loud. He finally set her on the ground and she clung to him, watching him with eyes full of joy. "Merry Christmas, Gabby," he whispered.

"Merry Christmas, Luke."

THAT EVENING THEY had their Christmas dinner, though it

was later than they had ever had it before. The house was full of joy, from Cade and Olivia's bliss in their new daughter, to Luke and Gabby who were obviously happy, but had yet to share their news with the family. The children had spent the day in the front room playing with their new toys, while the rest of the family had relaxed and had coffee and pie until finally pulling out food for the dinner.

Olivia even made it out of her room to join them, and they were all laughing together as Trevor shared one of Serena's latest endeavors that had ended in spectacular fashion. With the meal finished, they were all enjoying time as a family, and Luke had never felt more at home in his entire life. He finally belonged, and soon enough, it would be official.

With his chair scraping backwards, he stood and held up his glass, and everyone gave him their attention. "I'd like to make a toast to the proud mother and father in the house, and precious Marisol, who will bring even more warmth and joy to this already incredible family. And a toast to the entire family for taking in a stranger and giving him the home he has always wanted but never had."

"Hear, hear!" Raphael cheered and the others joined him.

"And finally," Luke said, glancing down at Gabby who nodded her support to him. "I'd like to announce that Gabby has agreed to become my wife."

There were gasps of excitement from all the women around the table, then squeals of delight as they congratulated Luke and Gabby. Luke sat down and grinned at Gabby, taking her hand and kissing her knuckles. He had never felt so happy in his entire life.

"It will need to be a spring wedding. Oh, just imagine, Gabby! We can use the bluebonnets in your hair, and we can—"

"Bluebonnets! The roses will be blooming by then. Remember the beautiful yellow rosebush we have? That yellow in her hair will be exquisite."

"As would the bluebonnets…"

The banter between Angie and Serena was interrupted when Raphael pushed back his chair and stood. "Congratulations to Luke and Gabby!"

Everyone raised their cups and toasted them. But Raphael wasn't done. He shuffled his feet for a few moments, then continued. "I suppose I have a bit of an announcement of my own," he said slowly, obviously picking his words carefully, and the table fell silent. "Trevor and I have spent a lot of time together, as you know, and I've learned a great deal about the Texas Rangers. Gabby, you won't be the only one who doesn't return to the ranch. At the start of the year I'll be signing up to join them."

"And a welcome addition you will be," Trevor said, raising his cup while the rest of the table sat in stunned silence.

"Raphael," Gabby began, but he interrupted her.

"I know you will be worried about me. I know all of you will. But this is what I want. I suppose I'm getting married, too. Just to the Rangers, and not to a lovely young lady."

"To Raphael." Luke raised his cup, and the rest of the family enthusiastically joined in.

Abuela spoke up. "Well, there is only one more thing we

need now."

"What's that?" Lorenzo asked, but *Abuela* merely winked as Trevor slowly stood and raised his cup.

"With all the excitement, I nearly forgot," he said, then winced when Serena kicked him under the table. "Of course, I could never forget this. It is my pleasure to share with the family that…well, that…"

"Spit it out, Trevor," Lorenzo prodded him.

"I'm pregnant," Serena said.

The gasps and squeals commenced again, and Trevor finished the toast amongst much laughter. Luke looked around at all of the happy faces and then over at Gabby, whose smile made his heart skip a beat. *Thank you, God, for answering my prayers.*

The End

If you enjoyed Texas Desire,
you'll love the next book in…

The Texas Legacy Series

Book 1: *Texas Conquest*

Book 2: *Texas Desire*

Book 3: *Texas Heat*

Book 4: *Texas Christmas*

Available now at your favorite online retailer!

About the Author

Holly grew up spending many lazy summer days racing her horses bareback in the Texas sun. But whenever Holly wasn't riding her horses or competing in horse shows, she was found with pen and paper in hand, writing out romantic love stories of the wild west.

Later, in her professional life, Holly worked just blocks from the Alamo in a unique setting where the buildings were connected with basements and tunnels. The exciting history of Texas, the Alamo, and working in a historic building dating back to the 1800's inspired Holly to write about the Texas Revolution, and has evolved into a series all about Texas becoming the great State it is.

Today, Holly lives in a small community just south of San Antonio, with her husband and two children. On the family's 80 acre ranch, surrounded by cattle during the day and hearing the howl of coyotes by night, Holly has endless inspiration for her writing.

Thank you for reading

Texas Christmas

If you enjoyed this book, you can find more from all our great authors at TulePublishing.com, or from your favorite online retailer.

TULE
PUBLISHING